The Stars at Night

The Stars at Night is a beautiful mountain romance that will transport you to a paradise. It's a story of self-discovery, family, and rural living. This romance was a budding romance that snuck-up and on two unsuspecting women who found themselves falling in love under the stars and while gazing at birds. It's a feel-good slow-burn romance that will make your heart melt.

-Les Rêveur

Hill is such a strong writer. She's able to move the plot along through the characters' dialogue and actions like a true boss. It's a masterclass in showing, not telling. The story unfolds at a languid pace which mirrors life in a small, mountain town, and her descriptions of the environment bring the world of the book alive.

-The Lesbian Review

The characters were very likable and dealt with realistic problems such as the sudden loss of a job or a loved one. I liked how Kyler and Lexie had meaningful conversations about many diverse topics. I especially loved how the author allowed her characters to get to know each other and develop a strong friendship while they explored the beautiful mountain setting whether biking, hiking, or driving. I also liked how the author pulled the reader into these scenes with her very vivid descriptive writing. The secondary characters, especially Lexie's brotl . . . is story. The support he . . . y Kyler, was heartwarmii

Overall, . . . d story. The very descri . . . ve you with

peaceful thoughts, a sense of tranquility, and a yearning to experience that type of setting in person.

-R. Swier, *NetGalley*

Gillette Park

This book was just what I was hoping for and wickedly entertaining. The premise of this book is really well done. Parts are hard to read of course. This book is about a serial killer who targets mostly young teenagers. The book isn't very graphic, but it still breaks your heart in places. But there is also a sweet romance that helps to give the book a sense of hope. Mix that with some strong women, the creepiness of the paranormal factors, and the book balances out really well. There is a lot of potential with these characters and I'd love to see their stories continue. If you are a Hill fan, grab this.

-Lex Kent's Reviews, *goodreads*

Hill is a master writer, and this one is done in a way that I think will appeal to many readers. Don't just discount this one because it has a paranormal theme to it! I think that the majority of readers who love mystery novels with a romantic side twist will love this story.

-Bethany K., *goodreads*

It was suspenseful and so well written that it was anyone's guess what would happen next! The characters—all of them, as you'll learn, were perfectly written.

-Gayle T., *NetGalley*

Gerri Hill has written another action-packed thriller. The writing is excellent and the characters engaging. Wow!

-Jenna F., *NetGalley*

...is a phenomenal book! I wish I could give this more than five stars. Yes, there is a paranormal element, and a love story, and conflict, and danger. And it's all worth it. Thank you, Gerri Hill, for writing a brilliant masterpiece!

-Carolyn M., *NetGalley*

After the Summer Rain

...is a heartwarming, slow-burn romance that features two awesome women who are learning what it really means to live and love fully. They're also learning to let go of their turbulent pasts so that it doesn't ruin their future happiness. Gerri Hill has never failed to give me endearing characters who are struggling with heartbreaking issues and beautiful descriptions of the landscapes that surround them.

-*The Lesbian Review*

Gerri Hill is simply one of the best romance writers in the genre. This is an archetypal Hill, slightly unusual characters in a slightly unusual setting. The slow-burn romance, however, is a classic, trying not to fall in love, but unable to fight the pull.

-*Lesbian Reading Room*

After the Summer Rain is a wonderfully heartfelt romance that avoids all the angsty drama-filled tropes you often find in romances.

-*C-Spot Reviews*

Moonlight Avenue

Moonlight Avenue by Gerri Hill is a riveting, literary tapestry of mystery, suspense, thriller and romance. It is also a story about forgiveness, moving on with your life and opening your heart to love despite how daunting it may seem at first.

-*The Lesbian Review*

...is an excellent mystery novel, sheer class. Gerri Hill's writing is flawless, her story compelling and much more than a notch above others writing in this genre.

-Kitty Kat's Book Review Blog

The Locket

This became a real page-turner as the tension racked up. I couldn't put it down. Hill has a knack for combining strong characters, vulnerable and complex, with a situation that allows them to grow, while keeping us on our toes as the mystery unfolds. Definitely one of my favorite Gerri Hill thrillers, highly recommended.

-Lesbian Reading Room

The Neighbor

It's funny...Normally in the books I read I get why the characters would fall in love. Now on paper (excuse the pun), Cassidy and Laura should not work...but let me tell you, that's the reason they do. I actually loved this book so hard. ...Yes it's a slow burn but so beautifully written and worth the wait in every way.

-Les Rêveur

This is classic Gerri Hill at her very best, top of the pile of so many excellent books she has written, I genuinely loved this story and these two women. The growing friendship and hidden attraction between them is skillfully written and totally engaging....This was a joy to read.

-Lesbian Reading Room

I have always found Hill's writing to be intriguing and stimulating. Whether she's writing a mystery or a sweet romance, she allows the reader to discover something about themselves along with her characters. This story has all the fun antics you would expect for a quality, low-stress, romantic comedy. Hill is wonderful in giving us characters that are intriguing and delightful that you never want to put the book down until the end.

-*The Lesbian Review*

Red Tide at Heron Bay

Other Bella Books by Gerri Hill

About the Author

Gerri Hill has over thirty-nine published works, including the 2020 GCLS winner *After the Summer Rain*, the 2017 GCLS winner *Paradox Valley*, 2014 GCLS winner *The Midnight Moon*, 2011, 2012 and 2013 winners *Devil's Rock, Hell's Highway* and *Snow Falls*, and the 2009 GCLS winner *Partners*, the last book in the popular Hunter Series, as well as the 2013 Lambda finalist *At Seventeen*. Gerri lives in south-central Texas, only a few hours from the Gulf Coast, a place that has inspired many of her books. With her partner, Diane, they share their life with two Australian shepherds—Rylee and Mason—and a couple of furry felines. For more, visit her website at gerrihill.com.

Bella Books, Inc.
P.O. Box 10543
Tallahassee, FL 32302

Printed in the United States of America on acid-free paper.

First Bella Books Edition 2021

Editor: Medora MacDougall
Cover Designer: Kayla Mancuso

ISBN: 978-1-64247-282-0

Red Tide at Heron Bay

GERRI HILL

BELLA
BOOKS

2021

CHAPTER ONE

Lauren paused outside her door to admire the flaming red bougainvillea that was in full bloom, then turned her face toward the bay, inhaling the familiar salty air. It was a cloudy morning, and the sunrise would go unnoticed, although it was still a few minutes away. The laughing gulls that soared over her head greeted her to the day and she smiled with contentment as she closed the gate to her walkway and headed to the small, paved road that would take her to the clubhouse and the cottages, all tucked into and between the coastal oaks that dotted the Rockport landscape. They had seventeen cottages on the property as well as a bank of rooms—mini-suites, her grandmother called them—that overlooked the pool and flower gardens. It had been her idea to paint the cottages all different colors—pastels of yellow, blue, lavender, mauve, and green. That was after her grandfather had passed, and her grandmother often said he would be "rolling over in his grave" at the sight of them. They were their signature now, though.

She opened the gate to the pool area and followed the sidewalk. Again, her gaze lingered on the colorful flowers—more bougainvillea, several colors of hibiscus, and an array of seasonal flowers. No one was about at this early hour and she pulled off her T-shirt and shorts, leaving her in the one-piece Speedo she normally wore. She went to the deep end and did a shallow dive, swimming underwater to the other side before surfacing. It was a ritual she did most mornings before heading to the office. She'd swim a few laps, then float on her back, mentally planning her day. Today, a day after the Fourth of July crowds left, she decided she'd do little more than tend to the flowers. They had a watering system set up for most of the gardens but some needed tending to by hand. It was a relaxing, therapeutic chore that she loved.

As she floated on her back, her gaze went to the clubhouse. An enclosed poolside entrance held the rack of towels and an icemaker. Through there, you could enter the kitchen and lounge. The clubhouse itself was used infrequently by the guests—birthday parties and such. The small workout room—with a treadmill, an elliptical, and a weight set—got more use. There were two large sofas in the lounge, separated by a bookshelf where guests were free to trade books. That was a popular thing years ago, before electronic devices took over. Now the books mostly collected dust. The game room saw a fair amount of traffic as couples would meet there to play board games or dominoes. The clubhouse was decorated much like the cottages, with coastal art and prints of shorebirds. A huge collage was dedicated to the aftermath of Harvey, the hurricane that decimated the oaks but surprisingly left little structural damage to the cottages.

She walked up the steps of the pool and dripped into the towel room, grabbing one and drying her long hair, then taking a second to dry her body. As she toweled off, something inside caught her attention. She frowned. The chairs around the table were toppled over.

She slung one towel over her shoulder and opened the door. She stopped in her tracks, her eyes darting around the kitchen and lounge.

"Oh my god," she whispered.

The chairs were tipped over, yes. So were both of the sofas and even the bookshelf. Books and magazines lay strewn on the floor and the colorful prints on the walls had been slashed with a knife. Her eyes were drawn to the front door, seeing the gaping hole in the glass where someone had smashed it.

She backed out of the room, hurrying over to her clothes and her cell. Her hands were shaking as she dialed 911.

"Yes, I need to report a break-in."

CHAPTER TWO

Harley glanced at the app on her phone—which was clamped to the handlebars—as she peddled her mountain bike along the wooded trail in Goose Island State Park. Eight miles so far. She'd wanted to do ten, at least, so she'd have to make the bay loop one more time before she headed back home. Sweat dripped into her eyes and she slid a finger under her sunglasses and wiped her face quickly.

She didn't ride the state park trail every day, but they all knew her by name now. After a year of living here, she knew most of them too, if only in passing. Of course, in the last year—after she changed her lifestyle—she'd gotten a lot fitter too. She remembered the first few times on the bike. Two miles felt like ten. Twenty minutes felt like an hour. Now? Now she could do ten, twelve, fifteen miles without laboring. Her morning exercise routine had become sort of an addiction. It beat the hell out of her other addictions, though.

She buzzed around a corner, the brush grabbing at her arm as she passed. The trail here was simply a cutout in the woods, with crushed oyster shells for the base. The woods encroached on the trail in spots, and she came out into a small clearing, where the trail split into threes. One would take her to the road next to the campground. One would take her to the giant live oak and the sitting bench. And one would continue on through the woods, coming out near the office and the entrance. She hopped on the one that would take her to the road, intending to ride the loop trail before heading back toward the bay. That might get her the ten miles she was hoping for.

The ringing of her phone took her attention from the trail. It was Commander Lawson. With a sigh, she answered.

"Shepherd."

"Good morning, Harley. I suppose you're on your ride?"

"Yes, sir. About done."

"I know it's early, but I've got something I want you to check out. Baker was dispatched to Heron Bay Resort. Looked like a break-in at first glance. Nothing seems to be taken, though. More vandalism than anything."

She wondered why something like that made him call her. This would be a case for Roscoe, not her. But she did not voice that opinion to him.

"It was a message written on a mirror that got his attention. Why don't you check it out?"

"Okay. It'll be a half hour or more before I can get there. I'm at Goose Island right now."

"No hurry. Like I said, nothing was taken. I'll let Baker know you're on your way."

"Where is this place, anyway?"

"You've been here almost a year—you still don't know your way around?"

"I know where the best seafood places are. Don't know the Heron Bay Resort."

"It's out on Highway 35, just south of the Copano Bay Causeway. Bunch of cottages, all different colors."

"Oh, yeah. I know the place. I drive by it every day on my way in."

"Baker said he's at the clubhouse, by the pool."

"Copy that. On my way."

She sighed as she hit the pavement. Instead of taking the long way along the loop, she turned left, heading back to the main road and the entrance.

She was one of four detectives on the Rockport police force. Assigned to CID—Criminal Investigation Division—they split the cases evenly, although Commander Lawson tended to favor her with the "good cases" as he called it. She knew it had more to do with her being friends with Chief Carrington than anything else. Or maybe her time spent in San Antonio gave her some clout in the small-town department.

Another perk was getting to take home one of the black SUVs the department owned. The police logo was written in blue and green sea colors, topped with a palm tree. Beat the hell out of driving one of the dull, unmarked cars and certainly beat driving her own old truck.

* * *

It was still early, and the temperature was pleasant, even for early July. Instead of taking Highway 35—the main business strip in town—she took Fulton Beach Road, following the bay. There wasn't much to see this time of year. The winter residents—the white pelicans and ducks and shorebirds—had long ago flown the coop. She spotted a great blue heron fishing in the shallows. Other than gulls circling over, the bay was quiet. If she continued to follow the road, she'd end up back in town and only a few blocks from the new police station—the old one having been flattened by Hurricane Harvey, along with most of the buildings along the bay. Instead, she turned right onto Chaparral, which came out near the edge of town on Highway 35, just a few blocks past Heron Bay Resort. Her favorite fish market was on the corner and she honked when she went past, seeing Jose unloading his catch. He smiled and waved at her.

"Got some snapper," he called.

She lowered the passenger side window all the way. "Save me one. I'll come by later."

"Will do, Harley."

Oh, she loved this little town. Her only regret was that it had taken her so long to get here. Back during college, it was only a two-and-a-half-hour drive from San Antonio. She came regularly with friends to enjoy the beach scene. As she got older, her visits became less frequent, and Rockport and the beach at Port Aransas was more a fond memory than anything else.

After the…well, the incident…she'd been ready to quit the police profession and go into something else. But her captain had interviewed for the police chief job here in Rockport—after the fallout from Hurricane Harvey had caused Chief Roselle to retire—and when he got it, he offered her the chance to join him. She jumped on it. Captain Carrington—now Chief Carrington—had been a friend for years. Their relationship had only strengthened since moving down here to the coast.

She slowed when she saw the sign for Heron Bay Resort. A white picket fence ran the length of the property along the highway, with two white pillars—a heron perched on each—forming the entrance. Large live oak trees—some still showing the damage from the 2017 hurricane—shaded the place, and she passed the office, a quaint yellow building with white trim, matching the design of all the other cottages that were crammed between the oak trees.

The driveway was tiny and only one vehicle could drive through at a time. The parking spots were small too, all in an effort to preserve the trees. She found it fascinating how many structures and fences in town were contorted to fit among the trees. It was only a last resort to cut even a limb off the old oak trees.

The police cruiser was blocking the road and she pulled to a stop behind it. David Baker was leaning against a tree, his phone to his ear. By the look on his face, he was talking to Shelly, the woman he'd been dating for a few months now. When he saw her, he quickly ended the call. Everyone knew that she and the chief were friends outside of work and no one wanted to be reported on. She didn't tell them that her relationship with Brian didn't revolve around the police force, and he'd never once asked for inside gossip. Brian was chief, but the commanders managed each division without interference from him. At least so far.

"Hey, Harley."

"Hope you have something fun and exciting for me today. Because if it is, then the bait shop burglary will be a cold case and not a day too soon."

He laughed. "Tired of dealing with Al?"

"I told him to get a damn security camera." Her expression turned serious as she motioned to the door. "What we got?"

"Thought it was plain and simple vandalism." He pushed open the door—with its broken glass—the cool air-conditioned air a contrast to the quickly warming day. "Then I found the message on the bathroom mirror."

The place was indeed trashed. Furniture toppled, seat cushions slashed, picture frames broken, their contents ruined. This looked a bit more violent than simple vandalism.

"Who found it?"

"The owner. Lauren Voss. I told her to wait out by the pool. She was pretty shook up."

She nodded. "Prints?"

"Dusted the doorknobs, countertops." He shook his head. "Smudges and multiples. According to Ms. Voss, this place sees all kinds of traffic."

"What did you call it? A clubhouse?"

"Yeah. Out back is the pool area. In here, there's a workout room, vending machines, full kitchen, a bathroom."

She looked around, seeing books scattered from the shelves, assuming it was a share or trade system. She moved one out of her way with her foot as she went toward the kitchen.

"And nothing was taken? TV?"

"Nope. Both TVs were smashed."

She glanced out the window toward the pool, seeing a dark-haired woman sitting at one of the tables, talking animatedly on the phone. She watched her for a second, then scanned the pool, noting how inviting it looked with all the flowers and greenery. She turned back to Baker.

"Okay. Let's see the message on the mirror."

Down a short hallway were three doors. She looked at him questioningly.

"One's a game room. Tables for board games and stuff." He opened that door, showing her the inside. The tables were flipped over, but the cabinets and shelves looked undisturbed. "The other, she said was a small meeting room." He opened that as well, revealing a room with about ten or twelve chairs. It didn't look to have been touched.

The bathroom door was standing open. She walked toward it, one eyebrow arching up as she read the message. A message written in what appeared to be blood.

Have you missed me? It's your turn to die.

"Well, that's certainly different," she murmured.

"That's probably blood, right?"

"Yeah."

She went fully into the room. Other than the message on the mirror—and the lone drop of blood on the countertop—the bathroom looked clean and tidy. A soap dispenser was beside the sink and a wicker basket held folded paper towels. A bowl of seashells decorated the counter, and a print—two white pelicans sitting on a pier—was hung above the toilet.

"We'll need to get a blood sample sent to the lab."

"You think it's human?"

"I hope not." She held up her phone, snapping a couple of shots of the message. "You got pictures of the mess out there?"

"Yeah."

"Okay. Let me interview the owner. What was her name again?"

"Lauren Voss." He winked at her. "She's kinda cute."

She gave him a smirk. "I can find my own dates, thank you." She pointed to the bathroom. "Dust in here for prints. Everything. Countertop, sink, fixtures…everything. We might get lucky."

CHAPTER THREE

Lauren frowned as a woman came out of the back door. "I need to go, Nana. I'll call you later."

She didn't know if she should answer the woman's smile with one of her own or a laugh. The woman was wearing a godawful ugly Hawaiian shirt—bright red with white flowers. She had on dark sunglasses, and her nearly black hair was cut in a fashionable style—longer on top, sweeping across her forehead, shorter on the sides and back. Crisp khaki pants, white sneakers. Black sports watch. Around her neck hung a police badge. Unbelievable, she thought. Did the woman think she was on *Hawaii Five-0*?

"Mrs. Voss?"

"Ms. Voss," she corrected automatically.

The woman held her hand out. "I'm Detective Shepherd."

Instead of shaking her hand, Lauren pointed to her face. "Do you mind taking your sunglasses off? I like to see who I'm talking to."

"Of course. Sorry."

The offending glasses were shoved on top of her head, revealing eyes that were as dark as her hair. Unexpectedly thoughtful, warm eyes that seemed to be reading her. Then the woman smiled, revealing tiny laugh lines at the corners of each eye.

"Thank you."

"No problem. So, the message," the detective said, pointing back toward the clubhouse. "You think it was meant for you?"

"I don't know. I don't know why it would be."

"Piss someone off lately? Got a disgruntled guest? Ex-husband? Ex-boyfriend?"

"No."

"No to which? No to all?"

She sighed. "I haven't made anyone angry that I know of. We don't have disgruntled guests. Most of the people who stay here are repeat customers. I don't have an ex-husband. I don't have an ex-boyfriend, unless you count James from high school. I do have an ex-girlfriend. She lives in San Diego and is happily married," she managed to say without cringing too much. Normally, just thinking of Leah made her cringe. She crossed her arms defensively. "So no to all."

"Surveillance cameras?"

"No."

"None?"

"No."

"At the office?"

"There are no cameras," she said a bit testily. "There's no need. We're a small-time family business, and most of our guests are retired couples or families and, like I said, repeats. During the winter months, half of our cottages are booked with Winter Texans. They come every year, stay in the same cottages for three or four months. We know them by name. It's a family atmosphere here."

"Okay. So you have no idea who could have done this?"

She shook her head. "I can't imagine that the message was meant for me. I don't live that kind of life. I rarely leave this place."

"Why is that?"

"We're too busy. I'm at the office by seven or seven thirty each morning. Since my grandmother—well, she lives in a retirement community now. She used to work in the office with me. It's just me now and one part-time office clerk. I stay plenty busy."

"So are you the owner or the manager?"

"My grandmother still technically owns it."

"So it'll be yours when she's gone?"

"Yes." She smiled, thinking of Nana. "She's eighty-six and still healthy enough to live alone. She moved to The Oaks Retirement Village last year because three of her good friends live there."

Detective Shepherd tilted her head. "Could someone have a vendetta against your grandmother?"

Lauren's eyes widened. "Nana? Lord, no. She's the sweetest woman you'll ever meet."

The detective put her sunglasses back on. "All right. Well, we'll question the guests, see if anyone heard something or saw something." She motioned to the suites behind the pool. "I'd like to start here. Are these motel rooms or—"

"Small suites. They all have mini-kitchens in them."

"Are they booked?"

"Last night, I think five were booked. Most of the holiday crowd left yesterday. I'll have to check the register to be sure."

The detective nodded and grinned. "That fireworks display was great, wasn't it?"

"Yes, it was." It was an annual event on the Fourth of July, but judging by Detective Shepherd's expression, it had been her first one. She assumed she wasn't a local then. Rockport wasn't that big. Surely, she would have seen her around town.

"Okay. We'll get started. If you could let me know which rooms are occupied. Or I suppose I could just knock."

When the detective moved to go around the pool, Lauren stopped her. "Are you new in town?"

"About a year. Why?"

"The shirt."

The detective smiled. "Thanks. Yeah, isn't it great? I have about thirty of them, I think." She nodded at Lauren. "I'll be in touch."

Lauren shook her head as Detective Shepherd walked off. She was an attractive woman with an easy smile. Yes, she would have noticed her had she seen her around town. She wondered at the significance of the Hawaiian shirt.

CHAPTER FOUR

Interviewing the guests had been a mixed bag. Some may or may not have heard glass breaking. Some thought they heard odd noises during the night but couldn't be sure. One lady said she saw headlights about two in the morning—she'd needed a bathroom break, she'd said. And Mrs. Etta Thompson, in Cottage Number Twelve, across from the pool, said she saw a truck drive through about four or so. No, she didn't know what kind of truck or the color. She'd been at the sink drawing water for coffee. Nate, her husband, was an early riser and expected coffee as soon as he woke. She assumed it had been a fisherman going out to an early morning hunt and hadn't paid it much mind, she'd said.

Harley walked the winding road that meandered between the oaks and the cottages. Three golf carts were buzzing around, loaded with towels and cleaning equipment. A man was hauling a long garden hose across the road, watering the shrubs and flowers along the cabins. Her vehicle was still parked at the clubhouse, but she'd seen Lauren Voss walk this very road earlier.

The sun was higher in the sky now and the July heat was making itself known. Under the shade of the oaks, though, the breeze was enough to be comfortable. She paused to admire the flowers which seemed to be crammed into every available space. All the cottages had little front porches and two matching rockers were on each. Tiny patches of manicured lawn separated the cottages, which were set haphazardly to accommodate the oak trees. Here and there were picnic tables, and cast-iron barbeque grills—the ones secured with a metal pipe—were at the corners of most cottages.

She stood in front of the office, her gaze going back down the winding road. It was a feast to the eyes—the colorful cottages, the flowering shrubs and greenery, the multitude of bright flowers. Inviting, yes. And quiet. Peaceful.

"Are you doing important detective work?"

She turned, finding Lauren Voss staring at her from the doorway of the office. She was wearing a green T-shirt with a Heron Bay Resort logo on it. A cute, colorful logo with a heron in the middle of a circle, a small fish caught in its beak. Harley smiled at her and motioned to where she'd been looking at the flowers.

"Pretty. I was thinking how inviting, how peaceful it looked."

"Thank you."

"You maintain the gardens?"

Lauren nodded. "Mostly. Gerald helps with the watering. I do the majority of the planting each spring."

"Impressive. Who's Gerald?"

"Handyman. Part-time gardener. Were you able to find out anything?" She held the door open. "Come inside where it's cooler."

Harley followed her into the air-conditioned room. The office was small and crowded. A tall countertop separated the entryway. Behind it was a desk with two monitors. Behind that desk was a long, skinny table against the back wall, cluttered with papers and brochures. A small room to the left showed a refrigerator and microwave and two filing cabinets. Lauren went there and brought back a chair.

"Sorry, it's a little cramped in here."

"That's okay." Harley sat down, waiting until Lauren sat behind the desk. She pulled out her phone, going to where she'd jotted down her notes. "A lady in one of the mini-suites saw headlights about two this morning. And from Cottage Number Twelve—"

"The Thompsons. They live there."

"Yeah. Etta." She looked up. "They live there? Like all the time?"

"It started out a couple of months during the winter. Then three or four months. That grew to six. They've been there since September."

"Where are they from?"

"Iowa. They started coming for a month each winter—I'd have to check with Nana but I want to say at least ten or twelve years ago. They stayed eight months last year."

"That sounds expensive."

"We have monthly rates during the winter months, but yes, it can get quite expensive during spring and summer." She smiled then. "We certainly don't complain that they want to stay longer."

"Well, she said she saw a truck drive past about four. She didn't get a good look at it. Assumed it was someone going fishing."

Lauren nodded. "A lot of our guests do fish."

"At four in the morning?"

"Not usually, no. Our pier is open all night—it's lighted—and people do fish after dark, but not all night long, no."

"You have a pier? One of those private piers along the bay road?"

"Yes. There is no parking there so if any of our guests use it, they have to walk from here. If someone was driving at four a.m., they weren't going to our pier."

"Do you live here on the property?"

"Yes. My cottage is at the very back, by the bay."

"So it's like all of these?"

"From the outside, it looks pretty much the same. It's larger. Bigger bedroom and bath. Larger kitchen. Has a tiny back porch whereas these only have a front porch."

"Very cute. I like the rockers."

Lauren smiled. "My grandmother's doing."

"So this is a family business?"

"My grandparents started it, oh, it's been fifty years, I guess. They started with only a few cabins and catered mostly to fishermen. The cottages came later. The pool was added about, oh, I don't know, fifteen or twenty years ago, I guess."

"How long have you been involved with it?"

Lauren arched an eyebrow. "Are you curious or is this part of your investigation?"

Harley smiled at her. "Curious."

The other woman leaned forward. "Why the Hawaiian shirt?"

Harley looked down at her shirt, still smiling. "You like it? It's comfortable as hell."

"You look like a tourist."

"No. I'd have shorts and flip-flops on if I was a tourist." She glanced at her notes again, going through the questions she'd pondered. "No locked gate? Guests can come and go at will?"

"No locked gate, no."

"Is this the only entrance? What about bayside?"

"We had that entrance closed off years ago. Where I live now, my grandparents used to live there. Nana got tired of the traffic going through. There's a walkway now for those going to the pier. A privacy fence blocks me in."

"You mention your grandmother—Nana. What about your grandfather?"

"No. He's gone." She frowned, as if thinking. "Six years this fall."

"I see. So, what about other family?"

"Curious?"

"No. This is actually a real question. See?" She held up her phone, showing Lauren the notes. "Got family that might be upset that you'll be getting the resort when your grandmother is gone? I imagine this piece of property is worth a pretty penny."

She nodded. "Yes, it is. I have an older brother. He lives in San Diego."

Her eyebrows raised. "Where your ex lives?"

"Yes. I used to live there too."

"Oh, so you're not from around here then."

Lauren sighed. "I am. I grew up here. My parents moved us to San Diego when I was in high school."

"But you came back? How old are you?"

"I'm fairly certain that is not a relevant question."

"Not really, no. Trying to get a timeline." She studied her. "I'm going to guess thirty-six maybe. Thirty-seven?"

Lauren's eyes widened. "Seriously?"

"I'm never good with ages."

"I'm thirty-three."

"Ah. Younger than me. I'm thirty-four." Lauren stared at her blankly. "Yeah. Not really relevant." She looked again at her notes. "So no disgruntled family member?"

"No. My brother thinks the Texas coast is for losers."

"Compared to the beaches in San Diego?"

"Yes. He hates it here. Too hot. Too humid. Too many fishermen."

"Parents?"

"My parents are deceased."

"Oh. Sorry," she said automatically.

"Car accident."

"So just the grandmother then?"

"My other grandparents—my mother's parents—live in San Diego as well. I'm not close to them. My brother is."

She rested her elbows on her thighs. "Why did you move back here? And when?"

"Look, my personal history doesn't have a bearing on this break-in or vandalism or whatever you want to call it." Her eyes narrowed. "What are you going to do about it?"

Harley shrugged. "Not much to go on, Ms. Voss. I'll tell you like I told Big Al...get a damn security camera."

Lauren Voss's eyes widened. "Excuse me?"

Harley stood up. "Al's bait shop got broken into. Again. He refuses to put a camera up." She shook her head. "Who the hell robs a bait shop? I mean, come on."

Lauren's mouth hinted at a smile. "I know Al. He is where I direct our guests when they're looking for bait. He's an old-timer."

"Right. But you're not."

"Cameras are threatening. Security cameras tell our guests that we don't trust them. I respect their privacy enough not to record their movements while they are here on vacation. It's common courtesy."

"It's common sense," she countered as she walked to the door. "I'll need to interview all of the employees who work here."

"Of course."

She stopped. "Oh, and can I get a list of all your guests from last night and their phone numbers?"

Lauren shook her head quickly. "No, you cannot. Not without their permission."

She had expected that would be her answer. "So can I sit here in the office with you, have you call them and let me talk to them?"

Lauren blew out a breath. "Fine."

She smiled. "Great. I'll be back after lunch."

"Lunch?" Lauren looked at the watch on her wrist. "It's barely eleven."

"Right. I didn't have breakfast. I'm starving."

"Don't you have some police work you should be doing?"

"Yeah. After lunch." She paused at the door. "Bring you something?"

"No, thank you."

"Okay. I'll be back about twelve thirty or so."

At that, Lauren raised both eyebrows. "An hour and a half lunch?"

"Jose is holding a snapper for me. Going to pick that up, take it home, and get it marinated."

"I see. Very important police work."

She laughed, ignoring the sarcasm. "Grilling out tonight will be the highlight of my day." Then she winked. "Other than meeting you, of course."

She was whistling as she retraced her route down the little winding road. Lauren Voss was a cutie. Dark hair—thick and wavy—that reached well past her shoulders. It had been damp when she'd first spoken to her out by the pool. Maybe she was a fan of early morning swims.

"Wonder if she wears a bikini?"

CHAPTER FIVE

"Nana, she's not taking this seriously," she said as she plopped down on her grandmother's sofa. "She's flirting with me, for god's sake! She's the detective assigned to this case and she's more interested in flirting than solving it."

"Is she cute?"

She glanced at her grandmother. "Yes, she is. That's not the point. And she had on this hideous red and white Hawaiian shirt."

"Oh, I love Hawaiian shirts. They're so colorful, aren't they?"

"She's a cop!"

"So what? They can't be fashionable?"

"Oh, Nana…the Hawaiian shirt is so not fashionable. Or is it? They seem to come and go every few years." She waved her hand in the air. "Never mind. That doesn't matter. She sat in the office with me for *hours*, calling all the guests. It was torture."

"What's her name?"

"Detective Shepherd."

"That's it? What's her *name*?"

"I didn't ask. And it doesn't matter. Someone broke into the clubhouse and trashed it. You should have seen the mess. And someone left that threatening message on the mirror. That's what's important."

"Well, I can't imagine that the message was meant for you, honey."

"I know. But what else could it be?"

"Has anything odd been happening that you've not told me about?"

"No. Nothing out of the ordinary."

"And no one saw a thing?"

"Nope. Etta Thompson was up at four and she saw a truck drive through, but that could have been anyone. I gave Detective Shepherd a list of all the guests who checked in with trucks. There were nine. She's going to follow up with them."

"Well, she seems to have a handle on it."

Lauren frowned. "She so does *not* have a handle on it."

"Have you had dinner? You seem a little testy."

Lauren stared at her grandmother. Was she testy? Maybe a little. Being cooped up in a tiny office with that woman for hours would make anyone testy. She wasn't sure why the detective got on her nerves, really. For the most part, Detective Shepherd was pleasant, friendly. Nonthreatening, really, despite her subtle flirting. Maybe it was the obnoxious Hawaiian shirt that did it.

"What are you having for dinner? Maybe I'll join you."

"Oh, honey, you can't. We're having a card game at Mary's tonight. We order up hamburgers from the cafeteria."

Hamburgers sounded better than anything she had at her place. Actually, she had little at the house. She hadn't been grocery shopping in weeks, it seemed.

"That's okay. I'll get something on the way home." She stared at her grandmother, with her snow-white hair and black-framed glasses. "Did you get your hair cut?"

She touched the hair above her ear. "I did. Do you like it?"

"I do. Quite a bit shorter than you normally wear it."

"I'll say." She held her hands out. "Got a manicure too. I rode with Gladys to the beauty shop, and she ended up talking me into a cut. Then we went next door to the nail salon. What a fun time that was."

She stood, going over to her grandmother's recliner and bending to kiss her cheek. "I'm glad you're getting out and doing things. Y'all have fun tonight. I'll see you tomorrow for dinner."

"Keep me posted on this detective person."

"You mean the case?"

"Well, that too," her grandmother said with a coy smile.

Lauren smiled at her. "She wears Hawaiian shirts, Nana. She's not my type."

"Ever since you and Leah broke up, you claim no one is your type."

"Yes. It's safer that way." She waved from the door, not wanting to get into *that* discussion again. "Bye."

She stood outside her grandmother's apartment door and sighed. How was it her eighty-six-year-old grandmother had more of a social life than she had? Working at the cottages dawn to dusk was really an excuse, she knew. Yet she used it, lying to herself that there was no time to date. Truth was, in the nearly three years that she'd been back full-time, she hadn't really made any close friends either. She didn't feel lonely, though. Not really. She came to visit her grandmother two or three times a week. And they had a standing dinner date each Wednesday at her grandmother's favorite seafood restaurant—Pelican Cove. They always chose one of the tables along the back windows that overlooked the bay. When the weather was nice, they'd sit out on the patio and she would fill her grandmother in on all the happenings at the cottages. It was a highlight of her week, she realized.

She finally moved away from the door, mentally going over her choices for dinner. Stop for fried shrimp or fish? Maybe get a burger at Fulton Pub and Grill? Pizza? No, she'd had pizza delivered on Saturday. A burger won out and she took Fulton

Beach Road along the bay, opening all the windows in her Prius to let in the gulf breeze.

Should she be more worried about the message on the mirror? Was it a prank? Not a very funny one, if it was. But still, it was a little disturbing, wasn't it?

Have you missed me? It's your turn to die.

What did that mean? And if it wasn't meant for her, then who? A member of the cleaning crew? They would normally have been the first to find it, the first to see the mess in the clubhouse. Their routine didn't waver there—tidy the clubhouse, clean the kitchen and bathroom, gather towels from the pool area. Every morning, first thing. Only, whoever left the message didn't know that she took an early morning swim most mornings. She frowned. Well, if they knew the staff's routine, why wouldn't they also know hers?

She blew out her breath. And that damn detective wasn't helping, was she? Why did the detective irritate her so? It couldn't only be the shirt. It was that smile, that "I'm so cute I can get anyone I want" look that she had. She turned into the Pub's parking lot, surprised at that thought. Maybe it was the dark sunglasses that shielded her eyes. No. It was definitely the shirt. It was a man's shirt—big and boxy. And yes, it looked comfortable. And it looked cool. She shook her head. Not cool, as in *cool*. No. But with the July heat, having a loose-fitting shirt would be better than something tight and tucked in.

The truth was the detective reminded her of Leah. And that was so not a good thing. By the time their breakup was finally over, she hated—*loathed*—all things Leah. Cute. Charming. Flirty. Sexy. At that, she rolled her eyes. She did *not* find Detective Shepherd sexy in the least. Good lord, the woman wore Hawaiian shirts, for god's sake. So not sexy.

She'd been so caught up in her thoughts, she'd completely forgotten to call in her order. Now, she'd have to order at the bar and sit and wait, something she hated to do. Because she was alone, people looked at her with pity, or some guy would come over and offer to buy her a drink. Always a guy. She had yet to have a cute woman offer to buy her a drink.

Her saving grace was that it was still early—a few minutes after six. She headed to the bar, which only had a few others there. At the end of the bar was a young couple looking at each other with flirty gazes. First date? No, their looks appeared to be too intimate. Second or third, most likely. Certainly too flirty to be a long-time couple. That never lasted. She stopped herself before she could roll her eyes. Since when had she become so jaded about love?

Yeah, that would be since Leah.

She sat as far away from the couple as she could, not wanting to listen to their sickening love talk. Robbie, the bartender and the only person she knew there by name, came over.

"Hey, Lauren. Did you order ahead? I don't see anything here for you."

"Hi, Robbie. No. I didn't get a chance. I'll have my usual cheeseburger—"

"Hold the pickles," he finished for her. "Steak fries or regular?"

"Let's splurge and do steak fries tonight."

"Are you going to eat here for a change?"

She smiled at him. "I don't think so. I'll have a beer while I wait, though."

"Bud Light. Coming right up."

She didn't often forget to call ahead so there usually wasn't a wait. Even so, sometimes she liked to sit and drink a beer and relax before taking her dinner home. Tonight, though, she couldn't seem to relax. She didn't know how she was supposed to act. Should she be afraid? Should she blow it off? Should she wait for the next message or sign or whatever? *Was* she in danger?

"Hey...I thought that was you."

She turned her head slowly, her eyes widening. "Oh my god. Really?"

Detective Shepherd sauntered over, wearing another godawful Hawaiian shirt—a green and blue neon with hibiscus flowers—that practically glowed under the bar's lights. Sunglasses were shoved on top of her head. It must have been too bright for the poor thing to walk from her car to the bar without them. This time, she couldn't stop, and she gave a dramatic eyeroll to the ceiling.

The detective laughed. "I just got this shirt the other day. You like it?"

"It's certainly bright. Perhaps I should borrow your sunglasses to hide the glow."

She sat down beside her, not waiting for an invitation. Robbie came over with her beer in a frosty mug and set it down. He surprised her by greeting the detective by name.

"Hey, Harley. What are you doing here on a Tuesday? I thought tonight was your shrimp night." He was already drawing her a beer.

"My shrimp partner canceled on me, so I thought I'd come over here instead."

Lauren stared at her. "Harley? You never told me your name."

"I didn't?"

"No. It's unusual. For a name, I mean."

"You think so? Well, as the story goes, my mom and dad were big bikers back in the day. Both of them." She laughed quietly. "You should see one of the pictures of my mom decked out in her leather and bandanas and all that stuff. Pretty badass. Anyway, my dad wanted a kid. So she told him she'd have one kid and one kid only. He got to pick the name." She shrugged. "Harley."

"That is kinda cute," she conceded.

"Yeah. But then after I was born, they settled down, sold the bikes, bought a minivan. Had three more kids."

Lauren couldn't help but laugh. "So there's three other little Harleys running around?"

"Afraid so." Harley pulled out her phone. "Found out who the four a.m. truck was. George Singleton."

Lauren nodded. "Yes. I know him. He comes twice a year."

"Said he went over to Port Aransas for a guided fishing trip. So the two a.m. headlights seem to be the only unexplained activity that night."

"Do you think I should be worried?"

"I'd be."

"You're not making me feel better."

"You want me to lie?"

She drank from her beer, then turned to her. "What do you think I should do?"

"Get security cameras."

"I told you, we—"

"Call them tomorrow. Get them installed ASAP," Harley said, ignoring her protest. "Other than that, there's not much else you can do. Be cautious. Make sure no one is following you, lurking around the place. Make sure you're inside before dark. Lock up."

"Dark?"

Harley leaned closer. "Boogeymen come out after dark." Her tone and expression were serious, then she smiled. "Not trying to scare you."

"Well, you are!"

Harley seemed to relax, and Lauren assumed she'd been teasing. She relaxed a bit too, although she thought tomorrow, she'd talk to her grandmother about adding security cameras. If her grandfather were still alive, she wouldn't even bother to bring it up. Now, she knew her grandmother would leave the decision up to her. When Nana had moved to The Oaks, she'd essentially handed over the running of the resort to her anyway. Still, all of her grandfather's reasons were valid. Perhaps if they could conceal the cameras and not make it so blatant that they were there, then—

"Why haven't I seen you here before?"

Lauren smiled at the detective. "Luck, I guess. Because trust me, I would have remembered a woman wearing obnoxious Hawaiian shirts."

Harley laughed, not indicating that she was offended in the least. "Obnoxious? Yeah, this one kinda is. So you don't come here often or what?"

"I usually call in my order and pop in to grab it."

"Take it home?"

"Yes."

"Why?"

She was about to say that she was far too busy to enjoy a leisurely dinner, but that would be lying. She lied to herself often though, didn't she? "People stare and give me sympathetic looks if I eat alone. Or worse, guys hit on me."

"I would be flattered. A guy hasn't hit on me in ten years or more."

Lauren laughed. "Maybe it's the shirts."

Harley's expression changed a little. "Yeah, the shirts are a recent thing. But I eat alone quite a bit too. Sitting at the bar eating alone is not quite as obvious as sitting at a table."

"Why alone?"

Harley raised her eyebrows. "Why do you eat alone?"

Again, the "I'm too busy to make friends" excuse popped into her head. "I've been back fulltime three years now. I haven't made very many close friends." How about *any?* she mentally corrected.

"Yeah, I've been here about a year. I've met a few people, but I wouldn't say we're good friends. I get invited to play beach volleyball with a group on weekends, but I don't always go. Mostly, I hang out with a couple of the single guys on the force. My closest friend in town is the chief, actually. And his wife."

"The police chief?"

"Yeah. He used to be my captain in San Antonio. I came here with him."

"So that's where you're from?"

"Yes. My family still lives there. It's about two and a half hours to my parents' house. My brother lives north of town, close to Spring Branch. My two sisters live pretty close to each other, closer to New Braunfels than San Antonio."

"You see them often?"

"I don't get back much, no. We chat on the phone all the time, though."

She was going to ask why she didn't go there. It was only a couple of hours, as she'd said. But it wasn't any of her business. And, of course, she didn't really care. Anyway, why on earth was she sitting here—at a bar—chatting like friends with a woman she'd met only yesterday? A woman wearing a hideous neon shirt that, by her own admission, irritated her a little. She was just so much like Leah. And beach volleyball? That was Leah's passion. She was growing to hate the detective by the minute. Thankfully, Robbie came by carrying a familiar white bag. Her dinner.

"Here you go, Lauren."

She slid her credit card over to him. "Thank you."

"Taking it with you?" Harley asked.

"Yes."

"You could stay."

Lauren actually considered her offer, but then she came to her senses. "I've got some...some spreadsheets to work on." It wasn't entirely a lie. The second quarter had ended in June and she liked to have the report done as soon as possible. Her statement, however, caused Harley's brows to draw together.

"You shouldn't be at the office alone, Lauren."

"No. I have my laptop. I'll be at home."

Harley stared at her for a moment, then waved Robbie over. "Got a pen?" She took one of the bar napkins, then wrote on it quickly. She slid it over to her. "My cell. Call me if you see or hear anything out of the ordinary."

Lauren took the napkin and nodded. "Thank you, Detective Shepherd. You've sufficiently spooked me enough, I think."

"Not trying to scare you, Ms. Voss," Harley said, adopting the formality that Lauren had initiated. "Reminding you to be careful is all."

She held the napkin up. "Let's hope I don't have to use this." She signed her credit card receipt, then picked up her card. "Enjoy the rest of your evening."

CHAPTER SIX

Harley walked slowly along the pier, listening to the quiet sloshing of water around the pylons. Like most of the piers here in the bay, it jutted out several hundred feet. Lights were spaced every thirty feet or so, but most were burned out. She liked it better in the dark anyway. At the end of the pier, a larger fishing deck had been built. The lights on only one corner of the deck were on and she moved away from it, leaning against the railing on the opposite side where it was dark.

The pier and deck had been heavily damaged by the hurricane. The owners of the RV park where she was staying had fixed the pier before anything else. The park catered to fishermen and without a pier, they had nothing to offer. The RV park itself was relatively small compared to most in town. That's one reason she chose it. That, and its proximity to the bay. It was small and rundown, to be honest. Unlike the parks closer to town—and farther inland—there wasn't a tree to be found. Unlike most other parks too, it wasn't well-cared for and manicured. The grass always seemed to need cutting and there were no flowerbeds to be found.

She sat down on the bench, her gaze fixed out over the dark water. There were several bays around Rockport, the largest two being Aransas Bay to the south and Copano Bay to the north. Here on the Lamar Peninsula—where her camper was parked— St. Charles Bay separated them from the wildlife refuge. A few clouds drifted about, hiding the moon for a bit before passing on. Maybe she should think about moving. Maybe she should buy a house. When she'd moved down here, she wasn't sure she would stay. Instead of buying, she got an RV—and a truck to pull it—and rented a spot here near the bay. But after nearly a year now, she supposed she'd stay in Rockport. The job had proven to be relatively stress free. With a population of ten thousand, violent crime—rape, assault, and murder—was pretty rare. They had their share of property crime, though—thefts and burglaries. It was enough to keep her busy and engaged, but not so overwhelming like San Antonio had been.

She looked up into the night sky, trying to picture his face. The image that came was of him laughing at her after she'd tossed a gutter ball during the final frame of their last bowling date. Travis had been such a happy man. Always smiling, laughing. Nothing ever seemed to get him down. She closed her eyes, missing him badly tonight for some reason.

He'd been her partner, her best friend. They'd been closer than family. And she missed him.

She stood up quickly, going from the darkness into the light. Moths flew in and out of the floodlight, and she followed its beam into the water, wondering why she hadn't taken up fishing yet. It would give her something to do in her free time other than rotate through the handful of bars she'd become comfortable with.

Like Fulton Pub and Grill. The Pub, as it was known to locals. What were the chances she'd run into Lauren Voss there? She went to the Pub at least twice a week and always on Wednesdays. Never Tuesday. Yet this week, Brian had a meeting come up and wasn't able to keep their standing Tuesday date at the Shrimp Shack. So instead of going alone, she decided to go to the Pub and hang out at the bar with Robbie.

Lauren Voss was a cutie, wasn't she? She got the impression, though, that Lauren Voss didn't particularly like her. It was almost hate at first sight. Well, Lauren had made it no secret that she didn't like Hawaiian shirts. That was too bad. Because she loved them.

With a sigh, she turned and headed back down the long pier, walking more slowly than before, not in any hurry to get back to her tiny RV—a twenty-five-foot bumper pull that she'd found on Craig's List. It served its purpose, she supposed, but it was small and cramped. Maybe she should think seriously about getting a house.

She was about halfway down the pier when she saw two guys step on, both carrying fishing rods. She recognized one as Tommy Butcher, her neighbor. He was sixty-seven, living on his Social Security check. He spent his days drinking beer and fishing and not much else. He'd offered numerous times to take her out in the bay and "show her the ropes" to catching flounder and drum.

"Hey, Harley," he greeted. "Taking your evening stroll?"

"Yep. What's on the menu, Tommy?"

"Gonna try to catch us some speckled trout." He jerked a thumb at the guy next to him. "This here is Richard. He was out last night at midnight and caught four nice ones off the pier."

She nodded. "Good luck then. Have fun."

"You should join us," he offered.

"Gotta be at work early, Tommy." She waved as she walked on. He was nice enough as neighbors went, but she had no desire to hang out with him.

When she got to the end of the pier, she turned around, looking back down its length, seeing the guys now at the other end, standing under the light. She shoved her hands into the pockets of her shorts and watched them for a moment, then crossed the road and headed to the rundown RV park that she called home. A dog barked at her in the darkness—the little yappy mutt that barked at anything that moved. She tuned it out as she climbed the steps to her rig. She slammed the door, then locked it.

She plopped down on the tiny sofa and took up the remote, flipping it over in her hand a time or two before turning the TV on. There wasn't anything that she watched on a regular basis and she flipped through channels, landing on an old *Friends* episode. With a sigh, she leaned back, planning to kill an hour or two with the gang.

CHAPTER SEVEN

Harley parked at the office. As she walked up, she again noticed the flowers, the greenery, the assorted shrubs and plants that lined not only the cottages, but the office as well. The sight was welcoming and the beauty of it made her smile. The office door was locked, however. She held her face to the window, seeing the inside dark and empty. She took her phone from her pocket, looking at the time. Seven-twelve. Instead of driving, she walked the winding road among the cottages, seeing no activity indicating that anyone was stirring this early. Most of the parking spots appeared to be occupied, though. It was a Wednesday in July and the place appeared to be booked solid. She wondered how much one of the cottages cost for a night. One-fifty? More?

As she approached the clubhouse, she heard a splash in the pool as if someone had jumped in. Instead of going to the front, she walked to the back, pausing at the gate. A dark-haired woman was in the pool, swimming laps with a lithe grace that barely rippled the surface. Harley pushed the gate open, walking around the spa, listening as the water cascaded over stones before landing in the pool. Pots stuffed with flowers were set among the rocks as they stair-stepped down toward the pool.

A gasp from the water made her look that way, and Lauren Voss held a hand to her chest.

"You scared the crap out of me!"

"Sorry." She raised her eyebrows. "Is this a ritual?"

"It is."

"Same time every morning?"

"Yes."

Harley shook her head. "You're too easy a target, Lauren."

"I'm not convinced I'm the target. If there even is one. Maybe it was a prank."

"Don't think it was a prank." She moved closer, staring at the body under the water, oddly disappointed that Lauren Voss was not wearing a bikini. "The message was written in blood."

"Are you sure?"

"Well, haven't gotten official lab results back yet. We have to send everything over to Corpus. They said they'd try to have me something before noon."

"Do you always wear sunglasses?" she asked unexpectedly.

Harley pushed them on top of her head. "Habit."

"You're one of those people who wear them indoors, aren't you?"

Harley smiled. "Is that a pet peeve of yours?"

"Yeah. That and obnoxious Hawaiian shirts."

Harley laughed outright, taking a quick peek at her shirt. She'd simply grabbed one off a hanger that morning, not bothering to look at it. She wore the same thing every day— khaki slacks, white Asics sneakers, one of her thirty or so Hawaiian shirts...and yes, the dark Ray-Ban sunglasses.

"This one is kinda tame today, isn't it?"

Lauren walked up the steps of the pool, and Harley's gaze was on the water droplets that streaked down her body. She finger-combed her long hair, then twisted the ends, wringing out some of the water. The black suit—a Speedo—was then quickly covered by a towel that Lauren wrapped around her slim waist. Another towel was used to tousle dry her hair.

"Did you come by for a reason?"

"Following up. Seeing how you made the night. Making sure there wasn't another incident." All true, of course. The fact that it was seven in the morning wasn't lost on her. Or on Lauren, apparently.

"Kinda early."

"You did tell me that you were in the office by seven or seven thirty," she countered. "Thought I'd swing by before going in. If everything is fine, then, I guess I'll be on my way."

Lauren met her gaze. "Everything appears to be fine."

Harley tilted her head slightly. "You don't like me, do you?" If Lauren was surprised by the question, she didn't show it.

"I haven't decided."

"Fair enough." She took a step away. "Sorry to have interrupted your swim." She paused before leaving. "I'll let you know if the lab results are anything significant."

Lauren nodded. "Thank you for checking on me this morning, Detective Shepherd."

At that, Harley smiled. "It was my pleasure, Ms. Voss."

* * *

After the detective left, Lauren hurried back to her cottage to change. Had she been rude to the detective? Perhaps a little. She'd simply been shocked to find her there at that hour of the morning. Truth was, she'd had a fitful night and didn't sleep well in the least. Every little noise had her wide awake and listening. So much so that at one point, she got up and opened her laptop, looking for an empty cottage. Number Six was available. But the prospect of walking the grounds in the middle of the night was too daunting and she'd closed the laptop and crawled back into her own bed.

It was a relief when daylight chased the night away. Three cups of coffee hadn't helped her mood, apparently. When—if—she spoke to Detective Shepherd again, she owed her an apology. After all, Harley had no obligation to stop by and check on her. None at all.

And she assumed that the break-in and vandalism would be forgotten all too soon anyway. There were obviously no suspects. Maybe she would take Harley's advice and get a security camera. One at the office and one at the clubhouse. Not at the pool, no. If she were a guest frolicking in the water, she wouldn't want a camera trained on her.

She opened a drawer, sorting through the multitudes of T-shirts, all bearing the Heron Bay Resort logo. She chose a blue one this morning and slipped it on. Flip-flops instead of the usual Teva sandals she wore. Her hair was still damp from her swim and she brushed it with her fingers before grabbing her phone and keys.

As she walked back, something white caught her eye in the flowerbed by the clubhouse. As she got closer, she saw that it was a gull. One of the large laughing gulls that patrolled the bay. She stopped, staring at its limp body. It was caught in fishing line, it looked like. She was about to reach for it, then stopped. It wasn't actually caught in line. The line was wrapped around its feet. Tightly. The line was then tied to a limb on the red crepe myrtle tree.

She backed up slowly, then looked around in all directions, feeling that someone was watching her. She clutched her phone tightly as she hurried on toward the office, thankful she'd added Detective Shepherd's number to her contacts last night.

"Miss me already?"

"There's…there's something here," she stammered. "I mean, I'm not sure it's related to the break-in or not, but—"

"Where are you?"

"Walking to the office."

"Okay. Go inside. Lock the door. I'll be right there."

"It's probably nothing. I mean—"

"I'll be right there. You're saving me from having to go explain to Big Al that I'm closing the case on his bait shop burglary."

The call ended and she slipped the phone back into her shorts pocket. Her hand was shaking slightly as she unlocked the door. She did as instructed—closing the door behind her and locking it.

Only then did she take a calming breath. Had she overreacted? The gull could have gotten tangled in fishing line. It happened all too frequently. But no. It appeared staged, didn't it? Someone tied the gull there intentionally.

Had someone *killed* the gull intentionally? She shook her head. No. It could have gotten tangled and then in trying to escape, it got wrapped in the tree. That's probably what happened.

That's what she hoped had happened. She ran a hand through her hair, then turned, gasping as a man peered at her from outside the door. She relaxed a bit when she recognized him as Fredrick Stenson. Only slightly, though. Mr. Stenson, as she'd told Nana, was a little on the creepy side. Since March, he'd been coming every two weeks, like clockwork, staying two nights each time. He rarely spoke more than polite babble as he checked in.

She opened the door now, eyebrows raised. "Good morning, Mr. Stenson. Can I help you with something?"

He shifted nervously, his gaze darting about, never looking directly at her, as was his custom. "Is it possible to extend my stay by a day?" he asked in his thin voice.

"I'll need to check our reservations." She was about to invite him inside, then thought better of it. Not that she was afraid of him. He was a small, slight man with thinning hair and black-framed glasses. If it came to a fight, she was fairly certain she could take him. But still, she was wary. "I don't have the system up and running yet. How about I call you once I check?"

He nodded and backed away. "Yes. Thank you."

With that, he turned and hurried back to his cottage, his head hung down. She blew out a relieved breath. There was something about the man that nagged at her. He was timid. Almost too timid. She could envision him as a child, locked in his mother's basement, only allowed out for church or something. That is, until he killed his mother and chopped up her body and stored it in the freezer. She sighed, wondering where that thought had come from.

CHAPTER EIGHT

Harley stood at the door, meeting Lauren's gaze through the glass. Lauren gave her a small, sheepish smile. She went inside, eyebrows raised.

"I think I probably overreacted."

"You did? Excuse to see me again?"

Lauren flicked her eyes to the ceiling. "Yeah, right. I just can't get enough of you and your shirts."

She smiled quickly, then moved her sunglasses from the top of her head back to her face. "There. All the things you hate." She motioned for Lauren to get up. "How about you show me what had you shook up. I'll decide if you overreacted or not."

Lauren led her back along the driveway. A few people were out and about. A man was loading luggage into the trunk of a car. A woman was walking two dogs and their leashes got tangled as the dogs barked at them.

"Good morning, Mrs. Franco."

"Lauren, good morning." The woman jerked on the leashes as she moved past them. "Hush now, boys."

"You allow pets?"

"Yes. One of the few places that do. We charge extra, but people don't mind paying."

They appeared to be heading to the clubhouse. "Do you have a pet?"

"I—" Lauren then shook her head. "No, I don't."

Harley, being the good detective that she was, noticed the hesitation. The polite thing to do would be to accept her statement and move on. But...

"You used to?" she guessed. She heard Lauren sigh.

"My...my ex kept the dog." She glanced at her quickly. "A black lab named Otter."

"Ah. That's a cute name."

Lauren smiled at that. "Yes. He was definitely a water dog. Couldn't keep him out of it." Her smile disappeared. "And yes, I miss him."

"Why did she get custody and not you?"

Lauren stopped walking. "I don't really want to talk about it." She pointed to a flowering tree. "There. The gull."

Harley shoved her sunglasses back on top of her head, stepping into the flowerbed to inspect the gull. Its feet were tied—fishing line—and it was attached to a limb. She turned the gull, seeing a spot of dried blood on its breast.

"I think it probably just got tangled and got trapped here," Lauren said. "Like I said, I overreacted."

"It's been shot."

"*What?*"

Harley stayed where she was, not wanting to disturb the ground any further. She looked down at her feet, wondering if she was stepping on evidence—another footprint perhaps? She lifted one foot but there was nothing there but the bulky mulch. She stepped out of the flowerbed, glancing among the flowers, but there was nothing disturbed. She took her phone out, snapping a couple of pictures of the bird and the tree.

"Did you call about that security camera yet?"

"No. But I will."

"Good."

"It was shot?"

"Appears so. Blood droplet on its breast. Had to be something small. Pellet gun, maybe. Anything bigger would have caused more damage."

"Oh god," Lauren murmured as she ran both hands through her hair. "What the hell is happening?"

Harley studied her. "Have you had any weird phone calls? Hang ups? Receive anything threatening in the mail?"

Lauren shook her head. "Not that I can think of. I'll ask Jessica. She works in the office Saturday and Sunday, but I think she would have told me if someone was calling and hanging up."

"Who is Jessica?"

"High school student. Was. She graduated in May. She's worked for us three years."

"Well, without calling all your guests again and asking if they saw anyone walking around with a dead gull, we'll assume it was left during the night." She looked at her pointedly. "Surveillance camera."

"Yes. I'll call this morning."

"Tell them it's urgent."

"I will." Lauren pointed at the gull. "What are you going to do with that?"

"Gonna take it to the lab, see if they can recover the pellet. Might help us."

Lauren crossed her arms across her chest. "Thank you for coming over. I was a little rude to you earlier. I'm sorry."

She shrugged. "When you don't like someone, it's hard to be nice to them. No need to apologize." She slipped her sunglasses back on, then started walking toward the office. "Need to get something to put him in."

Lauren walked beside her. "I never said I didn't like you."

"You never said you did."

"I said I hadn't decided."

Harley glanced at her as they walked. "I can tell that you don't. Why is that?"

Lauren sighed. "You remind me of my ex."

Harley smiled at her. "Oh? So she was cute and charming too?"

Lauren laughed. "The fact that you both *think* you're cute and charming is enough to label you twins."

"So your ex is in San Diego—happily married, I believe you said—and she stole your dog. I'm assuming your breakup wasn't amicable. I'll also assume that she broke your heart." She stopped beside her vehicle. "I've never broken anyone's heart. Never had a dog. Never been to San Diego. Never been married." She shrugged. "So really, all we have in common is we're charming." She winked. "And cute."

Laruen shook her head as she walked away. "Goodbye, Detective. Thank you again for coming by."

As Lauren went toward the office, Harley called after her. "Don't forget the security cameras."

CHAPTER NINE

Two days later, Lauren stood by, watching as a camera was mounted below the eave of the office. She'd settled on three wireless cameras. One at the entrance. One at the office. Another at the clubhouse. They were small and not conspicuous in the least. After much debate with herself, she'd decided to go all in with the plan, getting not only a hub that would sit in the office, but also cloud storage and an app on her phone where she could view the camera feeds at will. The debate had been whether she actually wanted to be able to see it at will. She had a vision of herself sitting in bed at night, phone clutched tightly as she watched the comings and goings on the camera feeds.

Then again, since the incident with the gull, there had been nothing out of the ordinary to happen. She'd not spoken with Detective Shepherd either. She'd received a text yesterday saying that the message on the mirror had indeed been written in human blood. She'd added that there was no DNA match to anything. Lauren assumed that would be the extent of it. Without any other happenings and no witnesses to the vandalism or the gull, she didn't imagine there was much of a case for the detective to work. And as such, she doubted she would see Detective Shepherd again.

Which was just as well. She'd spent the last three years trying to forget Leah, forget that time in her life. She certainly didn't need any reminders of that by having Harley Shepherd parading around in her Hawaiian shirts and dark sunglasses, her smiling face and stylish hair. No. If she never saw her again, it would be all the better.

Instead of going back into the office, she walked the winding road through the cottages to the small building that was laundry room, supply closet, and maintenance shed all in one. Even though Gerald was on site today, she felt like watering. She took out the long hose and hauled it over to the pool area. She attached it to a faucet, then proceeded to drench the flowers and plants along the spa, moving aimlessly toward the beds with the bougainvillea.

Peaceful and therapeutic. The yard crew was here today, and even the sounds of the mowers faded to the background as she moved among the flowers and lush greenery of the pool gardens. There was no one in the pool this early, and she watched as a tiny green lizard scurried from a bush, racing across the stone wall separating the spa from the pool. It slipped onto the overflow basin, nearly getting caught in the current, which would have sent it cascading over the side, riding the waves as it dumped into the pool. But no. As if he had done this before, he fought against the flow, making it easily to the other side and up again on the stone ledge. She watched until it disappeared into the leaves of the variegated hostas that grew along the spa.

Her phone rang, disturbing the peace, and she turned the nozzle off before pulling it from her pocket. It was a forwarded call from the office phone, so she answered appropriately.

"Heron Bay Resort, how may I help you?"

"Hello, Ms. Voss. How are you today?"

The sound of his voice always made her cringe. "Mr. Hallstead," she said curtly.

"I'm making my monthly call. Have you and your grandmother discussed selling?"

"As I've told you for the last year, the resort is *not* for sale."

"I thought maybe you may have had a change of mind. I heard you've had some trouble out there lately."

"Trouble?"

"A break-in of some sort."

She couldn't imagine where he would have heard it, other than from the police report in the weekly paper. Even then, it was listed as vandalism, not a break-in.

"Where did you hear that?"

"I have my sources. So? Ready to sell?"

"Mr. Hallstead, please stop calling. It's rather annoying." She disconnected without further conversation, allowing herself a growl as she turned the nozzle on again.

The man was a pain in the ass. Yes, he called nearly every month, offering to buy the resort. He was a large, portly man, loud and intimidating in person. Fortunately, he didn't come around that often. The first she'd heard of him, her grandfather had still been alive. Then he came around again after her grandfather had died. Nana had made the mistake of telling him she'd think about it. Ever since then, he'd been badgering them to sell. So much so that she'd threatened to call the police one time when he showed up in person—a lawyer at his side—with papers ready for them to sign. He had refused to leave, parking his ample butt in one of the rockers on the porch.

"Pompous ass," she muttered.

She didn't know much about him, other than he owned several car dealerships in the Houston area. Apparently, he didn't know what to do with his excess money and thought owning a resort would be fun.

"Jerk."

"Who are you talking to?"

The words whispered near her ear made her gasp and she spun around, spraying water all over a blue and white Hawaiian shirt.

Harley held her hands up in a sign of surrender, but Lauren had already drenched her. She turned the water off quickly, trying to keep the smile off her face.

"I'm so sorry," she managed as she let the hose fall to the ground. She couldn't hide her smile, however. Water droplets clung to the familiar dark sunglasses. The entire front of the shirt was wet and even Harley's slacks hadn't been spared. "Oh my god, that's too funny."

Harley slowly took her sunglasses off, but the eyes hiding behind them weren't angry in the least. They were twinkling, in fact.

"So that was kinda fun." Harley pulled at the wet shirt that was clinging to her skin.

"I'm really sorry. You startled me."

"Obviously. Good thing you weren't chopping weeds. You may have hacked me to death."

Lauren laughed at that. "Yes. Beware." She motioned toward the pool. "I'll get you a towel."

"Or two," Harley called after her.

She opened the glass door to the back room, grabbing two towels from the pool rack. Harley was standing out in the sunshine now, arms held out to her sides. Her gun and holster, which was normally hidden under the loose-fitting shirt, was visible now.

"Here you go."

Harley handed her sunglasses to Lauren as she toweled her hair dry. "So, who were you calling a jerk?"

"Oh, this guy who keeps calling, wanting to buy the resort."

Harley lowered the towel. "Someone I should be concerned with?"

Lauren shook her head. "He lives in Houston. Has too much money, I suppose."

"What's his name?"

"Detective Shepherd, he's someone who's been bugging us for years. Other than he's annoying—especially in person—he's harmless. What are you doing here, anyway?"

Harley used her fingers to comb her wet hair, then patted her shirt with the towel. "I'm headed across the bay, over to Lamar. Thought I'd pop in and check on you. Wanted to see if you'd gotten cameras installed, but I saw them working on one at the office."

"Got three of them, yes. What's going on in Lamar?"

"Good." She wiped her hair again. "Nothing's going on. I live there."

"On Lamar?" she asked before she could stop herself. She really didn't want to know.

"Yeah. Nothing fancy. I live in a little travel trailer in an older RV park that caters mostly to fishermen."

"On the bay?"

"Yeah."

She nodded. "I can see that, I guess. Although I would have pictured you for some beach cottage or something."

"I can't afford a beach cottage, and, well, when I moved here, I wasn't sure I was going to stay."

She was curious as to why, but she reminded herself that she didn't care. She reminded herself that she didn't like Detective Shepherd. So she gave her an uninterested look, hoping she'd take the hint and leave already.

"Anyway, since I haven't heard from you, I assume things have been quiet here."

She nodded. "Yes. No other incidents. Maybe it was a prank after all."

Harley took the sunglasses from her and put them on. "Human blood on the mirror. Hell of a prank, if it was." She gave her a quick nod. "See ya around, Ms. Voss."

Lauren stared after her, watching as she went through the gate and back to the driveway, walking quickly toward the office. With a sigh, she wondered at their exchange. She'd sprayed Harley with water, had laughed at her. Harley hadn't seemed upset in the least. In fact, she'd been more amused than anything. Yet, it changed, didn't it? Her fault. She'd reverted to formality between them. It was safer. It kept things in a strictly professional state, which is how she wanted it to remain.

With that, she picked up the water hose and resumed her task, pushing thoughts of Harley Shepherd from her mind. Well, she tried to, at least. She kept picturing the scene of her spraying water all over the Hawaiian shirt. She smiled as she pulled the hose along with her, giving the bougainvillea a drink.

CHAPTER TEN

She tipped her beer bottle against Brian's—Chief Carrington—before taking a swallow. He returned her smile.

"Got a call from Al Norris today."

"Big Al? What? Complaining about me?"

"Yeah." Brian took a shrimp from his basket and popped it in his mouth. "I missed this last week."

"Me too."

Brian was her Tuesday night dinner date at the Shrimp Shack. When he could make it, that is. He'd been her sergeant when she'd first started on the force in San Antonio. She'd been under his command the entire eleven years there, ending with him a captain and she a detective. After…well, after the thing with Travis…it affected him as much as her. Brian had grown up here in Aransas County. So had his wife. When he learned that Chief Roselle was going to retire, a man he had once worked for, he reached out to both Roselle and the mayor, putting his name in the hat to replace him. Harley hadn't considered a move at the time. Well, she *had* considered a move. Quit the force. She'd taken a leave—her head wasn't in the right place to work. Brian had taken her out for drinks one night, telling her of his plan. He offered to bring her along if he got the job.

"So you told him to quit wasting your time?"

"I did."

"Harley—"

"He's had five break-ins at the bait shop since we've been here. Five! Who the hell breaks into a bait shop? Yeah, I told him to get a damn security camera."

"What do they take? Cash?"

"No. There's no cash. He says they take bait. Whatever he's got in the freezer. Not the cooler and not the holding tanks."

"All of it?"

"No. That's just it. Not all of it. Some. A little. Or a lot. He always guesses at the pounds. And it's never the live shrimp or fish. Always the frozen."

"Seems logical."

She smirked. "Who steals bait?"

"So what are you thinking?"

"Drugs."

His eyebrows popped up. "What?"

"He's got two guys working for him. He buys a lot of his stuff from a bait boat. So maybe they're moving drugs. Get one of the guys who works for him to hide it in the bait."

"Then after hours, break in and take the drugs?"

"Yeah."

"Seems a little risky. First off, Big Al might find the drugs before they can pick them up. And if you're bringing drugs into the marina on a boat, why not offload them right there. Why have a middleman?"

"Because, as you know, we do patrol the marina. But, as a cop, are you going to go poking around in smelly shrimp and fish?" She bit into a piece of fried fish. "So your guys go out early for bait fishing. They hook up with another boat and get the drugs, bring them back to the marina. Off-load them with the bait. I'm only guessing, Chief. If it is drugs, it's small potatoes. Maybe marijuana that they sell locally."

"You don't think it really could be bait they're after?"

"Between the Rockport marina and the Fulton marina, there are six bait shops. I've been here a year. Al's is the only one who's had a break-in. And five times now."

He nodded. "Okay. I'll go with your gut. What do you want to do?"

She grinned. "Stakeout."

"Every night?"

She shook her head. "Every break-in has been on a Thursday night."

"They're not too smart, huh?"

"And I suppose if he actually gets a security camera, then the game is over."

"Judging by his tone today, he doesn't want a camera. He wants us to catch the little bastards and throw their asses in the bay. His words." Brian ate his last shrimp. "He's also not keen on you working his case any longer. Says you're obnoxious."

She laughed. "Damn. I've been called that a lot lately. Although when Ms. Voss said it, I think it was in reference to my shirts."

"Who is Ms. Voss?"

"Heron Bay Resort. Remember the message in blood."

"Oh, yeah. And a dead gull. Whatever came of that?"

"Nothing."

"No leads? No suspects?"

"None. And nothing else has happened. Been over a week since the gull. She seems to think it was a prank."

"What do you think?"

"Not a prank, no. It was too violent. Cushions slashed with a knife. Picture frames broken, prints cut up. And, of course, the message in blood."

"What was the message again?"

"'Have you missed me? It's your turn to die.'" she quoted. "I take it to mean he's killed others before."

"You think the message was meant for her?"

"Hard to know. I assume it was. Or it could be meant for someone who works there and who was likely to see it first. I interviewed the ladies on the cleaning crews and the one guy who works there. Just like Ms. Voss, none have had threats, none have enemies, none think they're a target."

"So dead end?"

"Pretty much. She did mention that some guy's been calling for a while, wanting to buy the place. Could be he's tired of asking and is trying to force her hand. Scare her to sell."

"You check it out?"

"She wouldn't give me his name. Said he was a rich dude in Houston but was harmless." She pushed her empty basket away and picked up her beer. "I haven't seen her since last week. I may swing by there tomorrow, see if anything's going on. Maybe she'll give up his name."

Brian smiled. "That's admirable of you."

She returned his smile. "To protect and to serve."

He laughed. "I take it she's better to look at than Big Al."

"She is. Only, like I said, she thinks I'm obnoxious. My shirts haven't grown on her yet."

He met her gaze, both of their smiles fading a little. "I think they're swell."

She put her beer bottle down. "I miss him."

He nodded. "Me too, Harley. Me too." He picked up his beer bottle again. "Marsha said I was to invite you over for burgers on Saturday. You up for it?"

Brian and Marsha were some twenty years older than she was, but they'd been friends so long, she didn't even notice the age gap. Marsha had been the one to drag her out of her funk after Travis died. She'd come over uninvited one weekend, clothes bag in hand. Said she wasn't leaving until Harley "snapped out of it" and "quit acting like the victim." Despite her protests, Marsha had stayed five nights with her. And yeah, she'd pulled her out of her stupor.

"I'd love to. I'll swing by the deli at HEB and pick up some potato salad."

"Great. She'll be happy to see you. Complains you don't come around enough anymore."

"I keep telling her to get a bike and ride with me."

He laughed. "Can you see Marsha on a bike?

CHAPTER ELEVEN

Harley rolled over, trying to find her phone on the tiny ledge beside her bed. She pulled it to her face.

"Detective Shepherd," she answered.

"Yeah, Harley. It's Ramirez. Commander said to call you. Got a body in the water."

She opened her eyes. "What time is it?"

"Four-something."

She sat up and rubbed her face. "Who the hell found a body at four in the morning?"

"Fishermen. Who else?"

"Okay. Where are you?"

"It's a private pier. Heron Bay Resort. It's down—"

"I know where it is," she said quickly. "Is it…is it a male or female?" She realized she was holding her breath, waiting for his answer.

"Guessing male, by the looks of it. It's still in the water."

"Guessing?"

He paused. "The head is missing."

"Jesus Christ. I'll be right there."

She flipped on the light, torn between wanting to hurry—which meant slipping on shorts and a T-shirt—and dressing appropriately. She splashed water on her face and took the time to brush her teeth. Her hair was a sleepy mess and she wetted it too, toweling it dry quickly. She pulled on jeans—she'd done laundry yesterday and hadn't ironed any of her slacks. She took a sports bra from the drawer and, without looking, grabbed a shirt and slipped it on as she went. She slammed the door on her trailer ten minutes after Ramirez's call.

From her RV to Heron Bay, it was only three miles. She stayed on Highway 35, breaking the posted fifty-five-miles-per-hour speed limit. She turned on Fulton Bay Road and drove toward the bay. She saw the flashing lights from the police cruisers several blocks before she got there.

"Harley, over here."

"Baker? What are you doing here? I thought you were on days."

"My day off, but I filled in for Striker last night."

She walked past him. "Who found it? Someone staying at the cottages?"

"Yeah. Two guys. Kinda shook up. One of them hooked him with their line." He laughed. "Thought he'd caught a whale or something." She glanced at him sharply and his smile disappeared. "Sorry. Not funny."

Like nearly all the piers here in the bay, this one had been rebuilt after Harvey came ashore and shattered the old ones like they were nothing but matchsticks. The lights weren't bright. They were a soft green, lining the pier all the way out to the fishing deck at the end. Her footsteps were silent on the boards and the wind off the bay was breezier than normal. She glanced up, seeing clouds blowing past, hiding the stars. Rain coming?

"He's down at the end there," Baker said from behind her.

"Where are the fishermen?"

"Wallace took their statement, then sent them back to the cottages. Told them you'd probably want to interview them later. He's got all their information."

Ramirez flashed his light at her, then pointed it into the water. She followed its beam, seeing a body floating. The waves were slamming it against one of the pylons.

"So it's anchored to something? Tied?"

"Probably anchored. The guy who snagged him said he had casted out this way." Ramirez pointed to the end of the deck. "Said he felt the pull when he was at the corner. Thought he'd hooked a monster, he said. His buddy was going to help him land it, had a flashlight—"

"And they freaked out," she finished for him.

"Yeah. So much so, the guy dropped his rod into the bay."

"Okay then. You call a dive team in?"

"The boat's coming from Port A. Said they'd try to be here by daylight."

She peered over the side of the railing. "In the meantime, the body is being beat to hell." She looked at Baker, then Ramirez. "You want to try to pull him up?"

"Oh, hell no," Baker said. "I'm not looking to get into the bay in the dark."

"What? It's only five or six foot deep here, right? Seven tops."

"You don't know for sure. They may have dredged out deeper when they built the pier. You can't get in the water, Harley."

"Is it high tide?" She knew Ramirez fished. "You keep up?"

"I have an app," he said. He flipped through his phone, then tapped on an app. "High tide is at four-fifty-six."

"Then let's get him out."

Yeah, probably not the smartest thing she'd ever considered doing. But still. She took off her holster and handed it to Baker. Then pulled her phone from her pocket. "Here." She paused, finding the leather wallet in her back pocket. "And here."

"You're crazy."

"Whatever evidence is on him is getting washed away by the minute. He'll be under water by high tide." She went to the ladder on the fishing deck. "Ramirez, follow me down."

"Yes, ma'am," he said without much enthusiasm.

The water was surprisingly cold. She used the board ladder to hold on to, not trusting the depth enough to jump in. She never touched bottom, though, even as she hung onto the last rung. She could feel the tug of the current as the waves came in. She grabbed hold of a pylon, then swam toward the body. Her foot caught on something and she nearly went under.

"What is it?"

"Not sure." She held onto the side of the pier, then moved her foot back and forth, catching it again. "A rope, I think. Maybe it's the anchor. Shine your light on him."

The headless body bobbed just below the surface now, the flesh at the neck jagged and torn. Small fish were feeding on him and she splashed water, scattering them. She moved closer, grabbing his arm, pulling him to her. She fought against the current, going back to the ladder. She held his arm up to Ramirez.

"Come down the ladder. Hold him. I'm going to see if I can find where he's tied."

"Oh, man," Ramirez mumbled.

She ran her hands across his torso, then his legs. At his ankle, she found it. It was a thick rope, and she tugged on it, feeling the weight on the other end. With both hands, she pulled, taking up the slack in the rope as the weight slid along the bottom of the bay. It was too heavy to lift, and she let it be.

"Can you untie him?"

"I could, but then we'll lose the evidence of the rope, the knot," she said. "Let's see if we've got enough slack in the rope to get him up on the pier." She looked up. "Baker, come help."

As she pushed the body from the water, Baker and Ramirez tugged from the ladder. Dead weight was dead weight, but this man was well over two hundred pounds. It was a struggle to get him up. Thankfully, the guys had the torso, not her. She didn't fancy looking at a neck where a head had once been.

"He's slipping!" Baker called.

"Don't you dare drop him on me!"

She had his legs between her and the ladder, holding him there as they pulled. Little by little, the body inched up the ladder, with them pulling and her pushing. At last, they tugged him away from the side and she climbed the ladder halfway, taking the rope and pulling on it.

"Help me," she said to Baker. He lay on his stomach, taking the rope from her. She grabbed it below his hands. "On three."

They hoisted the anchor out of the water. It was an oversized cinder block—the rope tied between both openings. They put it up on the pier beside the body.

"Ain't no laymen's knots," Ramirez said as she climbed the ladder back up. "This is a buntline hitch on his ankle. And the cinder block has a perfectly tied anchor hitch."

"So our killer is a fisherman or a boater?"

"Could be."

"Should I cancel the dive team?" Baker asked.

"No. Let them go in the water. Maybe they'll find something. You call Corpus already? They going to send an ME?"

"Yeah, I called it in."

"Okay. Secure the pier. Put up tape. Once it's daylight, we can see if there's anything here. He was probably dumped from a boat, though." She held her hand out. "Where's my stuff?"

"Over there," he pointed with his flashlight to the bench on the fishing deck. "Where are you going?"

"To steal some towels from the pool room. And to wake Ms. Voss."

CHAPTER TWELVE

Lauren had always been an early riser, even when she was a young girl. Her mother said it was because she was afraid she'd miss out on something. What her mother didn't know was that she got up early to join her father out on the back porch. He would let her have a little coffee, diluted with milk, and sit with him. She smiled at the memory. Actually, it was mostly milk with a splash of coffee. They would sit there, side by side, rarely talking. Him sipping his coffee and she holding a matching cup, sipping her milk. When the sky began to lighten, he'd nudge her up. "Don't want to be late for school."

She still enjoyed the early mornings, only she didn't sit out as much anymore. She'd watch the day come alive behind the screen on her laptop. She did a lot of her busy work then, uninterrupted by the phone and guests. Occasionally, she'd take her coffee out to the small back porch, but there was no view. The privacy fence her grandparents had erected circled the entire cottage, save for the walkway in front, and even that was guarded by a gate. No, there was no view. But she was a stone's throw from the bay, and she could hear the water, smell the salty air, see gulls and pelicans as they flew over. She occasionally walked over to the pier, enjoying a sunrise from time to time. Not often enough, she knew. One of the first things she'd told herself she'd do was replace the privacy fence to allow her a view of the bay. So far, that hadn't risen to the top of the list.

She put her coffee cup down and glanced at the clock on the microwave. A few minutes until five. She had time for another cup. Dawn came early in the summer. By six thirty, it was light enough for a bike ride, something she did all too infrequently these days. Getting a few laps in the pool was easier and that was what she stuck to most days.

She was watching as the Keurig dripped coffee into her cup when a knock on her door startled her. She looked across the bar, staring at the door as if she could see through it. Who in the world was knocking at this hour of the morning?

She moved toward it, then stopped. What if—? The knock was louder this time.

"Ms. Voss? It's me. Detective Shepherd." Another knock. "You up?"

She felt relief at the familiar voice. She paused again, though, running a hand through her hair. Bed head, no doubt. She wore a T-shirt, no bra. Cotton shorts. No shoes.

"Lauren?" The voice sounded concerned now. Obviously, the detective could tell there were lights on.

She opened the door then, about to ask what the hell she was doing there at five in the morning. The words never formed as she stared at her. She was soaking wet, head to toe. In her hand were a couple of white towels, the Heron Bay logo visible under the porch light.

"What in the hell happened to you?"

"Went swimming."

"In my pool?"

"In the bay. May I come in?"

"Yes, of course." She stepped aside. "Did you fall off a boat or what?"

Harley took her shoes off, leaving them by the door. Her socks squished as she walked and she stopped, taking them off as well. She has nice feet, Lauren thought absently, then shook that away.

"Would you like some dry clothes?"

"Oh, that would be great. Got any Hawaiian shirts?"

Lauren headed to her bedroom. "Sorry. I'll try to find my brightest, gaudiest T-shirt, though."

As she rummaged in her drawer—where was that ugly tie-dye shirt?—she wondered what Harley was doing there. And soaking wet, no less. They were about the same size—the detective perhaps an inch taller. She supposed her shorts would fit her. Instead of the hiking shorts, though, she grabbed a pair of the cotton ones that she normally wore around the house. She spotted the tie-dye, a shirt she'd purchased on a whim and had worn only once.

Harley was still standing by the door. Standing on the towels instead of dripping on the floor. Their eyes met and Lauren smiled at the sight of her. She was a wet mess, her hair tousled, and she looked about as attractive as anyone Lauren had seen before. That thought wiped the smile from her face in an instant. *What the hell?*

"The half-bath is there." She pointed to a door off the kitchen, then handed over the clothes. "I can put yours in the dryer, if you want."

"I don't think I'll be here long enough for them to dry. If you've got a trash bag or something, I'll put them in there."

"Yes. Okay." Again, she wondered why she was there. "You want coffee?" she called to the bathroom door.

"Please."

She started another cup, then got a trash bag out from under the sink. She glanced up when the door opened, another smile lighting her face.

"God, that shirt is awful."

Harley laughed. "I like it."

"You would." She handed her the plastic bag. "Sugar in your coffee or black?"

"Sugar. Just a little."

Lauren liked brown sugar in her coffee. She scooped out a teaspoon full, then wondered if that was too much.

"That's great," Harley said from behind her. "Thanks. I was freezing."

They both leaned against the counter, a few feet apart, sipping their coffee. Harley set hers down, then took a deep breath.

"So, a couple of your guests were out fishing this morning. Caught something."

She raised her eyebrows but said nothing.

"A body. A man."

She put her cup down too. "Oh, no. Someone drowned? Not one of our guests, surely."

"Don't know if it's a guest or not. Not drowned, though. Don't have a cause of death."

Harley's phone rang and Lauren's head was reeling. Was it one of their guests? Had they fallen off the pier? Even so, the water wasn't that deep. Well, down by the fishing deck it was. They'd dredged out a couple of deep spots so guests could anchor a boat.

"I'm over here filling Ms. Voss in." A pause. "They can look, but I'm guessing we won't find the head. If the killer wanted us to find the head, he would have left it on the damn body."

Lauren's eyes widened. *What?*

"No, I haven't called him yet. I will as soon as I leave here." Harley met her gaze. "Ten minutes."

When she put her phone down, Lauren grabbed her arm. "What is going on?"

"The body was decapitated."

"Oh dear god," she murmured. She released her hold on Harley, steadying herself by holding onto the countertop instead. "Where was he found?"

"Right off your pier, by the fishing deck. He'd been anchored in place with a large cinder block."

"Oh dear god," she said again. "Do you...do you think it's related to...to the message on the mirror?"

"There's no way to be sure, Lauren. We can assume, but really, it could be that whoever dumped him out there picked your pier randomly."

"Do you really believe that?"

A quick shake of her head. "No. I'm not a big believer in coincidence." She picked up her coffee cup again. "Your gate was unlocked, by the way."

"I don't lock it, no. A lot of the regular guests know I live back here. If they need something after the office closes, they come here." She rubbed her temples. "You don't think the man was one of our guests, do you?" *God, she hoped not.*

"I really don't know. He hadn't been in the water long. We'll run prints, of course, but..."

She nodded. Unless he was in the system, fingerprints would do them no good. And without a head...how would they identify him? She turned away from Harley and squeezed her eyes shut for a moment. A decapitated body found at her pier. Was it a coincidence? No. For one thing, murder was rare in Rockport. Dumping headless bodies even rarer. *God, please don't let it be one of their guests.*

"Are you okay?"

She opened her eyes again. "I'm scared. I think."

"Let's don't jump to conclusions. Once we know who he is, then we can determine a motive."

"And if there is none?"

Harley gave her a reassuring smile. As reassuring as someone wearing a tie-dye T-shirt can. "Don't panic just yet, Lauren. Let me do some digging first. And lock your gate from now on."

"Yes. Okay."

"Thanks for the coffee. And the clothes. I'll return them later."

"Keep the shirt. I never wear it."

"Oh yeah? Great! Thank you. I love it."

She smiled at that, following Harley to the front door where her bag of wet clothes was. She slipped her bare feet into the wet shoes, then picked up the bag.

"Why were you up so early?" Harley asked unexpectedly.

"I'm usually up by four thirty. Five at the latest."

"Why so early?"

She shrugged. "I like the mornings. I do office work."

"Not a night owl, huh?"

"Opposite of a night owl. I'm usually in bed by nine."

"That must cut into your nightlife. Hard to date with those hours, isn't it?"

"Are you fishing for information?"

She smiled. "Well, I am a detective."

"Yes, you are." She gave her a fake smile. "Goodbye, Detective Shepherd."

"Goodbye, Ms. Voss. I'll keep you posted."

"Thank you."

She watched her walk away, in her borrowed shorts and shirt and squishy wet shoes. She had nice legs too. At the gate, Harley turned back around, meeting her gaze for a moment. She closed the gate and Lauren went back inside. She locked the door, then leaned against it.

Was she worried? Scared? She blew out a breath.

"I believe I am," she whispered to the empty house.

CHAPTER THIRTEEN

"You think it's related?"

She paced in front of Commander Lawson's desk. "No way to know for sure, but my gut says it is. There's certainly no evidence to say it's linked."

The commander leaned back in his chair, watching her. "There was a murder the year before you got here. Found a dismembered body stuffed into the truck of car."

She nodded. "Drug deal gone bad. Heard about it."

"We average about one a year, I'd say."

"You think this is it? Drug-related?"

"It makes more sense than thinking some random sicko is targeting this woman for no reason at all. What was her name again?"

"Voss. Lauren Voss. I did a background check on her." She didn't know if it was warranted or not, but Lauren hadn't exactly been forthcoming with information. She'd most likely kill her if she found out. "Nothing stood out. Model citizen. She moved here from San Diego three years ago. I even went back to her time there. She's squeaky clean."

"You mentioned someone wanted to buy her out."

"Yes. But trying to scare her out is one thing. Murder? Don't think so."

"Find his name. Check him out anyway."

"I will. It's been over two weeks since the break-in. I want to go over her guest list for then and now. She said she has a lot of repeat customers."

"Good idea. Now where are we on IDing this guy?"

"No hits on his prints. Hopefully he'll be listed as a missing person. Until then he's John Doe."

"Caucasian?"

"Yes. And he had a wedding ring on."

"Then someone will report him missing."

"The dive team found nothing. The pier was clean. We'll be going over the surveillance cameras at both marinas."

"What about private marinas?"

"The closest one is across Copano Bay. I called them. They only have a camera at the entrance. None where the boats are kept. I'll take a look at that one too." She paused. "He was a big guy, over two hundred pounds—two-twenty-five, probably. The three of us had a hard time getting him out of the water."

"And? You think he had help?"

"Maybe. Even if you're going to just roll him out of the boat, you still have to get him up. I don't think one person could have managed that."

"The boat scenario is still an assumption at this point, but yes, I'll agree with you. Let's concentrate on the surveillance video."

"Will do."

"All right. Keep me up to date. The newspaper wants a statement from the chief today. And a news crew from Corpus wants an interview. We'll give as much of a description of the guy as we have. Maybe someone will come forward with his name." He cocked an eyebrow. "A bit different from San Antonio, huh?"

She nodded. "Small town, yeah. A murder is a big deal. Especially one as gruesome as this. Everyone is talking about it." She was about to leave, then stopped. "You're not going to mention Lauren Voss to the newspaper, right?"

"No, no. That really has no bearing, other than it was their pier." He leaned back in his chair. "You want to partner with someone on this? Or hand one of them off?"

"No. I'm good. If they're related, I'd just as soon have my hand in both of them." She paused, remembering he was the boss, after all. "Unless you think otherwise, of course."

He smiled at that. "I know your credentials, Harley. Even if the chief didn't say you were top dog, your work so far has proven that."

"He said I was top dog?"

"He did. He said you were the worst officer he'd ever had under his command, but absolutely the very best detective."

She laughed, remembering her early days on patrol. Yeah, Brian had written her up a few times. She and Travis, both.

"I have to agree with him," he continued. "There certainly hasn't been much excitement here for you, yet you treat each case with the same enthusiasm."

She shook her head. "Big Al might disagree with you."

"Big Al should take your advice and get a security camera. Forget about him. I'll assign someone else to that. Chief told me your thoughts on that. Drugs?"

She shrugged. "Seems the most logical. Thursday night stake-out was my plan."

He nodded. "I'll put someone else on it. You concentrate on this." He pointed at her. "And Harley, while I've gotten used to your Hawaiian shirts, you might want to lose the tie-dye and shorts, huh?"

She smiled and looked down at the T-shirt she'd yet to take off. "Yeah. Borrowed them after my swim in the bay. I'm heading home now to change."

Lauren had told her to keep the shirt. She would, she decided. Because no, she couldn't picture Lauren Voss wearing something like this. She was a bit too conservative for the splashy colors on it. Each time she'd seen her, she'd been wearing a solid-colored T-shirt advertising the Heron Bay Resort. Navy one day. A lighter blue another. And green that first day. She liked the shirts. The logo was a circle of rainbow colors, the heron was blue. Maybe she'd ask Lauren for one.

* * *

She'd gotten the call while she'd been showering. The voice mail was brief and to the point. Their guy had been identified—by his clothes—as Christopher Bryce of Corpus Christi. Forty-eight-years-old. He'd gone fishing on his night off. When he didn't return at eleven, his wife started calling his phone. At three, she called the police. Her description matched their victim—he'd been wearing jeans and a Corpus Christi Hooks T-shirt. The commander was sending Roscoe over to Corpus to interview the wife.

"Roscoe," she muttered. Roscoe Ventura—an old-timer who barely knew how to use a computer—was past retirement age but gave no inclination that he was ready to call it quits. He got assigned the simplest, mundane cases. Commander Lawson obviously thought interviewing the wife was mundane. Well, at least it saved her a trip to Corpus.

She left Lamar, crossing the causeway, the virtual border between Copano Bay and Aransas Bay. The causeway was some two miles long, and she enjoyed the trip each morning, watching for dolphins among the shrimp boats that cruised the waters.

Instead of going back to the squad room, she continued along the bay. It was hot. Not even noon and already over ninety degrees. She was used to the heat, obviously. San Antonio hit triple digits often. It was the humidity she wasn't used to. Driving along the water made it seem cooler for some reason.

She slowed when she approached the Heron Bay Resort fishing pier. The crime scene tape had been removed and there was no evidence that only hours earlier, a body had been pulled from the water. The pier was deserted, though. Apparently, it was too hot for fishing. She glanced to the right, seeing the walkway that would lead back to the clubhouse, pool, and the cottages. Lauren's house was tucked in here at the back, completely hidden by the high privacy fence which blocked any view she might have of the bay. She didn't have any news to share with Lauren, but she turned at the next block anyway, going up to Highway 35 and then back to the entrance to Heron Bay.

Lauren was in the office, talking to a man. Harley stayed outside, finding a shady spot under an oak tree. A sprinkler was going in one of the flower gardens, and she watched as two butterflies danced along the blooms.

"I'll keep asking. You'll say yes one of these days."

She turned at the sound of the man's voice. He was in his mid-twenties, she guessed. Handsome with an easy smile. She looked past him to Lauren whose expression seemed a bit exasperated. When she glanced back at the man, she found him staring at her. As their eyes held, she had an odd sense of déjà vu. She blinked it away as the man walked past her and she moved into the office. She arched an eyebrow questioningly, but Lauren waved it away.

"Bret Blevins. He's annoying."

"Ask you out?"

"Always."

"So he's a regular?"

"Yes. He comes at least once a month, sometimes more often. Stays two, sometimes three nights."

"Business or pleasure?"

"Pleasure, I'm assuming. I don't ask questions—he gives me the creeps. All I know is he says he has a fancy boat and wants to take me out fishing sometime. Or partying." She pointed to Harley's shirt. "I actually kinda like that one."

Harley looked down at the rather plain green shirt with small white flowers. "Thank you. See? I knew they'd grow on you."

Lauren raised her eyebrows. "So, what brings you around? News?"

"Got a name of the victim. Christopher Bryce. Ring a bell?"

Lauren shook her head. "No. Who was he?"

"Don't know much. Another detective is going to Corpus to interview his wife. He went fishing last night. Didn't come home."

"Do you think it's related to the break-in?"

"Hard to say. The dive team didn't find anything in the water. There was nothing on the pier. We'll delve into this guy's background, try to trace his movements yesterday. We'll—" Her phone buzzed and she pulled it out of her pocket. "Excuse me," she said quickly before answering. "Detective Shepherd."

"Harley, got a call from Corpus PD," Commander Lawson said. "They found the guy's fishing gear. His wallet and phone were there. Near Packery Channel."

"It's the murder scene?"

"No. They think they've found that too. Some guy reported that his boat had been stolen. They found it floating, unattended, in the bay. Lots of blood. They're still at the scene."

She glanced at Lauren. "Any sign of his head?"

"No. And they've got to wait on the lab to match the blood, but they're going over the boat thoroughly now."

"So CCPD is taking over this one?"

"Yeah. I've told them about our concerns here. It's probably a coincidence, though."

"I hate that word."

"Let's see what they come up with, Harley. They're going to keep us in the loop."

"What about Roscoe?"

"Haven't heard from him. I told him to get with you after the interview."

She sighed as the line went dead. "My commander," she explained. "The Corpus Christi Police Department will be handling the murder investigation, not us. They found his fishing gear near Packery Channel. Found a bloody boat. Makes sense. Kill him on the boat. Haul him out here and dump him."

"What does that mean for me?"

"Commander Lawson chalked it up to coincidence."

"The word you hate?"

"Yeah. So, listen, you'll let me know if see or hear anything unusual, right?"

"Of course."

"Okay. And I'll let you know if I learn anything."

Lauren nodded. "Thank you. I appreciate you taking more than just a passing interest in this case, Detective Shepherd."

Harley smiled at her. "Well, it's my job, ma'am," she said with a wink. She opened the office door. "See you around, Ms. Voss."

CHAPTER FOURTEEN

"It surely has nothing to do with you, honey, does it?"

Lauren sipped her frozen daiquiri—a mango-strawberry concoction that was simply too good. She shrugged at her grandmother's question. "There's no way to know for sure. It could be coincidence, although Detective Shepherd is hesitant to use that word."

"And the poor man had his head cut off?" Nana shook her head. "That's awful. Just awful. Who would do such a thing? Or is it like a drug gang or something?"

"I don't think so," she said, remembering the call she'd gotten from Harley only an hour ago. "He was forty-eight-years-old. Married with two kids. The Corpus police are doing the investigation, but Detective Shepherd said it seemed like a totally random act of violence."

Nana picked up her glass of wine. "Have you found out her name yet?"

"Yes. It's Harley."

"Harley? Like the motorcycle?"

"Yes."

"Oh, she sounds dashing then. Is she?"

"Nana, dashing? Because her name is Harley?"

"Well, I'm just saying—"

"She's not dashing. Well, she thinks she is, but no. Remember the obnoxious Hawaiian shirts? That hasn't changed."

"I think female police officers are attractive."

Lauren frowned. "Do you know any?"

"Well, on TV they're always so attractive."

Lauren smiled at her. "On TV?"

"Yes. How old is your Harley?"

"Nana, she's certainly not *my* Harley. I told you, I don't even like her."

"Yes, yes. Obnoxious." She sipped her wine. "So? How old?"

"She's thirty-four. And she volunteered the information—I didn't ask." She held her hand up. "I didn't ask because I don't care. All I care about is finding out who vandalized the clubhouse and whether or not this poor man's murder is linked to it or not."

"Oh, well let's hope not. How terrible would that be?" Nana smiled then. "So tell me more about Harley. You said she showed up at your door soaking wet at five this morning. She's one of those feisty policewomen, isn't she?"

Lauren rolled her eyes. "You watch too much TV."

"I can picture her jumping off the pier, fully clothed, to save this man."

"You don't even know what she looks like."

"Dashing. More handsome than pretty, I'll bet." Nana looked past her, her eyes widening. "Oh, I see fried shrimp coming our way."

"Here you go, Mrs. Voss."

"Thank you, Jenny."

"More chardonnay?"

"I think I will have another glass, yes."

Lauren eyed the plate Jenny placed in front of her, the seafood special. Nana always got the fried shrimp platter, then would give Lauren two in exchange for the stuffed crab.

"Lauren? Another daiquiri?"

"I shouldn't, but it's too delicious to stop with one." She dunked a plump shrimp into the tartar sauce before taking a bite. "I never get tired of this."

Nana handed her the ketchup bottle. "I always say I'm going to skip the baked potato, but I never do. It's dripping in butter."

"That's why it's so good."

"At my age, you have to be careful."

Lauren laughed. "Nana, you're eating deep fried, double-battered shrimp. Butter is the least of your worries with this meal."

"Oh, but it's so good, isn't it?"

Thankfully, the discussion about the murder—and the dashing Detective Shepherd—came to an end and Nana told her about the happenings at The Oaks. Lauren, in turn, filled Nana in on the comings and goings at Heron Bay. It was a familiar routine and she looked forward to their weekly dinners. It reminded her that she didn't go visit Nana nearly enough, although Nana's social calendar was much fuller than her own. Nana wasn't lacking for company, she knew that.

Maybe it was her who was lacking? Yes, she supposed that was true. Other than this outing with Nana, she did little else each week. How dull and boring she must be. Why did Harley even bother to flirt with her? Because flirt was what she did. Sometimes subtle, sometimes right out in the open.

Harley was kinda cute, she supposed. Certainly not dashing, as Nana expected, but attractive. Then she mentally shook her head. No. Harley was way too much like Leah. She did not need to think of her as attractive.

"Mary's son is picking her up next week. Taking her all the way to Portland."

"Her granddaughter lives there, right?"

"Yes. She'll be gone two weeks. I guess our weekly card game will be put on hold."

"Why don't you find a replacement for her?"

"It wouldn't be the same. The four of us have been playing together for fifty years. Oh, how time gets away, doesn't it?"

"Yes, it does."

"Why, I can remember being your age and thinking I had all the time in the world. Then you wake up one day and you're eighty-six and feeling every bit of those years."

"Nana, you're in excellent health."

"Oh, I know. A blessing, I tell you that. The others all have some ailment, or this hurts and that hurts. Why, I feel like I need to make something up just to stay in the conversation," she said with a hearty laugh. "I used to think that if I made it to eighty, I'd have had a good life. Now? Ninety is four short years away and I think maybe I should go ahead and shoot for one-hundred."

Lauren touched her hand. "I hope you do. I can't imagine my life without you in it."

"I do worry about you being alone. What with your mom and dad both gone and—"

"And Lance and I not having a relationship," she finished for her.

"Oh, your brother just needs to get over it. Why would I leave him any part of Heron Bay? You are the one who came back to stay with us each summer, not him. He had no interest in the place at all." She waved her hand in the air. "San Diego this, San Diego that. The *best* beaches, the *best* surf, the *best* people. Well, phooey, I say. And after George died, it was you who came to help me, not him. He couldn't even be bothered to come to the funeral." Nana took her hand. "I don't know what I would have done without you, dear."

"To be fair, Nana, if my relationship with Leah hadn't ended, I would still only be down here part time."

"Yes, well it did end, and you moved here permanently, like it was meant to be. As you know, I never liked her to begin with."

"You were only around her a handful of times."

"And that was enough." Another wave of her hand. "Such a haughty attitude she had, much like your brother."

"Well, I'll have to agree with you on that."

"Snooty, I called her."

"Yes, you did, and yes, she was." She pointed to her plate, hoping to end this vein of conversation. "I'll trade you a couple of these scallops for another shrimp."

Later—after she'd dropped Nana back at The Oaks—she drove along the bay, windows opened. It was a pleasant evening, the breeze cool for July. This drive always cleared her head, whether it was day or night.

When Harley had asked if there were any disgruntled family members, she'd denied it. Truth was, Lance had been more than a little miffed when he'd found out that Nana had left the resort to her. They'd had—well, to say they'd had *words* was too mild a statement. Nana, of course, had been livid when she'd found out. Because, as she said, Lance never bothered to come down to see them. And no, he hadn't made the funeral because he'd had some project at work that he couldn't get away from. Leah hadn't been able to make the funeral either. She'd had a very important beach volleyball tournament that she couldn't possibly miss.

Lauren shook her head. She should have seen the writing on the wall, but she ignored it. She apparently ignored a lot of things when it came to Leah. To hear Leah tell it, Lauren ignored her as well. And maybe she had. She'd still spent each summer in Rockport with her grandparents. That never changed. Her job afforded her that.

She smiled, remembering the Clintons, the wonderful older couple who owned the tiny coffeehouse in Seaport Village. She started working for them when she was in high school. They'd gotten used to her leaving each summer and when she was in college, she kept the job, still leaving each summer for Rockport. When she'd begun looking for a "real" job after college, they'd made her an offer she couldn't refuse.

She bought the coffeehouse at a bargain price, changed the menu to include breakfast and lunch, and added alcohol. Business started booming. Even then, after she'd met Leah and with a new thriving business, she still came down here each summer. It was her connection to her parents, and it was her down time, where things were much slower than in San Diego.

After her grandfather died, she'd thought perhaps that Nana might sell Heron Bay. That would have been devastating, she knew. Heron Bay was where she'd grown up. Heron Bay was home. Rockport was home, something San Diego had never been.

When her relationship with Leah soured—that was a good word, wasn't it?—she knew, if she was going to keep her sanity, she'd need to move back to Rockport. Selling the coffeeshop had been easier to do than she'd thought—both in terms of the time it took to sell and the emotional toll it took on her. By then, she'd simply wanted—*needed*—to get away. She probably could have held out for a better price, but considering what she'd paid for it to begin with, she'd made out like a bandit.

She drove the bay road past their pier, the green lights glowing along the water. She spotted a few fishermen on it. She assumed the word had spread among the guests about the body found that morning. Several had come into the office asking about it. She'd been happy to tell them that the victim was from Corpus and not there. That seemed to appease most of them.

She rounded the corner of the bay, going back to the highway. When she pulled into the drive at Heron Bay, she noted how welcoming it looked at night. Several of the large oaks at the entrance had white lights strung around their trunks. Porch lights were on at each cabin and solar garden lights were scattered among the flowerbeds.

She drove around to the clubhouse, hearing laughter and splashing coming from the pool. She smiled, loving the familiar sound. The tiny driveway wound around to her own private cottage and she parked next to the privacy fence. When she went through her gate, she remembered Harley's warning to lock it and she did, slipping the chain between the slats of the gate and snapping the padlock closed.

She felt restless as she went inside her quiet—lonely— cottage. She stood in the kitchen and took a deep breath, wondering if she should try to kill an hour or so or just go to bed.

Bed won out.

CHAPTER FIFTEEN

Harley tapped on Brian's door, waiting only a moment before his voice muttered a "come in."

"Hey, chief."

He raised his eyebrows. "Harley. What's up?"

"Wanted to see if maybe you could pull some strings."

"The headless guy? Not sure I've been here long enough to pull strings. What's going on?"

She sat down. "That's just it. Nothing's going on. They have no motive, no suspects, no witnesses. Nothing."

"That's what I hear too. So there aren't any strings to pull, Harley."

"If they have no motive and it's just a random killing, then it has to lead back to Heron Bay. It's got to be connected to the vandalism."

He nodded. "I tend to agree with you. But like them, we have no evidence, no witnesses, no nothing." He held his hand up when she would have spoken. "I talked to them directly, Harley. They've traced his last movements. They've gone out to interview fishermen, seeing if anyone saw him. They've looked at the available surveillance…there's nothing. His background, his job…nothing. Normal guy. Stable job. Happy family. Poor guy was just going out night fishing on his day off."

"There was no blood found where his fishing gear was, right?"

"They found nothing there, no."

"So what? The killer offers him fishing on the boat? Or makes him get on the boat at gunpoint? What's the assumption?"

"The victim was a large man. The assumption is, yes, that he was forced on the boat. If he went willingly, as a ruse for fishing, he would have taken his gear. It appears to be random."

"Okay. Random killings are made by madmen."

"What are you suggesting?"

"That message on the mirror. 'It's your turn to die.' He's killed before. Maybe many times."

"A serial killer?"

"Why not?"

He leaned forward. "I know this is close to home, Harley. Are you sure you want to go there?"

"What happened in San Antonio—the circumstances were completely different."

"But a serial killer nonetheless." He leaned back again. "Let's don't jump to conclusions, Harley. We have one victim. It's a gruesome murder, yeah. But nothing about it indicates it's a serial killer."

"I don't want to *not* jump to conclusions and have that innocent woman end up dead."

"Why would he target her? There has to be a reason."

"Does it? Most serial killers target by looks, by similarities."

"Most serial killers don't leave messages and bodies to toy with their victims."

She sighed. "I know. I checked the FBI database. There's nothing similar."

"So why do you think it's a serial killer?"

"He cut a man's head off, for god's sake! That wasn't his first kill."

He spread his hands out. "So what do you want to do?"

"Can we have a patrol car park there at night?"

"At Heron Bay? We can probably arrange to have one cruise by several times a night. Don't think we need to have one parked there all night, though. You know how many officers we have out on patrol each shift. Don't think we can spare one to just sit there all night."

She nodded. "If we could patrol more, even cruise through the place a few times each night, that might help."

He nodded. "We can do that. I'll get with Commander Deeks." He studied her. "You taking this one personal?"

She shrugged. "The most excitement we've had in a year."

"Okay, Harley. Then do what you've got to do. You know Lawson will give you free rein."

She nodded. "I've got a bad feeling on this one, that's all." She stood up. "We still on for Saturday?"

"Yep. Come around six. It'll be cool enough for the patio then."

"Thanks, Brian." She paused. "You mind if I bring a friend?"

He looked startled by the question. "Of course not."

She smiled. "I'll see if I can find one."

* * *

She didn't really have an excuse to stop by Heron Bay Resort, but she pulled in anyway. It was on her way home, she reasoned. It would be the proper thing to do—stop by and check on things. She parked at the office, but it wasn't Lauren she found behind the counter.

"Hi, may I help you?"

Harley smiled at the girl, assuming she was the high school student Lauren had mentioned. "Hi. Looking for Ms. Voss. Is she around?"

"She's outside watering. I can call her," she offered.

"No, that's okay. I'll find her."

She put her sunglasses back on, then headed down the drive, looking for Lauren. She found her at a blue cottage, Number

Nine. She was holding a garden hose, watering the flowers. Her back was to her, and Harley walked quietly, a smile on her face as she approached.

"Boo!"

Lauren gasped and spun around, spraying her with water. Harley jumped out of the way before she got drenched. She had to have seen that coming.

"Oh my god! *You!*"

"Yeah. You'd think I'd have learned by now not to sneak up on you when you're armed." She took her sunglasses off and wiped at the water on her face.

"I'm sorry."

"No, no. My fault."

Lauren turned the nozzle off. "Why are you sneaking up on me, for god's sake?"

"There's a thirteen-year-old boy hiding inside me sometimes, I think." She put her sunglasses back on. "So? Everything okay?"

"Yes."

"Good. So listen, since we don't know if the message on the mirror was meant for you or not, and since we don't know if this murder is linked to you or not, I've requested to have a patrol car come by. They'll cruise the bay road and then do a pass in here." She shoved the sunglasses on top of her head. "You don't have a problem with that, do you?"

"No, of course not. I mean, it's not like they'll be coming through here that often, right?"

"A few times during the night, that's all."

"Okay. That's fine. I guess it would make me feel a little better. I'm not sure what the guests will think about it. I don't want to scare off my customers."

"If anyone asks, you could say that you asked us to do it as a courtesy, since the vandalism and all."

"Okay." Lauren stared at her. "And what else?"

"What else?"

Lauren pointed at her. "You have something else on your mind. I can tell."

"You think so?"

"Yes. What is it?"

She nodded. "Okay. I'd like to take a look at your books."

"Whatever for?"

"Well, not your books. Whatever you call it. Your register. I want to compare your guest list from the night of the break-in to Tuesday night." She held her hand up before she could protest. "I don't want phone numbers or personal information. Just want to see if you had guests that were here on both nights."

"You surely don't think someone from here—one of our guests—is responsible? That's ridiculous, Detective. I told you, the people who stay here—"

"Yeah, yeah. They're all family people and repeats. Saints, all of them." She gave a fake smile. "I'd still like to take a look, Ms. Voss, if you don't mind."

"And if I say I do mind?"

"Then I'll take that to mean that you really don't care if we catch this guy or not."

"You know that's not true!"

She narrowed her eyes. "Then let me see your register," she said, enunciating each word succinctly.

Lauren blew out her breath. "You're impossible to deal with."

"Funny. I was about to say the same about you."

They stood staring at each other, then Harley smiled. "You're contemplating turning the hose back on, aren't you?"

At that, Lauren smiled too. "How did you know?"

"Because you had a little evil glint in your eyes."

Lauren's expression lightened. "Okay. You can see the register. But—"

"Just going to compare names, Lauren. That's all."

"If there are some—which I'm sure there will be—I don't want you interrogating my guests." She headed toward the driveway and Harley got into step beside her. "I know these people."

"Do you honestly know *all* of your guests? Don't you have some strangers that come?"

"Yes, of course. But I still meet every one of them." Instead of going toward the office, Lauren led them around back and toward the clubhouse. "I chat with them. I try to remember names so that I can address them if I see them out on the grounds. I just can't imagine that any one of them would have trashed the clubhouse. Not to mention what happened the other night. I'm telling you, it's not one of the guests."

"Where are we going, anyway?"

"To my cottage. Jessica is working in the office. I'd rather not discuss anything in front of her."

Lauren's cottage was far enough away from the clubhouse and pool area to afford her some privacy, but the wooden fence still puzzled her.

"Why the high fence? Your grandparents put it up?"

"Yes. Nana said she wanted to be able to close the world out sometimes. I have intentions to remove the part along the bayside but so far haven't gotten to it yet. Of course, with the road separating me from the bay, I may hate it when it's gone."

A black Prius was parked by the fence and the gate to her house was unlocked. Harley shook her head. "Do I need to come by and make sure you lock this damn thing?"

"I locked it last night. You think I should keep it locked all the time?"

At least the front door was locked, and she waited as Lauren turned the key and pushed the door open.

"I would, yes."

Lauren went to the small desk and opened a laptop. "I'll start locking it when I leave then. I'm back and forth so much, it's a pain, that's all."

Harley leaned over her shoulder, watching as she pulled up a calendar view for July. "It happened the night of the fifth."

Lauren pulled up a page that listed each cottage and the guests for that date. "There were four empty cottages, so thirteen occupied. The mini-suites had seven rooms occupied."

"Do you only have the person who booked the room, or do you also have names of guests?"

"It depends. If it's a family, then no, they don't list the kids' names. If there are two adults, say, then yes, we request names. That's mostly for liability." She shrunk that screen and pulled up another from Tuesday night. She put the two side-by-side on the screen. "I'll read off the names from the fifth. You compare them to this one," she said, pointing to the box on the right.

They were standing close, their shoulders touching as they both bent over the laptop. Lauren's hair hung loose between them, and as Harley watched, Lauren tucked it behind her ears. Harley turned away as she glanced at her. She turned her focus to the screen as Lauren started reading off names. The fourth name was a match.

"He's on my list too. Fredrick Stenson."

Lauren nodded. "Kind of a creepy guy, yeah."

"Tell me about him."

"He's small in stature, kinda nervous when he talks to you. Won't meet your eyes. I'd guess he's in his forties, maybe older."

"What else? What's he doing here?"

"He works for the Parks Service, I think. He told me he was an ornithologist—fits the stereotype perfectly. He's doing a study at the wildlife refuge. He's been coming since March. Every two weeks."

Harley typed some quick notes on her phone. "He's still here?"

Lauren checked, then shook her head. "No. He left yesterday."

"Okay. Continue."

It was eight more names before they got another hit. "That one."

"Bret Blevins? He's the guy you met yesterday morning."

"The annoying one who keeps asking you out?"

"Yes. He usually comes once or twice a month, but I guess he came up for the holiday too. We were so busy that weekend, I don't remember seeing him." She went to another screen. "He checked out early that morning before the office opened. Left the keys in the box."

"On the fifth?"

"Yes."

"Is that unusual?"

"Not really. Sometimes he leaves later and will come in. I'd much rather he leave early, to be honest. Saves me having to pretend to enjoy his company when he stays to chat."

Harley again took notes, although—even though she'd only met him briefly—he didn't fit the profile of a killer. Well, unless you compared him to Ted Bundy. She shook that thought away.

"Continue, please."

They had two more hits, but Lauren dismissed them. Both were older couples who had been coming for years. The Thompsons, who Harley had already met, and the Lucernes, who had come with their grandchildren for the holiday weekend, then had come back three days ago, planning to stay until August.

"So we've got the creepy bird guy and the annoying handsome guy."

Lauren frowned at her. "You think he's handsome?"

Harley shrugged. "Well, as far as guys go, he was kinda cute, yeah. I would think most women would say he's handsome." Then she laughed. "I mean, you know, if you like that sort of thing."

"Yes, I suppose he is handsome. His flirting is so tiresome, though."

"Tell him to stop."

"I have made it quite clear he's not my type. It hasn't seemed to deter him. But I can't actually be rude to him. He is a customer."

"You still shouldn't have to put up with being sexually harassed. That's what he's doing, right?"

"Yes. He makes innuendoes all the time. They are always accompanied by a wink or a laugh to keep it light and to make me think he's teasing."

"But he's not?"

"No."

"You want me to talk to him?"

Lauren laughed. "You? Are you going to try to scare him?"

"I could pretend to be your girlfriend. Make sure he sees my detective's shield and my big gun," she said with a wiggle of her eyebrows.

She was surprised that Lauren didn't laugh off her suggestion. "That's not a bad idea, actually."

"Really?"

"He leaves at different times, but he always checks in between noon and one. You'll have to wait until August to scare him off, I guess."

"When is he leaving?"

"Tomorrow morning. But like I said, sometimes it's before we open, sometimes it's later in the morning."

"So I'll pop by in the morning. Maybe we'll catch him when he's dropping the key off." She paused. "I don't suppose I could have both of their addresses and phone numbers, huh?"

Lauren met her gaze. "What are you going to do with them?"

"Run a background check."

"Is this normal? I mean, should I be asking you for a warrant or a subpoena or whatever you call it?"

"They're not technically suspects. I just want to see where they live, if they have a criminal record, or anything like that. I will need a warrant to pull their phone records, though, but I'll see what their background check shows before I do that."

She sighed. She supposed she needed to trust Harley. She was, at least, following up and trying to find a killer. "Okay."

CHAPTER SIXTEEN

Lauren took her swim earlier than normal, wanting to be at the office by seven. Harley had texted her at five—while she was having her second cup of coffee—saying she'd skip her bike ride and be there at or before seven. That, of course, made her curious as to what bike ride she was skipping. Was that Harley's form of exercise? Like she took a morning swim, did Harley hop on a bike? As she walked to the pool, she thought a bike ride sounded like fun and once again she wondered why she didn't go out more. She was right here at the bay. Lots of people took early morning walks and yes, bike rides. Maybe she'd do it tomorrow. Something different.

It was barely daybreak and the pool was—as expected—deserted. Occasionally, someone would come out for an early swim, but it was usually later than her early and she was often on her way out when they were getting in. She slipped off her shorts and T-shirt and kicked the flip-flops to the side. She tucked her hair behind both ears, then, before diving in, she glanced around, her gaze traveling over the colorful flowers that surrounded the pool. She took a deep breath, then did a shallow dive into the pool, swimming underwater to the other side before surfacing. She did several laps, alternating between freestyle and backstroke, her two favorites. When she stopped to rest, she nearly gasped as she realized a man was standing there watching her. She tried not to show her surprise as she slicked the hair back away from her face.

"Good morning, Mr. Blevins."

"I've told you, it's Bret." He pulled his shirt over his head. "You don't mind if I join you, do you?"

Before she could answer, he was in the pool, swimming toward her under the water. He surfaced some four or five feet away, thankfully. Yes, he was a handsome man. His body was fit and muscular and sported a healthy tan. She moved away from him, intending to get out, but he called to her.

"Don't let me interrupt, Lauren. I only came in for a quick dip. I have an early flight today and need to get to the airport."

She knew from his time here, that he flew in and out of Corpus, but she had no idea where he flew back to. She had never been curious enough to ask.

"I need to get out anyway." She looked at the watch on her wrist. It was ten minutes until seven.

"Listen, I wanted to invite you to a party."

She got out, feeling his eyes on her. "A party?" she asked as she quickly toweled dry.

"Yes. Next time I'm in town. I'm having a little party out on my boat. Be my date?"

She shook her head. "Sorry. Not interested."

"You keep saying that. What's a guy got to do?"

"I told you, you're not my type. At all." She heard the gate open, and she let out a relieved sigh when she saw Harley.

"Who's your type then?" he asked as he floated on his back.

She met Harley's gaze, watching as she sauntered over, her bright Hawaiian shirt matching the splashes of red flowers around the pool. She wondered if Harley had heard the question.

"Good morning, sweetheart."

Lauren smiled at that. "Good morning, Detective. You're early."

She stood stock-still as Harley came closer, leaning in to kiss her. On the mouth, no less. She hoped she was able to hide her shocked expression when Harley pulled away.

Harley made a show of revealing her holster and weapon as she glanced to the pool. Like the first time they'd met, her detective's shield was hung around her neck. "I see you have company." Harley nodded at Bret Blevins. "Good morning. Lovely day, isn't it?"

"It was," he said dryly.

Harley tilted her head and frowned. "Have we met before?"

"No." He disappeared under the water, moving away from them.

"Perfect timing," Lauren whispered to her.

"It's a gift I have," she said with a wink before putting her sunglasses on. "So yeah, I'll have to miss our breakfast date. Got time for a quick chat?"

"Of course." Lauren didn't turn as she heard Bret getting out of the pool. She gathered her clothes and followed Harley out the gate. When they were on the other side of the clubhouse, she smacked her on the arm. "You *kissed* me!"

"Well, yeah. Isn't that how you greet the love of your life?" Harley rubbed her arm. "And that's the thanks I get for saving you from this guy?"

Lauren blew out her breath. "I'm sorry. Yes, thank you for saving me. He'd just invited me to a party on his boat." She wrapped the towel tighter around her waist, then used the other to dry her hair as they walked. "If he doesn't stop hitting on me after this, I'm going to have to be rude to him."

"Threaten to call your girlfriend cop on him. That should do it. Because I'd be happy to have a little chat with him. He's got shifty eyes. I don't trust him."

"Did you really think you'd met him before?"

Harley gave a slight shrug of her shoulders. "Something about him was familiar. Maybe it's his shifty eyes."

"Speaking of that, did you run your background checks?"

"No. I went home after I left here. I'll do them this morning."

Lauren paused at the gate of her cottage. "Bike ride?"

"Huh?"

"Your text."

"Oh. Yeah. I ride along the bay and then to the state park. Ride their trails. Got a loop I do in the neighborhoods back around the lakes."

"What lakes?"

"Oh, that's what they call them. I think they're holding ponds to prevent flooding. There's this little golf course around the lakes—nine holes—and the houses butt up to the greens. Lots of deer around. It's a relaxing ride. Nothing strenuous, by any means."

"I've never spent much time on Lamar. When I would visit in the summers, my grandparents would sometimes take me to the state park. My grandfather liked to fish, and they have this long pier out there. Or they did."

"From what I hear, Harvey wiped it out. They're still repairing stuff from that storm. The pier is not quite finished yet."

Lauren nodded. She knew all too well the damage the hurricane had caused. "Well, thank you for coming to my rescue. I should get changed and get to the office."

"No problem." Then she grinned. "It was my pleasure."

Lauren rolled her eyes. "I can't believe you kissed me."

"Thank you for not slapping me. That would have totally blown my cover."

She closed the gate, and they stood looking at each other across from it. "You'll let me know if your background checks turn up anything?"

"Of course." Harley turned to go, then stopped. "Hey, so, do you feel like burgers on Saturday? Well, that's tomorrow. About six? I'll pick you up."

Lauren frowned. "What? No."

"Dinner. Burgers. Patio. Beers. The chief invited me."

Her eyes widened. "The police chief?"

"Yeah."

"At his house?"

"Yeah."

Lauren blinked several times, remembering that Harley said the chief was her closest friend in town. But then she shook her head. "No."

"Why?"

"Because I don't even like you," she blurted before she could stop herself.

"Oh, that's right. I remind you of your ex." Harley leaned closer. "Was she *really* as charming as I am?"

Lauren tried not to smile. She really did. But yes, Harley *was* charming and to say she didn't like her was a lie. The problem was, she didn't *want* to like her. And the more they saw each other, the less she could hold on to that belief.

"She was certainly as conceited as you."

Harley showed mock horror. "Conceited? Ms. Voss, I am a very humble person. Modest, in fact." Then she smiled. "So. Burgers. I'll pick you up at six." She spun on her heels and walked away.

Lauren called after her. "I did *not* agree to that."

"See you at six."

Harley had already turned the corner around the privacy fence by the time she'd yelled "no" to her. She stared at the empty space where Harley had been for a long moment before turning and going into her cottage. The word "obnoxious" came to mind, but she dismissed it. That seemed too harsh a word to use now. Maybe arrogant fit better. But a cute arrogant, not the vain kind.

As she dressed, she wondered if Harley was indeed planning to come by at six tomorrow. And if she did, would she go with her?

She was still going over her exchange with Harley as she walked to the office. Bret Blevins was there, dropping his keys in the box that hung on the outside wall. She had half a mind to dart behind a tree to avoid him, but he turned before she could do that.

"Oh, there you are. I figured you'd be around." He pointed to the road. "Saw your girlfriend leave. A cop? Really?"

"Really."

When he smiled at her, she noticed that the normal levity in his eyes was missing. "So you're gay?"

"I thought I'd made that clear already."

"I didn't believe you."

She shrugged as she went past him to the door. She took out her keys, then paused, wondering if he would follow her inside. Wondering if it was safe if he did? So she turned around, deciding to have a conversation with him that she should have had months ago.

"Mr. Blevins, it was quite apparent that I wasn't interested in you. Yet you continued to pursue it. So much so, that it made me uncomfortable. It may have seemed all fun and games to you, but trust me, it was not."

"I'm sorry you feel that way. I was just playing around. Teasing. Having fun, yes."

"It wasn't fun. It was harassment."

He held his hands up. "Whoa now. Don't go throwing that word around. I thought we were friends."

"We're not friends, no." She squared her shoulders, keeping her expression serious. "Have a safe flight," she said a bit dismissively.

When she unlocked the door, she immediately closed and locked it again. He stood there, looking at her through the glass. Then the cocky smile she was used to lit his face and he gave a mock salute before leaving.

Her hands were shaking as she flipped the sign from "closed" to "open" and went about the business of getting ready for the day. Yes, she should have had that talk with him long ago instead of enduring his constant flirting and innuendoes.

And why hadn't she? Was it only because he was a paying customer, and she didn't want to offend him? Or had she secretly been afraid of him? Well, maybe not so secretly. On days when she knew he would be checking in, she'd often get one of the ladies from the cleaning staff to come by the office or get Gerald to do his watering around that time, just so she wouldn't have to be alone with him.

She looked up then as she saw his rental car drive past. He stared in her direction for a brief moment and she actually breathed a sigh of relief when he was out of sight. She would have a month's reprieve before he returned. And with any luck, he'd start staying somewhere else.

The office phone rang, and she pushed Bret Blevins from her mind, getting back to the business at hand.

"Good morning. Heron Bay Resort. How may I help you?"

CHAPTER SEVENTEEN

Harley crossed the wooden bridge, then stopped next to the big oak tree to rest. She balanced on her bike, holding on to the tree with one hand while the other grabbed the water bottle from the wire holder. She squeezed water into her mouth, then lifted up the end of her T-shirt to wipe the sweat from her brow. It was a hot and humid morning—as usual—but the normally constant breeze from the bay was missing today. The woods were downright still, and she slapped at a mosquito that landed on her arm.

She tapped her phone, bringing the app to life. She'd been on the bike for an hour and nineteen minutes. She'd surpass her hour and a half goal by the time she got back to the RV park. After another drink of water, she peddled on, keeping to the trail instead of going out to the paved road. At the park entrance, she saw Ami, the cute clerk with the sometimes pink, sometimes purple highlights in her hair. Ami was standing out front, apparently giving directions to someone towing a boat, and she waved at her as Harley passed.

"See ya tomorrow," she called as she buzzed by.

She wasn't really in a hurry to get back, but she was getting hungry. She'd been on her bike by seven and the weekend fishermen had been vying for the few pull-out spots along the bay. The public boat ramp near the RV park had already been crowded when she'd gone by that morning and even their own pier had men milling about with their fishing gear. Maybe the moon was right or the tide or something, but there seemed to be an inordinate number of people about.

Her RV spot was tiny, and she was crammed between two bigger rigs. There was barely five feet separating her and her neighbor on the back side. On her door side, she had about eight feet of space between her and her neighbor, Tommy. She leaned her bike against the old wooden table that she'd confiscated from another site when the renter moved out. She had two lawn chairs shoved against it but more often than not, only one got used, unless Tommy popped over to have a beer with her.

Inside, the AC hummed, and she took off her bike helmet and tossed it on the table. She stood at the fridge, wondering what she could concoct for breakfast. There were three eggs left. Some pico de gallo, beans, and Spanish rice from her takeout dinner the other night. She rummaged in the small freezer, finding the package of tortillas she kept in there. That had been a habit she'd brought with her from San Antonio. Always have tortillas on hand. Because when in doubt, make a taco.

She was able to stretch her sparse ingredients into two tacos. She took them outside to her little sitting area, which was still shaded this time of the morning. She needed to make a run to the grocery store to pick up potato salad for dinner tonight. On her phone, she jotted down some items she needed—like eggs— to restock her fridge. She didn't keep much on hand as the only time she normally cooked was on the weekends. Not that she couldn't cook or didn't like to cook. She did. But her little RV with its tiny kitchen and fridge didn't allow for much. A two-burner stove and just a microwave for an oven—there was only so much she could do. It was simply easier to pick something up or eat out. Of course, she did enjoy grilling some fresh fish or a steak. That was usually her Saturday night activity.

She finished her first taco and took a swallow of water. Was she really planning on stopping at Heron Bay? Would Lauren go with her to dinner at Brian and Marsha's? She'd be surprised if she did, but yeah, she'd swing by just the same.

She picked up the second taco, but before she bit into it, she relived that brief kiss again. God, what had possessed her to kiss her? It had been too easy, really. She could tell by the look in Lauren's eyes that she was uncomfortable there with Bret Blevins. Lauren's eyes had been filled with relief when she saw her, and it seemed the most natural thing in the world to kiss her.

She smiled, then took a bite of her taco. She was damn lucky Lauren hadn't slapped her face in the process! Of course, she did get a good punch in on her arm.

She liked Lauren Voss. And, if she had to guess, she'd say that she was starting to grow on Lauren as well. Maybe she would go to dinner with her after all.

CHAPTER EIGHTEEN

Lauren had spent the morning in the laundry room—Rebecca had called in sick yet again, and she wondered if she needed to replace her. She'd been with them for over four years and had always been dependable. But the last several months, she'd been missing work more and more. To hear the other ladies tell it, Rebecca had a new boyfriend who liked to party. Apparently, Friday nights were a party night because when it was Rebecca's turn to work on a Saturday, she invariably didn't make it.

Really, she didn't mind washing the linens and towels. It was mindless work and she'd been doing it enough years—since the summers she'd been in high school—that she had a system down. By noon, she'd finished with the day's laundry. Anything else that came in today would be washed in the morning.

Even though they were usually fully booked on the weekends, housekeeping was usually light. Each guest had the option of having only towels replaced or having both towels and linens changed. And, of course, full maid service, if they wanted. She'd found that given the option, most chose only towel service. Fridays and Sundays were the busiest days for the cleaning crews, and everyone was scheduled on those days. They took turns getting Saturday off and they each had an additional day off during the week. Most of the ladies had been with them for years, many having been hired by Nana long before she'd gotten there. She supposed she'd have to have a talk with Rebecca, something she probably should have done already.

Now, with Jessica holding down the office, she thought she'd spend a couple of hours hauling the garden hose around, watering flowers. More mindless work but infinitely more relaxing than being inside with the noisy washers and dryers. Mindless work which gave her time to think.

The thoughts running through her head alternated between the man found out by their pier and the detective who had somehow slipped into her life. And she had, hadn't she? Harley came by enough that when she didn't, Lauren found herself looking for her. Which was ridiculous. And a dinner date? No. She had no intention of going out to dinner with the woman.

Harley hadn't actually used the word "date," though, had she? Burgers was all. And at the police chief's house? No, she had no business going there. She pulled the hose with her as she crossed the drive, going to water the clusters of hostas that were planted under the center oak tree.

She had nothing else to do tonight, though. At that, she rolled her eyes. Did she *ever* have anything to do on Saturday nights?

But did she really want to see Detective Shepherd in a casual, social setting? What did it mean? Why had she asked her? Well, that was obvious, wasn't it? Harley flirted with her all the time. In fact, that very first day she had. So, if she went with her this evening, what signal would she be sending Harley?

She shook her head. No. Don't go, she told herself. She did not want to start anything—*anything*—with Harley Shepherd. Well, maybe if she made it clear to her that she was only going as a friend, nothing more. Because, yes, friends were few and far between.

Later, though, as six approached, she fretted over what to wear. How casual? The police chief? Should she dress up? What had Harley said? Burgers. Patio. Beer. So yes, casual, not dressy. Khaki shorts would do, she supposed. Should she wear a blouse? Or a T-shirt? No, it was too hot for a blouse. She sorted through her nicer T-shirts—meaning shirts that weren't advertising the Heron Bay Resort—settling on a sea-green one with two white pelicans on the front. Sports sandals or her nicer leather ones? Maybe she'd wait to see what Harley was wearing. The sports sandals were much more comfortable.

At two minutes after six, a knock sounded. She walked barefoot toward the door, pausing only a second before opening it. She laughed at the sight before her.

"Oh, no, you did not."

Harley grinned. "What?"

"Run out of Hawaiian shirts?"

"I like this one."

It was the godawful tie-dye T-shirt that she'd given her the morning the headless body was found. She was wearing dark hiking shorts and yes, sports sandals. She thought again that Harley had nice feet, and she quickly raised her gaze.

"Let me put my sandals on, then I'll be ready."

Harley followed her into the cottage and closed the door. "I'm hoping you unlocked your gate for me. It hasn't been unlocked all day, right?"

"I unlocked it about a half-hour ago," she called from the bedroom. She came back out. "Since I didn't hear from you, I assumed your background checks didn't turn up anything."

"Unfortunately, no. The bird guy is indeed just that. And it's *Doctor* Fredrick Stenson. Besides the study he's doing here, he's also doing one in Florida, where he stays when he's not here."

"And Bret Blevins?"

"He's very wealthy. You might want to reconsider going out with him," she teased.

She shook her head. "Like I said, he gives me the creeps. He came by the office after you left. I finally had a talk with him. I hope I got through to him this time."

"Well, I don't think he's our guy. His father made a boatload of money in the oil and gas business. Bret's on his payroll, but I couldn't find out exactly what he does if anything. He's got a small yacht that he keeps at the marina. He flies in and out of Corpus. Goes mostly to Houston, where his father's company is headquartered or to San Antonio. His father has got several active wells south of there, near Pleasanton. They've got an office there too. He's twenty-seven, never married, no kids."

"If he's that wealthy, why in the world does he stay here at Heron Bay? I mean, I know 'resort' is part of our name, but really, we're not even close to being a fancy resort. There are plenty of places in town that cater to his kind."

"Maybe he likes the quiet, the privacy."

"I always thought he never fit in with our normal guests." She moved about, turning lights out. "So he's rich. Why does that tell you he's not the guy?"

"Our victim—Christopher Bryce—was last seen leaving his truck with his fishing stuff in hand at seven that evening. He was still alive at nine thirty because he took a call on his cell. That was the last activity. His wife started calling him about eleven. At three that morning, when she still hadn't heard from him, she called the police. Your guests found his body at the pier a little after four."

"What does that mean?"

"Most likely, he was killed between nine thirty and, say, two. Your Dr. Stenson didn't leave the wildlife refuge until dark—almost nine. Credit card receipts showed he got a late dinner—takeout. Phone records show he was on a call—to a colleague in Florida—until almost midnight. No evidence that he left the resort."

She blew out her breath. "And I assume Bret Blevins has an equally sound alibi?"

"He was on the island, hopping about. Got a credit card hit at a restaurant there at eight. The amount suggests it was for two people, maybe even three. Got another hit at a bar a couple of hours later. Last hit was at one thirty at another bar. No cell phone activity though."

"Could have been someone else using his card," she suggested.

"Sure. But I don't have enough to request to pull surveillance video. Getting a warrant for their phone records and credit card info was iffy as it was since CCPD has the lead on this." She walked outside. "I think he's just a spoiled rich guy who thinks he can have anything he wants. Meaning you."

Lauren locked the door behind them, then went out through the gate, locking it as well. "And so there are no suspects?"

"We're not actually the ones working the murder, but no, they have no suspects yet."

Parked beside her Prius was the black SUV that Harley normally showed up in. "You drive that on your own time too?"

"Gives more of a police presence in town." She held the door open for her. "We don't have to drive them. My other option is an old truck I bought to pull the RV. Hard to be cool driving around in that thing, though."

Lauren laughed. "Oh, yes. You do have a reputation to maintain."

They headed to the north part of town, taking Pearl Street past Memorial Park. Harley then turned right into one of the newer subdivisions. The coastal oaks were smaller here than along the bay, but the area was wooded and park-like.

"I wasn't certain you'd come, you know."

Lauren turned to her. "Neither was I."

"It's not going to be a big party or anything. Just us."

"Really? What's the occasion?"

Harley shrugged. "Like I said, we're friends. His wife is like my second mother. I think burgers on the patio was her idea since I haven't been over in a while."

"They're your closest friends?"

"Yeah. I've known them a long time. We've...we've been through a lot together."

Lauren raised her eyebrows at her hesitation, but Harley didn't continue. Instead, she pulled into the driveway of a brick home with a well-manicured lawn. A privacy fence on both sides hid the backyard and she followed Harley up the walkway to the front door.

"Warning you now, Marsha will talk your ear off. She's really nice, though. I think you'll like her."

The front door opened and a smiling woman, probably in her mid- to late-fifties stood there. Her hair was platinum blond, and Lauren wondered if it was real or a wig. Harley was drawn into a tight hug and given a kiss on the cheek, then the woman extended her hand to her.

"Welcome. I'm Marsha Carrington."

"Lauren Voss. Nice to meet you."

The woman smiled broader. "When Brian told me that Harley might bring a friend, I thought surely he was joking. Our Harley never brings someone over." Marsha glanced at Harley. "She's cute."

"Yeah, she is. She's not crazy about me, though. She hasn't decided if she likes me or not."

Lauren looked between them, not sure if that statement required a comment.

"Oh, give her time." Marsha looked back at Lauren. "She'll grow on you. Now, come in. How about something to drink?"

Lauren followed them into the house, through a comfortable-looking living room and past the kitchen—where Marsha paused to drop off Harley's tub of potato salad—then out to the covered back patio. Like most covered porches in town, it had a ceiling fan to stir the air. Against the side wall was a small refrigerator, and when Marsha opened it, it was the proverbial beer fridge.

"If you want something else, Lauren, I've also got wine or, if you don't drink, I have bottled water."

"I'll have a beer, thanks."

"Where's Brian?"

"I sent him to the store. In all my shopping for burgers, I forgot the tomatoes. If it were just us, I wouldn't have bothered, but with a guest—we must have tomatoes," she said with a smile. She took three beers from the fridge. "Come sit. Tell me how you met."

"Someone threatened to kill her. I've come to the rescue."

"*What?*"

Lauren rolled her eyes. "There was a break-in at the cottages. I—"

"What cottages?"

"The Heron Bay Resort. My grandmother owns them. I manage it."

"Oh, how wonderful." She slid the beer bottle over to her. "I love all the colorful cottages. When my niece and her family came to visit over Spring Break, they stayed there." She waved a hand in the air. "Sorry. Go on."

"Well, someone broke into the clubhouse and trashed the place. They left a message on the mirror."

Marsha looked at Harley with raised eyebrows.

"A threatening message. Written in blood. Lucky me, I got the call."

Lauren shook her head. "We don't know if it was for real or just a prank or something."

"There was the dead gull and then the headless man. Let's don't assume prank."

"Oh, my goodness. That was *your* pier where they found the body? How awful for that family."

"Yes. But we don't know if it's related to the break-in or not."

"I think it is," Harley interjected. "We have no proof, though." She held her hand up. "But let's don't talk police stuff. How have you been?"

"Oh, nothing new with me, Harley. I still volunteer at the museum twice a week." Marsha turned to her. "The Texas Maritime Museum. Brian and I both grew up in this area. I remember going there for school outings when I was young."

She nodded. "Yes. I've been a few times too. Not in years, though."

"Not much has changed. A few new artifacts are added occasionally, but it's mostly the same. I still find the history fascinating." She laughed. "All of that and I'm terrified of being out on or in open water."

"You are?"

"Oh, yes. I love the bay, don't get me wrong, especially walking around the marina and having lunch out near the pier by the park. I'm just not comfortable being *on* the water. Brian loves it, though. His brother has a boat, and they go fishing once a month or so. What about you? Do you like the water?"

"Like you, I like being *at* the water. I've actually never even been on a boat."

"Really? Have you always lived here?"

"I grew up here. My parents relocated to San Diego when I was in high school. I still came back each summer to stay with my grandparents." She paused, glancing at Harley. "After my grandfather died, Nana needed help, so I came back." That was technically true. Although it was three years before she officially moved back. "My grandfather loved to fish, but he was mostly a pier fisherman or from the surf if we went to Port A."

"Harley loves to eat fish, but she hasn't taken to fishing yet. Brian keeps trying to get her out on the boat."

Lauren laughed. "You would think with all your Hawaiian shirts, you'd love all things water-related."

"I like beach volleyball," Harley teased with a wiggle of her eyebrows. "Especially girls in bikinis. But yeah, I love to get fish at the market when it's fresh off the boat and grill it. The actual fishing part doesn't interest me, though. And like you, I've never been out on a boat either. Not here, anyway. The lakes around San Antonio, yeah. Water skiing."

The patio door opened, and Lauren turned, seeing who she assumed was Brian Carrington, the police chief. She didn't know what she was expecting. This man had a youthful appearance with dark brown hair that was cut clean and short. A neatly trimmed moustache and goatee had a hint of gray, however.

As his gaze met hers, she saw the surprise there. She supposed it was true that Harley didn't bring friends around, which made her wonder if there were friends. She hadn't mentioned anyone other than the group she played volleyball with occasionally. What had she said? She'd met a few people, but they weren't close friends. The same could be said about her. Other than Nana, there really wasn't anyone in her life.

"Wow, Harley. So, you found one, huh?"

Harley laughed. "Yeah. This is Lauren Voss."

He hesitated before shaking her hand. "Ms. Voss, how are you? I'm Brian."

"Lauren, please. Nice to meet you."

He glanced at Harley. "This is *the* Lauren Voss, I'm assuming."

"It is."

His tone was a little guarded and she wondered if Harley was breaking some sort of police rule by having her there. She supposed she was still technically involved in an ongoing case, although she had little hope of ever finding out who vandalized the clubhouse. And unlike Harley, she wasn't certain that the body at the pier was related to her. Or maybe she simply hoped it wasn't connected.

He made no further mention of it, however. He got a beer and sat down with them. They passed the hour chatting and she never once felt out of place. Both Brian and Marsha were friendly and talkative, always including her in the conversation. Harley was her usual teasing and playful self and Lauren found herself drawn to her far more than she wanted to be. Maybe it was the two beers that relaxed her, but she found herself responding to her and she had to remind herself that they were *not* on a date.

"Well, I suppose we should get those burgers on. If you two will get the grill going, I'll ask Lauren to help in the kitchen. You don't mind, do you?"

"Of course not."

"How about we do the charcoal grill instead of gas? I like that better for burgers."

"Whatever, honey. You'll be doing the cooking."

Without thinking, Lauren squeezed Harley's shoulder as she went past her. As their eyes met, she jerked her hand away. No, she did not want to send Harley mixed signals. She didn't want to send her any signal at all, in fact. Whatever was wrong with her?

It hadn't seemed warm outside, but as soon as she went inside the house, the cool air was welcome.

"It's so humid out, isn't it?"

"Yes. You'd think we'd be used to it by now." Lauren followed her into the kitchen. "I do sometimes miss San Diego weather."

"Oh, I'm sure." Marsha took a bowl of ground meat from the fridge. "It was admirable of you to leave your home to help your grandmother."

"I'll confess, I went through a bad breakup. Getting away from there was the best thing for my sanity."

"Oh? Well, it's good that you're dating again. Harley is—"

"Dating? Oh, no. No, no…it's not like that. We're friends, that's all."

"No? That's a shame. I haven't seen that light in Harley's eyes in so long, it surprised me to see it now. I thought for sure you were dating." She smiled at her. "There's a spark in her eyes today. She had such a bad go of it after her partner died."

Lauren's eyes widened. "Her partner died? I had no idea. She never indicated that there was anyone in her life. In fact, she—"

"Oh, no, no. Her *work* partner. Travis. Not a girlfriend or anything like that. I've known Harley for years. The women in her life have been, well, fleeting is a good word, I guess. It was rare that she brought someone around with her. She spent all her time with Travis. Those two were as close as I've ever seen two people. Like an old, married couple without the sex." She laughed. "They'd finish each other's sentences. Knew what the other was thinking." Her smile faded. "She hasn't gotten over it, of course. Probably never will."

"It?"

Marsha looked at her. "I gather she hasn't told you?"

"Like I said, we're just friends and new ones at that."

"It's probably not my place to go into it all. Maybe if she brings you around again, we'll talk more." She sighed heavily. "It was so tragic. I wasn't certain Harley was going to make it through. Brian too. That's why when this job came up, he jumped at the chance to get away. And of course, he wasn't going to leave Harley behind. She's like family to us."

"Why the Hawaiian shirts?"

Marsha laughed. "Oh, that girl. It was an old joke between her and Travis. She hated the shirts. Loathed them, in fact. Told him he looked ridiculous when he wore them. So for every birthday, he got her a Hawaiian shirt. Every damn year. And she had to wear it at least once." She laughed again. "They'd go out together, both with their Hawaiian shirts on. Quite a sight, that's for sure. Then she'd promptly get rid of it and not have to endure another one until her next birthday. He simply teased her with pictures of them then."

"So why now?"

"It was Brian's doing. He got her one. They had a big cry over it when she opened the present, then they laughed and let old memories in. It was the first time she'd laughed, you see, since Travis had died. Next thing we know, she'd ordered twenty or thirty of the things and always wore them." She handed her the tomatoes. "Wash and slice those, would you?"

"Sure."

"The tie-dye today is a change, but it fits her. Fits her now, anyway. For all the fun she and Travis used to have, she was always so serious about life. After the…well after the incident, after we moved her down here with us, she changed. She and Travis were gym rats, they liked to say. Nothing else. Down here? She hasn't set foot in the gym. No, she bought a fancy bike and rides that thing nearly every morning, I think. It's freeing, I'm sure. It all changed her outlook on life."

"She seems so…so cheerful, I guess is the word I'm looking for. In fact, I told Nana that she wasn't taking this case serious enough. That was the vandalism, I mean." She smiled. "I accused her of flirting with me instead of doing police work."

"Oh, don't ever doubt her dedication to the job, Lauren. She'll go above and beyond, that one. But cheerful, yes. That's a good word to describe her now. So many awful things happened in San Antonio. It zapped the life out of her."

"Is that why she doesn't go back?"

"I see she told you that much. No, she hasn't been back. She's close with her family and they talk on the phone all the time. Her parents came down to visit a couple of times. So did one of her sisters. But it'll probably be a while before she'll want to go back. Maybe in a few years, once her memories have faded some."

"Was he…killed in the line of duty?"

A shadow passed over Marsha's face. "That's a story for another time."

They were quiet as Marsha shaped the ground meat into patties and she sliced first the tomatoes, then the onions. She was now beyond curious about Harley's life. Her previous life, anyway. She couldn't picture Harley as the serious person Marsha said she used to be. Even from that very first time they met, Harley's eyes had been smiling—twinkling, almost. She was often teasing, playful. The wild, Hawaiian shirts simply added to that. Was that why she wore them? They made her smile?

CHAPTER NINETEEN

"I had a good time, Harley. Thank you for inviting me."

"I'm glad you came." She again parked next to Lauren's car, then walked beside her as they made their way along the fence. "I haven't made many friends in town."

"Me either, actually." Lauren's keys jingled as she unlocked her gate. "Truthfully, I haven't really tried."

"Why?"

"I'm not sure. At first, I was busy with this place. While Nana kept it up the best she could, the flowers and gardens had fallen into a weedy mess. Gerald wasn't working here then. My grandfather kept it up more than Nana, so when he passed, everything kinda fell apart."

"But you didn't move right away," she reminded her.

Lauren paused at the gate, as if trying to decide if they should take the conversation inside or not. "I spent the summers here. Four months, usually. And I worked dawn to dusk in the gardens, it seemed. My relationship with Leah was hanging by a thread by then, so I was torn between the need to get back to try to salvage it and my desire to stay away from the constant bickering and fighting." She ran a hand through her hair. "In hindsight, our relationship should have ended years earlier. Of course, at the time, I couldn't see that."

"So it wasn't an amicable breakup?"

Lauren gave a bitter laugh. "God, no. It was awful. Whatever love I still clung to disappeared very quickly." She held her hand up. "And I don't want to talk about it."

"I understand."

"What about you? Had your heart broken?"

"Me? No." She took a step away. "Not by a woman, anyway." She pointed to the cottage. "Go ahead. I'll wait and make sure you get inside, then I'll lock the gate behind me."

Lauren met her gaze in the shadows, then nodded. "Okay. See you later, Harley."

"Goodnight, Lauren."

Maybe it was being around Brian and Marsha, but she was feeling a little blue tonight. Travis wasn't ever far from her mind, but tonight he seemed to be hovering over her. She shoved her hands into her pockets, but instead of going to the SUV, she headed to the bay instead. She knew the gate code for the Heron Bay pier, and she unlocked it, walking slowly across the wooden planks. The green lights were soothing, and she paused to listen to the water as it lapped against the pylons. No one was out fishing, and she had the pier to herself. As she walked down its length, she glanced to her right, picturing Christopher Bryce's headless body bobbing in the water. She pushed that thought aside as she continued on.

It was much like the pier at her RV park, with two fish-cleaning stations instead of one. At the end was a large deck and she sat down on one of the benches. She leaned back and closed her eyes, letting in memories that she usually tried to keep locked up. Because she got angry when she let them in. Angry at Travis. She still had a hard time believing how selfish he'd been.

How could he do that? Why would he leave her?

It made no sense. No matter how many times she went over it in her mind, it made no freaking sense. He was strong. They'd seen a lot of shit in their days, but he never let anything get to him. She was the one who took everything to heart. She was the one who worried over cases and their outcomes. Not him.

Then why? Why that case?

"Are you okay, Harley?"

She was startled for a moment, but the quiet voice whispered past her, disappearing into the breeze. She turned her head, finding Lauren standing near the light, the green glow giving her an almost ghost-like appearance.

She sighed and turned her gaze back to the dark bay, seeing ripples in the water as it flowed beneath the lights. Lauren surprised her by coming closer. She paused only a moment before sitting down beside her.

"I'm a good listener."

She leaned her head back and closed her eyes. "I feel so alone sometimes." She hadn't intended to say the words out loud. Saying them out loud made them true. Saying them out loud made tears form in her eyes. "I lost my best friend."

Lauren leaned back too, letting their shoulders touch. "Tell me."

She swallowed, wondering at the request. What did Lauren want? Why was she even out here? She opened her eyes again, blinking several times to clear them. Did it matter? Lauren was here, offering an ear, offering some quiet companionship.

"He was...he was my partner. We had this case. A serial rapist. And murderer. Seven women over about thirteen months' time. All of them on the south side of the city, in older residential areas. We had DNA from semen, but there were never any prints. We had no suspects. All we had was a little stuffed bear that he'd leave at each scene." She closed her eyes for a second, picturing the damn things in her mind. "Travis and I called him the Teddy Bear Rapist. But we got lucky one day. It was a little after three in the morning. We had been driving around all night, every night for weeks, it seemed. Got a call. New parents were up with their baby and they saw two men jump the neighbor's fence."

She blew out her breath, her mind flashing back to that night, the way Travis had kicked the front door in, the commotion in the bedroom. The gunfire. The silence.

"We thought there was just one guy. We never thought there were two. Anyway, when we got there, she'd already been raped. She was tied to the bed, like all the others had been. The guy cut the woman's throat a second before Travis shot him. The other guy jumped out the window. Disappeared. The DNA we had from semen didn't match the guy Travis shot."

"So the rapes continued?" Lauren asked quietly.

"No. They stopped." She cleared her throat. "Four days later, Travis shot himself with his service weapon." The words were spoken matter-of-factly, but she heard Lauren gasp beside her. She turned, blinking away tears again. "And I get so goddamned mad at him every time I think about it. He wasn't that kind of guy, you know. Yeah, he was drunk on his ass. That was Travis's way of handling the stress."

She stood up quickly and walked to the edge of the pier, leaning against the railing. "He could have called me. If he was thinking about shooting himself in the goddamn head, he should have called me. Christ!"

She heard Lauren come up behind her, felt hands on her shoulders, rubbing lightly. She hung her head, letting tears fall. She hadn't cried in so long. Not since those first few dark days after it happened. Anger had replaced her tears back then. For a while. Then she'd just gone numb. She'd wanted to cry, but she couldn't. It was the worst feeling—when the tears wouldn't come.

They came now, though, and she let them. They came in waves, like high tide splashing the pier, and her hands gripped the railing hard, holding on against the onslaught. Lauren's touch never wavered, continuing her gentle, comforting strokes on her back. The breeze from the bay dried her tears as they fell, making way for new ones. She stood there for the longest time, with Lauren's soft touch on her. When her grief subsided, she felt drained—and still so alone. She wondered if she turned, would Lauren hold her? Would she pull her close and hold her tight? How long had it been since someone had touched her like that?

She didn't dare turn, though. She didn't want to be disappointed. Instead, she stood up a little straighter and cleared her throat. "Sorry about that."

Lauren gave her shoulder one last squeeze, then came up beside her, leaning against the railing much like she was. Their gazes were not on each other but on the bay.

"Tell me about the Hawaiian shirts."

Whatever she thought Lauren might say, that certainly wasn't it. She turned then and so did Lauren. Their eyes met and she wondered what Lauren saw in hers. "You hate my shirts."

Lauren smiled. "They're growing on me."

"I used to hate them too. It was a joke. Travis had a few of them and whenever he wore them, I gave him hell. So he started giving me one on my birthday." She laughed. "And he'd find the ugliest ones. We always went out for our birthdays and he made me wear it. He'd take a bunch of pictures and torment me with them for the rest of the year." Her smile disappeared. "My birthday was four months after he died. It was the worst day, yet the best day."

She moved away, going to the edge of the pier. "I hadn't been working. Brian was my captain and he put me on leave. I couldn't work. Hell, I could barely function. After about three months, Marsha came over. Stayed a week with me, told me I was acting like the victim and I needed to get back to living. She gave me the kick in the ass that I needed. Then when my birthday rolled around, Brian came over with a bottle of scotch and this present." She shook her head. "A damn Hawaiian shirt. I cried my eyes out that night. Then we drank scotch and told stories and...and the next day I had a hell of a hangover. But I felt alive again. For the first time since he died, I felt alive again."

Lauren was leaning against the railing, facing her. She smiled. "And thus, your Hawaiian shirt habit was born?"

"Yeah, something like that. The damn shirts make me a little happy, I guess."

Their eyes held for a long, quiet moment, then Lauren surprised her by moving closer. She stood still, letting Lauren wrap her arms around her and pull her into that tight hug she'd wanted earlier. She closed her eyes, relaxing against Lauren as she pulled her closer.

"I'm sorry about your partner."

When Lauren released her, Harley searched her eyes, seeing a gentle empathy there that made her feel...what? At peace? Like she wasn't all alone after all?

"Thank you, Lauren. For coming out to check on me. For the talk."

"You don't talk about him?"

"Sometimes. Brian and I go out for shrimp on Tuesday nights. We'll reminisce occasionally. But I don't like to think about it too much. It makes me angry and sad, both." She shoved her hands into her pockets. "He loved me. I know he did. So to think he'd do that, without calling me to talk it out—I just can't wrap my head around it." She sighed, not wanting to get into it again. "I should go."

They moved back along the pier in silence. At the road, they paused as a car drove past, then continued to the path that would take them back to the cottages. It was a warm and humid July night, yet the breeze made it comfortable. When they got to Lauren's gate, she held it open for her.

"Sleep tight."

Lauren smiled at that. "Thank you. Goodnight, Harley."

"I'll lock up." She waited until Lauren disappeared inside the cottage, then closed and locked the gate.

She felt a little lighter now, a little less lonely. She'd made a new friend, it seemed.

CHAPTER TWENTY

Lauren had resisted calling Harley yesterday, even though she'd pulled her phone out several times to do just that. She didn't have an excuse to call her and saying that she was checking on her sounded far too intimate for what their relationship was. They were barely friends, new friends. What business was it of hers to check on Harley's state of mind? She had hoped that Harley might pop over, as she sometimes did. But as she made her final rounds yesterday evening, there'd been no sign of her. She'd dutifully locked her gate and locked herself into her cottage for the night, eating a tasteless frozen dinner made only palatable by a glass—or two—of wine.

That's why she was pleasantly surprised to see the familiar figure in an equally familiar Hawaiian shirt walking up to the office door at seven sharp that morning. She'd been pouring herself a cup of coffee and as Harley came inside, she motioned to the pot.

"Want a cup?"

"Sure."

Harley leaned against the counter, watching her. "How are things?"

"Fine. What about you?"

Harley nodded. "Okay. No news to report."

"I mean, how are things with *you*," she clarified as she put a teaspoon of sugar in before handing Harley the cup.

Harley gave a quick smile. "I knew what you meant. I'm… okay. After our talk, I felt better, so thanks for that. Like I said, I try not to think about it too much."

She nodded. "I won't bring it up again."

Harley took a sip from her coffee. "This is good. Different from the other morning. I guess you know a lot about coffee."

Lauren raised her eyebrows questioningly.

"The coffeehouse thing."

Lauren put her cup down. "I don't remember telling you about that."

"Oh." Harley shifted a bit uncomfortably. "I, well, I may have done a background check on you."

"You *what*?"

Harley stared at her. "Maybe I shouldn't have told you."

Lauren narrowed her eyes. "You had no right to invade my privacy like that. I'm not a suspect, am I?"

Harley held up a hand. "Hey, it wasn't like that."

"Wasn't it?"

"I am a cop, you know."

"Yes, and you apparently enjoy doing background checks on people!"

Harley faced her, holding her gaze. "You had a random break-in. You had a damn headless body dumped at your pier. So yeah, I ran a background check just to make sure there wasn't something out there."

"And did you find any skeletons?"

"No. There was nothing abnormal. Squeaky clean, in fact."

"Well, that's good to know." She picked up her cup again. "You're right. You shouldn't have told me. Because it pisses me off."

"I'm sorry. But you have to admit, at the beginning, you weren't very forthcoming. I had to pry information out of you."

"That's so not true! I answered every one of your questions."
Hadn't she? Had she been evasive?

"Why did you and Leah break up?"

"That has nothing to do with this case." She sat her cup down again. "And if I wasn't forthcoming with everything, it was because you were asking personal questions that you had no business asking."

Harley simply stared at her, waiting.

She sighed. "Why do most couples break up?"

Harley shrugged. "Is this a test? I'll go with…let's see. They grow apart?"

Lauren rolled her eyes.

"Okay, so no." She grinned. "She was cheating on you?"

Lauren sighed again.

"Do I win?"

"Yes. But her cheating on me didn't start until we were already on shaky ground. I'll at least give her that." She added more coffee to her cup, wondering why she was divulging this to Harley. "I came down here in May, like always. In fact, I couldn't wait to get away. And our calls were infrequent and quite chilly. I went back after Labor Day in September and there was someone living in my house, playing with my dog, cooking in my kitchen." She paused. "And sleeping in my bed."

"Wow."

"Yes. Wow. Leah had packed my stuff—my *personal* stuff. All of our joint things—furniture, dishes, household items, whatever, she and—" She gritted her teeth. "She and Randi—with an I—intended on keeping." She closed her eyes for a second. "Along with Otter."

"So the house wasn't in both your names?"

"It was not. She was in the process of buying the house when we started dating. I moved in a few months later." She held her hand up. "And I don't want to talk about it."

Harley leaned her elbows on the counter. "Did you have a broken heart?"

"No. Well, at the time, yes, I suppose I thought I did. I'm not sure why, really. Like I said the other night, we hadn't been getting along and there was constant arguing over something. I was just so pissed off that she'd had the nerve to move someone into our house while I was gone. *Her* house," she clarified.

"What did you argue over?"

"Anything and everything. She played on a beach volleyball team and they had tournaments practically every weekend. I wasn't into that and she couldn't understand why I wasn't interested. She said I worked too much. She hated that I came here every summer. She said I loved this place more than her. She became a vegan. I didn't. None of her friends liked me." She waved her hand in the air. "On and on."

"So then—"

"Enough. No more talk about Leah. It's been three years." Then she smiled. "Tell me about you."

"Nothing to tell. I don't really date."

"Why not?"

"At first, there was the job. And Travis. Most of my downtime was spent with him or my family."

"No love life at all?"

Harley smiled quickly. "Well, whatever love life I had, I wouldn't call it dating."

"What about here in Rockport? Do you have any 'not exactly dating' girls here?"

Harley shook her head. "No. I haven't been on a single date since I've been here." She met her gaze. "Why? Are you offering?"

"Me?" She shook her head. "No. God, no." The office door opened, and she was thankful for the distraction. She looked past Harley. "Good morning, Mrs. Burris. Heading out already?"

"Yes. We need to get back for our granddaughter's birthday party. We had a lovely time, as always."

"Did you have success on your fishing trip?"

"Not me—I caught a few small redfish, but they weren't keepers. Jeb now caught two nice speckled trout. He'll grill those up for us one day this week."

Harley moved to the door. "I should get going, Lauren. Thanks for the coffee."

Lauren nodded at her. "See you later."

"There's a police vehicle out there. Is something going on?"

Lauren shook her head. "No, no. That was Detective Shepherd. We had a break-in at the clubhouse earlier in the month. She was following up."

"Oh, no. It's always so quiet around here." She frowned. "Something we should worry about?"

"No, no. Not at all. They didn't actually take anything. It was more vandalism than a break-in." Well, if you ignored the message on the mirror, that is. "Probably kids or something." She took the key from her. "Any plans to come back this summer?"

"Not until September, I think, Lauren. We take our annual trip to Colorado next month."

"Oh, that's right. Well, I'm sure you'll enjoy the cooler temperatures."

"Yes, we will." Mrs. Burris tapped the counter with her knuckles. "See you in September, dear."

Lauren hung the keys on the rack, then logged the departure into the system. Her glance went to Harley's coffee cup and she picked it up, taking it to the little sink in the back to rinse it out. She paused in her task, staring blankly at the wall. She hated to admit it, but she liked Harley, obnoxious Hawaiian shirts and all.

"God, but I don't want to date her," she murmured, as if reminding herself that she wasn't *supposed* to like Harley Shepherd. She wondered why Harley didn't date. What had Marsha said? Harley rarely brought a woman—a date—with her. Harley was attractive, yes. Other than her taste in clothing, she had no glaring flaws. She was likeable. Nice. Her partner's death obviously had scarred her, but her dating habits were apparently in place before then.

She didn't know why she was worrying over it. Some people simply didn't need to have someone in their life. Like her. She was content with the way things were. Why complicate things with dating?

Was she content, though? Hadn't the tiny slivers of loneliness been growing? Little cracks in her armor here and there, wistful moments while having a solitary dinner—like last night—that she wished there was someone in her life. If not a lover, then at least a good friend. She had neither at the moment.

It was something she didn't like to think about—how truly alone she'd be when Nana was gone. While she and her brother had never really been close, their relationship had deteriorated to the point that they barely spoke and only when she initiated it.

She pushed that thought aside too. Sure, Nana was eighty-six, but she was in excellent health. Hopefully, she wouldn't have to worry about that for many years yet.

She and Harley were becoming friends, though, weren't they? Would Harley still pop over from time to time, even after all this police business was finished? Could they maybe have dinner together sometime? She knew that Harley and Brian went out for shrimp on Tuesdays. And she had her standing dinner date with her grandmother on Wednesdays. Maybe Harley would be up for a burger at The Pub on Thursday or Friday. She quickly shook her head. Not Friday. Dinner on a Friday would indicate it was a date. Thursday would be safer. She rolled her eyes at her thoughts and went back out front. Dinner on a Friday would not signify a date.

One of the white golf carts—used by the cleaning staff—buzzed by loaded down with clean towels and Angela, the driver, gave her a quick wave. The yard crew was already here, and she heard mowers going. Gerald was walking by with two sections of PVC pipe. Hopefully that meant he was going to fix the water leak in the flowerbed by Number Seven. It wasn't a huge leak, but it was enough to be annoying. She'd been after him to fix it for weeks now.

The phone rang and she pulled her attention from the activity outside, picking it up automatically.

"Good morning. Heron Bay Resort. How may I help you?"

CHAPTER TWENTY-ONE

The sun was a good fifteen minutes from rising, but there was plenty of light in the sky for her to zip along the bay on her bike. The breeze was cool, and she slowed as she came upon a heron fishing just offshore, his sleek neck curved, ready to strike. He paid her no mind as she went past, and she smiled into the wind, acknowledging how good she felt this morning.

She and Brian had their usual dinner date last night, but he'd surprised her by bringing Marsha along. Marsha's family all still lived in the area and Tuesdays were her normal night for dinner with her parents. That got canceled so she joined them for shrimp. With Marsha there, there was no police talk and no mention of Travis. Although Marsha was beyond curious about her and Lauren's relationship.

"There is no relationship," she had insisted.

"Then you need to ask her out. A real date."

"I don't think she'd go for that."

"I think she would. I think she likes you."

Harley skipped the park this morning, going instead around the lakes and the golf course. Should she ask Lauren out? Like a real date? She shook her head as she turned onto Lake Circle. Despite the affection Lauren showed her the other night out on the pier, she didn't think she'd warmed up to her that much. She still remembered the flash in her eyes when she'd told her she'd done the background check on her. Yes, a flash, a bit of anger, but that had disappeared quickly, hadn't it? They'd been talking about dating and her lack of a love life when they'd been interrupted. She'd been teasing when she asked if Lauren was offering. Hadn't she?

Maybe. Or maybe they should just work on this friendship they'd started.

She peddled a little faster, deciding to go back to the loop and go by the Big Tree. She'd then take the road along the bay back to her RV. It would be a good workout, a little over an hour total, and she'd have time for a cup of coffee before she headed into work.

* * *

Harley hadn't intended on stopping, but when she'd slowed as she passed the Heron Bay Resort, she spotted Lauren outside the office, the familiar garden hose in her hand as she tended to the flowers. Without much thought, she found herself turning onto the driveway. Lauren turned at the sound of her vehicle, offering her a smile.

"Good morning, Detective Shepherd."

"Ms. Voss," she greeted as she shoved her sunglasses on top of her head. "Gonna be a hot one today, they say."

"Yes. That's why I'm getting a head start on my watering."

"You water the flowers every day?"

"This time of year, yes. I don't mind. It's relaxing. Gerald helps too, but he only works three days a week. And a lot of the beds have automatic sprinklers."

Harley walked up beside her, admiring the colorful blooms around them. "So, there's not really much going on with the case. Corpus PD verified that he was killed on a boat. Everyone is surmising that the killer drove the boat up the bay, dumped the body, then went back and left the boat."

"And still no witnesses or anything?"

"No. Where his fishing gear was found, it was out in the channels. At night. No surveillance cameras near there. It's been all over the news in Corpus. They've had a few fishermen come up, say they saw this and that. One guy, he fishes all the time. Said he saw a van out that night that he didn't recognize." She shrugged. "That's about the extent of it."

"I saw the interview with his wife. It was so sad. His kids are still in high school. The girl was so upset, she couldn't even talk."

"I know." She hadn't seen the interview, but Marsha had told her about it. She made it a point not to watch the news.

"So they'll probably not get justice, will they?"

"Probably not." She paused. "Not unless he kills again and slips up this time."

"God, let's hope that's not the case. At least not here in Rockport. I don't think our little town can handle another one."

"Yes. Violent crime down here is usually drug-related and doesn't affect the common masses. A case like this, where the guy was apparently at the wrong place, wrong time, gets everyone's attention." She cleared her throat. "So I usually go over to the Pub on Wednesdays for dinner. You want to join me tonight?" she asked casually.

But Lauren shook her head. "Can't. I have dinner with Nana on Wednesdays."

"Oh." She shrugged. "Maybe some other time then." She put her sunglasses back on, hoping to hide her disappointment. "I should go. See you around."

When she opened the door to her vehicle, Lauren called to her.

"Harley? How about tomorrow?"

She lifted her sunglasses, meeting Lauren's gaze. "Tomorrow?"

Lauren nodded.

"Okay. It's a date."

Lauren shook her head quickly. "No, no, no. Not a date. Just dinner."

Harley walked over to her again. "Of course it's a date. We've already kissed."

"That was a fake, pretend kiss that lasted all of one second. So we have *not* kissed."

"We haven't?" She met Lauren's eyes, trying to read them. Was that a little bit of a challenge she saw there? Was Lauren daring her to kiss her? Right here, out in the open, standing on the manicured lawn with flowers all around them? "When I think of that kiss, it always lasts way longer than one second."

It dawned on her then how badly she did indeed want to kiss Lauren. She wondered if Lauren could see that want in her eyes. Perhaps so, because when she leaned closer, Lauren didn't pull away. No, she met her mouth with just a touch of urgency. That surprised her. Pleasantly. Their lips moved together, slowly, and she heard the tiniest of moans escape Lauren's mouth. God, she wanted to deepen the kiss—yes, she did, because there were all sorts of wonderful things happening in her body. If they weren't out here among the flowers and if Lauren weren't still holding a garden hose, she would be tempted to pull Lauren flush against her. It was then she realized they weren't even touching, nothing but their mouths. Lauren's hands were between them, the water hose drowning the flowers without concern. She pulled back then, again meeting Lauren's eyes. They were dark and filled with wonder, as were hers, no doubt.

"That was, like, ten seconds long. So, it's a date," she said quietly, her voice a little husky. "I'll pick you up. Yes?"

Lauren still looked stunned, but she nodded, never breaking their gaze. "Okay. Yes. A date."

CHAPTER TWENTY-TWO

"It's not a date, Nana."

"You just said it was."

"I should have phrased it differently. It's dinner. That's all. We're becoming friends. Nothing more," she said with emphasis. She would *never* tell Nana that they kissed. And she would certainly never tell her that that simple kiss had sent chills up and down her body, something she hadn't felt in more years than she could remember. Or that she'd actually considered—for a brief moment—tossing the garden hose aside, pressing herself close to Harley and—

"Are you playing hard to get?"

Lauren shook off the mental picture of her and Harley in an intimate embrace and managed to roll her eyes for emphasis. Why had she mentioned the date at all? "Dinner. At the Pub. We'll probably sit at the bar and have a beer and a burger. Not really a romantic date, Nana."

Nana picked up her wineglass, looking at her over the rim. "At your age, you'd think you wouldn't be so picky."

"Picky? First of all, I'm not being picky. I'm simply not interested in dating. I am plenty busy with the resort. I don't have time to date. And secondly, if I were going to date, Harley Shepherd would not be my choice. She's too much like Leah." *Wasn't she?*

"Oh poo. If that were the case, you wouldn't even be friends with her. To hear you tell it, Leah was the bride of Satan."

Lauren laughed. "Did I make her out to be that bad?"

"Wasn't she?"

"Yeah. At the end, yes, she was downright evil." She sighed. "Leah and I hung on too long. We had too many differences and not nearly enough in common. She liked crowds and people and social events. I—"

"You are a homebody," Nana finished for her. "Even when you were in school, you didn't have very many friends, did you?"

"No." Oh, that's not to say there were no friends. She had a group she hung out with, both in high school and college. There just wasn't ever that one good, close friend. Had there ever been? How sad, really. Here she was, thirty-three-years old and Nana was her only true friend. When she and Leah had still been together, of course she'd considered Leah her best friend. She'd never been Leah's best friend, though. Not even close. Leah had hordes of friends. Very few of them had warmed up to her and vice versa. She found them shallow, superficial. They, in turn, mocked her Texas roots and her simplistic life. Even Leah had called her unsophisticated on more than one occasion.

"So it's good you're making a friend now, then." Nana folded her hands together. "When do I get to meet her? She's dashing, isn't she?"

Lauren laughed. "Will you quit saying that? You'd think you have a crush on her the way you go on about her. But no, I don't think you'll get to meet her. What? Should I bring her over to your place one day?"

"She could join us for dinner next Wednesday."

Lauren shook her head firmly. "No. This is our time. Now, tell me what's been going on. Has Mary left for Portland already?"

Nana seemed to forget about Harley as she filled her in on the latest gossip. By the time their dinner arrived, she too had put Harley from her mind.

Later, though, as she drove home, she contemplated her dinner date tomorrow. And yes, despite her words to Nana, it *was* a date. The look in Harley's eyes—the kiss—indicated that yes, it was a real date. Would it be so bad, really? She hadn't been on a date since she and Leah first met. She'd been twenty-six and had been quite infatuated with her, to be sure. Leah was charming and attractive, and Lauren had fallen for her in short order. They had their very first fight four months later when she'd "abandoned" Leah, to use her words. Even a new romance hadn't kept her away from Rockport for her annual summer visit. Leah had surprised her by showing up at the resort in July and they'd spent a week acting like newlyweds. That was the one and only time, however. Subsequent years produced more arguments, but Leah never came again.

When their relationship finally did end, she never entertained the idea of dating. She'd still been too raw from all the petty fighting and the tug of war they'd waged over Otter. Three years had slipped by, and now a police detective, of all things, had come into her life. A police detective who had come to Rockport to heal. A woman who wore gaudy Hawaiian shirts because they made her smile. On the surface, yes, Harley reminded her of Leah. But she suspected that beneath it all, they were nothing alike.

Should she go on a date with her? Should she take a chance? She smiled a little as she turned into Heron Bay Resort. She *was* going on a date, wasn't she? She'd already agreed to it.

Besides, she liked Harley Shepherd. Harley made her days seem a little brighter whenever she popped over. Popped over to flirt with her.

Harley—and her sweet, almost tentative kiss—made her heart spring to life. It had been many, many years since she'd felt that fluttering in her chest. Yes, she liked Harley and it was definitely a date.

She was actually looking forward to it.

CHAPTER TWENTY-THREE

A sound—or something—woke her. Lauren rolled onto her back, blinking in the darkness. Something wasn't right. She listened, hearing nothing but the usual hum of the ceiling fan in the quiet bedroom.

But no. It wasn't quiet. She heard night sounds and the bay—sounds she'd hear while sitting on the porch. She turned her head slowly, her eyes widening as the breeze ruffled the curtains at the window. She hadn't had her windows open since April, when the weather had still been cool. Certainly not in July.

The fact that her bedroom window was wide open finally penetrated her sleepy brain. Her heart pounded to life, threatening to choke her, yet she remained paralyzed with fear, only barely resisting the urge to yank the covers up over her face, as if that would protect her. She slowly sat up, eyes darting around the dark room. Her bedroom door was closed. That caused her breath to catch. She always slept with it open.

She silently counted to three, then tossed the covers off. She grabbed her phone off the nightstand, then hesitated. Hide in the closet? Memories of old horror movies came back to her—they *always* hid in the closet—and she moved into the bathroom instead. She quietly locked the door, then, with trembling hands, she called the one person she knew would help her. Harley. As it rang, she sank down to the floor, against the far wall, her eyes glued to the door. A sleepy voice answered.

"Lauren? Everything okay? Or are you missing me?"

"Harley," she whispered as loudly as she dared. "I…I think someone's in my house."

"*What?*"

"I woke up and the bedroom window is wide open. And I never close my bedroom door. But it's closed now. I'm scared to death."

"Oh, Christ. Where are you?"

"I'm hiding in the bathroom."

"Stay there. I'm on my way. Five minutes."

Before she could urge Harley to *hurry*, the line went dead. Five minutes would be an eternity. She stared at the phone, noting the time. Three thirty-three. The witching hour. Nothing good could possibly happen at three thirty-three in the morning. Not with her window open, the colorful curtains blowing lazily from the gulf breeze as if they hadn't a care in the world.

She leaned her head back against the wall, her hammering heart still loud in her ears. She wanted to close her eyes and pray, but she didn't dare take her gaze from the door. Here she was, in her sleep shirt and undies, hugging her knees tightly. As she stared, she swore she saw the knob turn. She stood up, her chest so tight with fright that she was afraid she'd pass out—or have a heart attack.

Yes! It did turn. She heard the jiggle of the door as someone attempted to open it. *Oh dear god.* She tried to focus, tried to think of what she could use for a weapon. A can of shaving cream? A dull razor blade?

Silence again. She stepped backward, her mind racing through scenarios of what would happen. Him crashing through the door. Him kicking it in. Maybe shooting his way in.

Regardless of how, he'd get her. Easily. What would he do? Use a knife? Would he kill her here, leaving her for Harley to find? Or would he take her with him? Would she end up like that poor man, her head removed and dumped in the bay?

She was shaking with fear, so much so that her teeth were chattering, and her phone slipped from her hands to the floor. The sound of it hitting the tile was loud and seemed to vibrate in the small room. She snatched it up, then backed up against the wall.

Her eyes widened as the doorknob turned again. *Oh my god.* A hard thud against the door made her jump and she could no longer take a breath, she was trembling so. Another thud. Then another. Would the door hold? Would Harley get there in time?

No. She didn't think Harley would make it. She suddenly didn't think *she* would make it.

CHAPTER TWENTY-FOUR

Harley sped across the causeway, the early morning fog over the bay making for a dreary, spooky morning. She gripped the steering wheel hard as she turned sharply, her tires skidding as she spun into the resort's driveway. The white lights that were wrapped around the oak trees seemed to be twinkling, and she slowed, noting that most of the cottages had cars parked in front. She passed the clubhouse, ignoring the "road ends" sign and drove as close as she could to Lauren's cottage.

The first thing she saw was the gate standing open. She pulled her weapon as she peered through the fog, looking for any movement. The chain had been cut and it dangled from the post, the lock still intact. She moved closer, her footsteps quiet. The front door was ajar, a little less than halfway open. She used her foot to push it, opening it fully.

"Lauren?" she called. She listened, hearing nothing but silence. She didn't sense a presence there. She slid her hand along the wall, finding the light switch. She turned it on, her gaze moving quickly through the living room and kitchen. Nothing seemed amiss.

She moved into Lauren's bedroom, pausing only a second before turning the light on. She steeled herself for what she might find. She let out a relieved breath to find the bed empty. The window was indeed open, the screen missing. She absently noted the curtain fluttering against the sill as she turned, looking at the bathroom door. She turned the knob, but it was locked.

"Lauren?"

"Oh my god! Harley?" The door jerked open, and Lauren flung herself into her arms with so much force, it sent her careening backward and they landed on top of the bed. "I have never been so glad to see someone as you." Lauren buried her face against her neck. "I don't think I've ever been this afraid in my life. In fact, I know I haven't."

"It's okay. I got you." She held her tightly, only dimly aware that Lauren was dressed in next to nothing.

Lauren lifted her head then. "I'm so sorry." She sat up, then her eyes widened. "He's gone, right? You checked everywhere, right?"

"Not yet...no." She got off the bed, then pointed at her. "You stay here."

"The hell I will!"

Harley pulled her off the bed, then eased her into a tight hug. "I'm right here. You're fine." But she could feel Lauren shaking.

"Don't leave me alone. Please."

"Okay, I won't." She moved toward the window, taking a look outside but she saw nothing in the shadows. There were two shrubs beside a little porch, but they weren't big enough to hide under. "I don't think anyone is here. I'll check the closet, under the bed—"

"The spare bathroom."

"The spare bathroom. Everywhere," she said.

And she did, searching in whatever hiding place someone could have been, all the while Lauren nearly clung to her as they moved throughout the house. Nothing looked out of place or disturbed. When she was satisfied that he was indeed gone, she relaxed, holstering her weapon before turning to Lauren.

"Tell me what happened."

Lauren ran both hands through her long hair, then tucked it behind her ears. "Oh, Harley…I'll need a strong cup of coffee for this." She pulled open a drawer and stared inside, apparently trying to decide on which coffee pod she wanted. She finally picked one out. "A dark roast. What about you?" Then she paused. "You weren't, like, planning on leaving or anything? Right? You're not going to leave me?"

Harley gave her a half smile. "Not leaving, no. Dark roast is fine. I'll need extra sugar."

Lauren turned the Keurig on, then got two cups out for them. She popped one of the pods inside the coffeemaker and Harley thought her hand was still shaking a little. She found herself staring at Lauren—the exposed long legs, bare feet, the T-shirt that barely reached her hips, the black panties that peeked out. She jerked her gaze up, startled to find Lauren watching her. She swallowed a bit nervously.

"Not that I'm not totally enjoying this…but it would be a lot less distracting if you'd put some shorts on or something."

Lauren tilted her head as their eyes met, then she gave her a slight smile and a quick nod. She went toward her bedroom, then stopped.

"Umm, do you mind coming with me?"

Harley stood in the doorway, leaning against the jamb, watching as Lauren pulled gray cotton shorts from a drawer and slipped them on, but left her feet bare.

"Better?"

Harley let her gaze travel over Lauren again, noting the T-shirt must be something Lauren slept in.

"Not necessarily better, no, but safer, I suppose."

Lauren walked over to her, holding her gaze. She cupped her cheek with a warm hand. "I've just had the most traumatic night of my life, yet I find myself wanting to flirt with you." Lauren's gaze dropped to her lips for a second, then she again met her gaze. "Should I get properly dressed? Bra? Shoes?"

"I think I can control myself."

Lauren laughed quietly at that and dropped her hand. "Thank you, Harley. You really are my knight in shining armor, aren't you?"

Harley shrugged. "You don't think I would have done this for anyone?"

"You live at least five minutes away, if not longer. Yet you were here in what? Three minutes?"

"I may have broken a few traffic laws, yes."

They went back into the kitchen, and Lauren added sugar to the cup that had brewed. She handed it to her, then started a second cup. She had just taken a sip when Lauren turned quickly to her.

"Wait a minute. You're in a T-shirt. Not one of your Hawaiian shirts."

"I just grabbed something when I got out of bed." She looked down at the faded blue T-shirt, an old one she'd had in San Antonio advertising a bar she and Travis used to frequent. She'd slipped it on as she'd run out the door.

"And shorts and flip-flops. You look nice."

"Nice? Not like a cop?"

"You always look nice."

"You hate my shirts," she reminded her.

Lauren wiggled her eyebrows. "I like this one."

"The fact that I'm braless or—"

"Yes. But it's four in the morning and far too early to be flirting."

Is that what they were doing? Flirting? Or was it just a way to relieve some of the tension after the trauma Lauren had been through?

Lauren put a little sugar in her cup as well, then took a sip, her eyes closing with a sigh. "I don't know what made me wake. With the window open, maybe the sounds were different. I thought how quiet it was and then I thought, no, it wasn't quiet. I could hear the bay, I could hear night sounds. Sounds that shouldn't be there." Lauren took another sip of coffee, then put her cup down. "The breeze was blowing the curtains into the room. I sat up and saw that the bedroom door was closed. I leave it open at night."

"Was he in your room?"

Lauren shook her head. "No. At least I don't think so. I...I panicked. I grabbed my phone and ran into the bathroom, locking the door. Then I called you. Then I waited." Her hand was shaking again when she picked up her cup. "The doorknob turned. It seemed like it was right away, but maybe a few minutes had passed." She visibly swallowed. "Then he was trying to break in, hitting the door. I don't know, like he slammed against it with his shoulder or maybe he was kicking at it." Lauren met her gaze. "I was terrified, Harley. I thought he was going to break in and kill me. I didn't think you would get here in time."

"I don't mind saying, I was a little terrified myself. I was afraid of what I'd find."

Lauren seemed to relax again. "Then he just stopped. There was silence and then I heard what I assume was him kicking the screen out. Then I heard your voice." Lauren smiled sweetly at her. "It was like an angel's voice. My hero."

Harley felt a blush light her face which caused Lauren to laugh. "I'm sorry. Is that putting too much pressure on you?"

Harley finished her coffee, then slid the cup toward her. "Wouldn't mind another."

"Of course."

"We'll need to dust for prints. I need to report this."

Lauren touched her arm with her hand. "Can we keep it quiet? I don't want to upset the guests with a bunch of police cars here." Then her eyes widened. "Oh my god. I didn't even think. What if he's on the grounds somewhere? What if he broke into another cottage? I mean, what if—"

"I think, for whatever reason, he's after you, Lauren. The chain on your gate was cut. Bolt cutters. He would have had to have known it was chained. Bolt cutters aren't something people normally carry around with them. But yes, I can dust for prints. I won't need to call someone in to do that."

"Okay, good."

"Has anyone besides you touched your window, for instance? Does the cleaning staff come in here?"

Lauren shook her head. "I maintain it myself. Don't look too closely, though. I can't remember the last time I actually dusted the place."

"Okay. Let me go get my kit. I'll do the gate, the front door, your bedroom door, the window."

"You're going outside?"

She heard the panic in her voice. "Do you want to come with me?"

"I feel like I'm being rather clingy, but—"

"So we'll go out and get my kit. You can hold the flashlight for me. I'll teach you how we do it. It's really simple."

"Thank you, Harley, for understanding."

CHAPTER TWENTY-FIVE

"Where is she now?"

Harley motioned out the door. "Out at my desk. She's still a little shook up."

"But no prints?"

"No. He wore gloves. The few clean prints I got all matched Lauren's. And she's got three surveillance cameras at the resort. Nothing on any of them."

Brian leaned back in his chair. "So what's your theory? Linked to the vandalism?"

"I don't know." She ran a hand through her hair. "Some crazy guy stalking her at random? She swears there's nothing in her past that could have triggered this. And I told you I did a background check on her. There was nothing out of the ordinary."

"What about that guy you said wanted to buy the resort?"

"No, I haven't checked him out. I will."

"What about that guy you said harasses her? You cleared him on Christopher Bryce, but what if that was simply a coincidence that it was her pier? We could be looking at two separate things here. That murder may have absolutely nothing to do with her."

"Yeah, I could see him being a stalker. Cute rich guy who thinks he's God's gift to women. He might be put off by her turning him down." She nodded. "If he was anywhere near here, I'll take another look at him. I also had her call to request a couple more security cameras—one at her house and one on the path to the bay. He had to have come in from the bayside. There was nothing at the entrance. The whole resort itself has a tall privacy fence around it. Doubt he climbed over it."

"I've driven by the Heron Bay Resort many times, of course, but I've never been there so I don't know the layout. There's a motel and RV park on one side, isn't there?"

"Yes. I actually almost rented a spot there when I moved here. The other side is a small subdivision. I think there's five homes there. But like I said, the privacy fence is tall, ten-foot at least. Not impossible for someone to scale it, but unlikely."

Brian nodded. "So now what?"

Harley grinned. "I'm thinking she may need twenty-four-hour protection."

Brian laughed. "And you're volunteering?"

She thought back to that morning, the frightened look in Lauren's eyes, the tight grip she'd had on her arm. And the sleep shirt she'd been in with no bra, the black panties. She smiled broader.

"Yeah, I'm volunteering." Then her smile faltered a little. "She hasn't actually asked, but I doubt she'd decline the offer." Would she? No, Lauren hadn't seemed to want her out of her sight. "I guess I'll run her back. Now that it's daylight and people are around, I think it'll be safe."

"I'll get with Deeks," Brian said. "I know we've increased our patrol around there, but I'll make sure that hasn't lapsed."

"Thanks. I'll be in touch."

She found Lauren where she'd left her, sitting beside her desk. Her legs were crossed, and she was staring at the far wall, apparently lost in thought.

"Hey, you okay?"

Lauren looked at her, relief showing in her eyes. "Yes."

"You want to get out of here?"

"Where to?"

"Take you back?"

The relief vanished, and panic took its place. "To the resort or…or my house?"

"I was thinking the office. People are out and about, I suppose. Your staff will be there. Gerald?"

"Yes, he'll be there too." Lauren took a deep breath, as if for courage. "I guess I can't hide, can I?"

"I'll hang around for a bit, if you want."

Lauren met her gaze. "And what about tonight?" she asked quietly.

Harley smiled at that. "I think we had a date planned, didn't we?"

Lauren smiled too. "And after that? Will you stay with me?"

"Why, Ms. Voss, is that a veiled innuendo?"

"Not so veiled, no." Her smiled faded. "I'm scared to be alone, Harley."

"I know. I can stay with you if you want," she offered as nonchalantly as possible. "Your sofa isn't lumpy, is it?"

Their eyes held and Lauren's smile returned. "You're too sweet, aren't you?"

"Am I?" She wiggled her eyebrows playfully. "Maybe I have ulterior motives."

"Do you now? Then why are you suggesting the sofa?"

"Seeing as how we've not had that first date, I thought suggesting your bed would be a bit forward." Harley motioned with her head toward the door. "Come on, I'll buy you breakfast. How about tacos at Jorge's?"

"The food truck? Oh, I love that place. Deal."

By the time they got there, the morning rush had subsided and there was no line. They each got two tacos, both ordering the spicy chorizo and egg. For her second one, Lauren toned it down with potato and egg, but Harley got another spicy one— carnitas and rice with extra jalapenos.

"So you like spicy food, huh?" Lauren asked as she bit into her first one.

Harley nodded, biting into the chorizo and egg before pulling out into traffic again. "I like spicy, period. Besides, I grew up in San Antonio. Not liking Mexican food wasn't an option. We had it three or four nights a week."

"Your mom cooked?"

Harley took another bite. "My mom is a great cook. She didn't work—well, other than hauling us all over the place—so she was always there when we got home from school. She cooked every day except Sunday. We either went out for a big lunch then or my dad would cook something on the grill."

She heard Lauren give a satisfied moan as she took another big bite of the taco. "I didn't realize how hungry I was," she explained with a mouthful. She wadded up the wrapper when she finished and tossed it into the bag before taking out her second one. "I don't picture you as a cook."

"No? Well, when you see my little RV, you'll really think I don't cook. Which I don't. I do breakfast sometimes, that's about it. And I've got a grill outside. I love to do fish on it."

"Will I get to see your RV?"

"Actually, we can go there now, if you want. I wasn't really teasing earlier. I think I should stay with you tonight. And I kinda need to put some real clothes on."

"I wasn't aware that you were teasing," Lauren said as she reached over to wipe the corner of her mouth. "You had a little salsa there. But yes, I want you to stay with me. There's no way I could stay there alone."

"Okay. So we'll swing by my place and I'll pick up some clothes and stuff." She pointed at the bag. "I'll take my second one, please."

* * *

Despite Harley warning her that the RV park was a little run down, Lauren was shocked at the condition. Most of the RVs were older and most appeared stationary, some even on blocks with the tires removed. She couldn't imagine what had drawn Harley to this place.

"Why here, Harley?"

Harley pulled the SUV in front of a beige trailer that was crammed between two larger ones. Lauren turned to look at her, eyebrows raised.

"Like I said, I wasn't sure I was going to stay in Rockport. This place is relatively cheap," she said with a laugh. "As you can probably tell." Harley paused before getting out. "The bay. Being right here at the bay, being able to walk along it at night—I needed the peace that it afforded. Plus, I bought a mountain bike and I'm close to the park, so…"

She got out without finishing her thought and Lauren did as well. She heard country music playing and there was a dog barking a few trailers away. Other than that, there didn't seem to be anyone around.

"Do people live here fulltime?"

"About half. This is kinda like a little fishing village." Harley took keys from her pocket and unlocked the door. "On weekends, it's pretty full."

She saw a bike chained to the corner of the RV and her gaze traveled over the little table and two chairs that occupied the tiny strip of grass between her place and the next trailer. Before she could comment on the modest sitting area, Harley motioned her inside.

"I'd offer to give you a tour, but this is about it," she said, motioning to the miniature kitchen and the small living room. "Bedroom is tiny. Bathroom is even smaller." She put on some lights, then closed—and locked—the outside door. "Give me about ten minutes." Harley gave her a quick smile. "Feel free to snoop around."

Lauren nodded as she watched her go through a door at the back. She did as Harley had given her permission to do— she snooped. The kitchen first, opening one of the few cabinets, finding exactly two plates, two bowls, one coffee cup, and a tumbler. For whiskey? The other cabinets were sparsely filled— some pasta, a bag of rice, a few cans of beans, and an assortment of vegetables. She wondered if Harley had stocked this when she moved and had forgotten about it.

She went into the living room, which consisted of a sofa, not much bigger than a loveseat. There was a nice TV and a small, mismatched table beside the sofa where a remote sat and an upside-down book. She turned it over, the title tugging at her heart.

Grief: How to Heal and Accept Your Loss

She picked it up, opening it to a page with a bookmark. It wasn't a bookmark, though. It was a photo. She plucked it out, staring at Harley first, then at the man who had his arm around her shoulders. Harley's hair was a little longer than she kept it now. They were both wearing gaudy Hawaiian shirts and she wondered if maybe it was taken on Harley's birthday. Travis was a little taller than Harley, his hair as dark as hers, and their smiles were wide and happy, making her smile in return.

She slipped the photo back into the book, then put it back the way she'd found it. Was Harley still grieving? Still hurting? If she didn't know about Travis, if she only went on Harley's actions, her appearance, her personality, she'd say no. The Harley she'd met was flirty and playful, teasing and smiling. There was no hint that beneath the surface she was hurting. Not hurting enough to still need a self-help book to get her through it.

She heard the shower turn off and she sat down on the sofa and crossed her legs, her gaze traveling around the room, seeing nothing personal there. No knick-knacks, no pictures. There was nothing on the walls. Of course she didn't know much about RVs. Could you hammer a nail in and hang something?

"You okay?"

She turned, finding Harley with her head sticking around the door. Her hair was wet and the one bare shoulder she saw indicated that Harley was naked. She met her gaze, conscious of a flutter in her chest. Good lord, she'd just had the most traumatic night of her life, and the sight of this woman in near undress was causing her libido to flare.

"Yes," she finally answered, her voice a little thick. She motioned her away with her hand. "Put some clothes on, huh?"

Harley smiled at her, that familiar flirty smile that she'd grown to recognize. "Be right out."

She leaned back against the sofa and closed her eyes, not trying to temper the smile that was on her lips. She liked Harley. Why had she ever thought that she didn't?

"She reminded you of Leah," she murmured quietly.

Oh, yeah. Leah. She opened her eyes then and sighed. She needed to let that go. That was three years in the past and no, Harley was *nothing* like Leah. Harley was more genuine, more caring. Well, she was a cop. She assumed that "caring" came with the job. But with Harley, she imagined that what you saw was what you got. She was unpretentious, that was for sure, and perfectly comfortable in her gaudy Hawaiian shirts, seemingly not caring in the least what anyone thought of her or her shirts. At the beginning, Harley had simply laughed off her mocking of them. And she liked that about Harley, she realized. She was amiable, mild-mannered, and easy-going. Completely the opposite of Leah.

Well, that was a little unfair, she supposed. Leah was certainly likeable, judging how she'd been drawn to her in the first place. Leah had tons of friends. The difference was, Leah wouldn't be caught dead in an obnoxious Hawaiian shirt, lest someone think poorly of her. Leah was all about perception and—as she'd learned from living with her—perfection. Leah *wanted* to be charming and dashing so she played that part as it suited her. With Harley, on the other hand, it seemed to come completely natural to her. There was no pretense. No acting.

The door opened, stopping her musings, and as Harley came out carrying a small duffel bag, Lauren gave a hearty laugh.

"What?" Harley was trying to keep a smile from her face. "What's so funny?"

"Oh my god, you are too cute."

Harley grinned. "I take it you like my shirt?"

"I didn't think you could possibly top that gaudy neon one you were wearing that night at the Pub. But this one? Wow. Just wow."

The shirt in question was bright orange with yellow somethings plastered on it. Pineapples, maybe? Palm fronds littered any remaining space and purple parrots clung to each one. It was absolutely hideous, and she couldn't possibly stop smiling.

"Yep. This one will cure what ails you." Harley picked her keys up off the counter. "You ready?"

"I suppose."

Harley opened the fridge and Lauren couldn't help herself as she peeked over her shoulder. In the brief moment it took for Harley to pull out two water bottles, she spotted a carton of eggs, a squeeze bottle of mayo, and a white Styrofoam takeout container. So she really didn't cook, did she?

They drove back across the causeway, and Lauren looked over into the bay, absently watching as brown pelicans soared over the water. She kept an eye out for dolphins, but none showed themselves. Soon Harley was turning left into the resort, and Lauren felt a bit of her apprehension return. As if reading her mind, Harley reached over and touched her arm.

"I'll hang around for a while. Maybe walk the grounds, enjoy the flowers."

Lauren smiled at that. "With this shirt you have on, I won't be able to tell you apart from the flowerbeds."

Harley gave a fake laugh. "Ha ha. Very funny. I'll have the flowers envious of my shirt."

They stood in front of the office, and Lauren was aware of Jessica watching them. She turned her back to her, looking at Harley instead.

"Thank you again. I know you're going above and beyond." She moved a little closer to her. "I'm awfully glad you came into my life, Detective Shepherd."

Harley nodded. "I wish we'd met in the normal way, though. Instead of, you know, having to deal with some crazy guy." She pointed down the driveway. "I'll walk around a bit."

"Okay. Let me know when you leave, huh?"

"Sure. I'll—" Her phone interrupted, and Harley answered quickly. "Shepherd here."

Lauren saw the frown on Harley's face and noticed that Harley was already moving toward her vehicle.

"Be right there." Harley met her gaze. "I've got to go. I'm sorry."

"What is it?"

"A woman's been killed. In her home." Harley motioned to the office. "Go on inside. Try to keep someone with you at all times. I'll be back as soon as I can."

Lauren just stood there, watching her as she walked away. When Harley opened her door, she paused and turned back to her. She didn't know what look she had on her face, but it caused Harley to quickly retrace her steps. Without a word, she pulled Lauren into a tight embrace. Lauren's arms went around her waist and she tried to absorb the strength that Harley emitted.

"You'll be fine."

Lauren nodded. "Yes. But hurry back."

Their eyes met and Lauren thought for a moment that Harley was going to kiss her right there in front of Jessica and whoever else might be watching. She was oddly disappointed that she didn't.

When Harley drove away, she turned and went into the office. Jessica looked at her questioningly.

"You've met Detective Shepherd. We've…well, we've become friends. We—" Then she stopped. Why did she feel the need to explain her relationship with Harley to Jessica? She was eighteen years old and probably couldn't care less.

She went around the desk to the coffeepot. "So, everything okay?"

"Yes. No problems."

She added a little sugar to her cup, then turned. "When do your college classes start?"

"The end of the month. Why?"

Lauren leaned her hip against the desk. "You feel like working more these next few weeks?"

"Oh, sure. That'd be great."

Lauren smiled at her, hoping that would be the case. "Instead of just Thursday through Sunday, how about every day except Wednesday? There's only two and a half weeks left of the month but, well, I've got some things to take care of," she said a bit evasively, "and I'll be in and out. It would help out a lot if I knew you were here to manage the office. I know August is our slowest month anyway, but—"

"I can work, sure, Lauren. The extra money would come in handy."

"Great. And when your classes start, you can still work weekends, right?"

"And Thursdays still. I don't have class that day."

Lauren sipped from her coffee. "That's fine, as long as it doesn't cut into your study time. College is different than high school, even though I know you were almost at the top of your class."

"Number three," Jessica said with a hint of disappointment, as if three wasn't nearly high enough.

"Are you going to live in the dorm or stay at home and commute?"

"I'm going to live at home. The dorm cost too much. Maybe in a year or so I'll get an apartment in Corpus or something."

Lauren nodded, remembering her first year of college. She couldn't wait to get out on her own and away from home. She had soon realized just how expensive life was and after the first year, she'd gone crawling back. A year later, she was forced out on her own again—when her parents both died in a horrible car accident. She pushed those thoughts away with a quick shake of her head.

"Thank you, Jessica. I don't know what I would do without you." Out the window, she saw Gerald pulling a garden hose along with him. "Be right back. Going out to talk to Gerald."

It was a sunny and breezy day, and she shielded her eyes from the sun as she went outside. She stepped out of the way as a car pulled in front of the office. She turned, an automatic smile on her face. It vanished as soon as she saw the driver.

Bret Blevins.

She silently groaned as he got out, and she had to force herself to stay put and not hurry over to Gerald.

"Why, Ms. Voss, good morning," he said pleasantly. "Good to see you again."

"Mr. Blevins," she said a bit curtly. "Has it been a month already?"

He laughed. "No. I can't seem to stay away from Rockport, though."

Without saying more, he went into the office and closed the door. She let out a sigh of relief that he hadn't wanted to stop and chat. Maybe their conversation the last time had finally gotten through to him. Really, she'd hoped that their talk had made him uncomfortable enough that he would find someplace else to stay on his visits to Rockport. Especially if he was wealthy, like Harley said he was. There were actually some very fancy— and expensive—cottages in town. Why in the world had he been drawn to Heron Bay?

CHAPTER TWENTY-SIX

Harley parked behind a police cruiser, one of three that lined Water Street. It was a one-way street next to the bay with the houses only feet from the road. It was an odd mix—some old and shabby, some new and colorful. There was a two-story hotel that advertised luxury suites and a pool. Next to it was a rundown, drab wooden-framed house with a torn screened porch. Inside the porch was a bright yellow table with equally bright chairs. She heard music coming from the house as she walked past.

Next door was a small stucco-type house, light green in color. Baker stood out front and motioned her over.

"Damn, Harley, that shirt."

"You like it?" She went past him into the house.

"You'll certainly stand out in a crowd," he said behind her.

She nodded at Salazar, who pointed down a short hallway. "Is Craig here yet?"

"On the way."

Craig was their one and only forensic expert. Unfortunately, he didn't actually have a lab to work in, so he was at the mercy of CCPD. For what they usually needed him for, he did a fine job.

She went into the bedroom where three other officers were. She stopped up short, her heart lodging in her throat. It was in slow motion that the scene unfolded in an eerily familiar fashion—the woman tied to the bed, duct tape covering her mouth, the bloody sheets, the opened window, the stuffed bear sitting on the bedside table. It was enough to suck the very breath from her.

"Harley?"

She heard her name, but she couldn't pull her eyes away from the damn bear. Its shiny black eyes stared back at her, its mouth lifted in a smile. The same bear that she'd seen seven times before. Those seven crime scenes started racing through her mind, no longer in slow motion. No, they flashed before her eyes as if she were watching a movie screen, scene after scene pausing only a split second, long enough for her to see it, then gone, on to the next bloody scene and the next and the next.

"Harley?"

She closed her eyes—and her mind—chasing the images away. She turned to the sound of her voice, finding Baker there. She blinked at him, finally nodding.

"You okay?"

"No," she said truthfully. She moved toward the bear, staring into its eyes. "It's the same goddamn teddy bear."

"What?"

"Nothing." She shook her head, trying to clear her mind. "Who is she?"

"Veronica Higgins."

"Hey, Harley," someone called from the hallway.

She turned, finding Salazar at the door. "Yeah?"

"There's something in the bathroom. A message on the mirror."

She frowned, then looked over at Baker, remembering the message on the mirror at Lauren's clubhouse. What was it? *Have you missed me?*

Oh Christ...was it the same guy?

Across the hallway, Salazar pointed to an opened door. She moved past him, seeing the plastic shower curtain—a beach scene with twin palm trees. She was almost afraid to look at the mirror, afraid to see the message. She turned then. When she read the words—written in blood like before—she nearly stumbled, and she had to rest a hand against the wall to steady herself.

I killed Travis.

She stared at the words, reading them over and over. Her head felt heavy, and she couldn't seem to think, to make sense of it, to—

"What do you think that means? He killed someone else today? Some guy named Travis?"

She pulled her eyes away from the words, turning to Salazar. "No," she choked out.

She nearly pushed him from the bathroom as she moved past. She went down the hallway and out the door, ignoring the curious stares of the others. Once outside, she looked out over the sunny bay, feeling the breeze lift the hair around her face. She stared into the water, watching the ripples dance in the sunlight. Two pelicans were floating lazily by and on a small sandbar, a dozen or so gulls were congregated, gossiping about the morning's happenings, no doubt.

She closed her eyes, hoping to rein in her emotions, but all it did was chase the peaceful picture from her mind. The scene in the bedroom—the woman—took its place, followed by a bloody image of Travis. She opened her eyes again, looking out to the bay, but this time, she saw nothing. Not the water nor the gulls.

She took her phone out, listening while it rang. He finally picked up and she looked up into the heavens.

"He's here, Brian. The goddamn son of a bitch is here. And I think it's me he's after. Not Lauren. It was never about Lauren."

CHAPTER TWENTY-SEVEN

Harley sat quietly at the kitchen bar, watching as Marsha added grinds to the coffeemaker before adding water. The act of making coffee was more of a distraction than anything, she knew. It was after one on a hot and sunny August day—well past coffee time. She stood then, moving over to where Brian kept his liquor. She pulled out a bottle of whiskey. She wasn't surprised to find a glass shoved her way. She poured only a splash in it, then knocked it back, feeling it burn her throat as she swallowed. She closed her eyes, letting the whiskey clear her mind...if only for a few moments.

The doorbell rang and Marsha hurried to answer it. It would be Lauren. She should have gone and picked her up herself but, well, she'd been in no shape to explain anything. She'd sent one of the officers over to get her.

Brian was the one who insisted she come here. He'd gone out to the scene, needing to confirm for himself that what she'd said was indeed true. He'd stared at the bear, much like she'd done. "It's the same damn bear," he'd murmured to her.

If the others were curious as to why the chief was at a crime scene, they didn't ask any questions. Brian had gone into the bathroom without her. She didn't want to see the message again. She didn't need to. It was permanently imprinted on her brain. *I killed Travis.*

She felt hands on her shoulders, and she turned, finding Lauren looking at her with compassionate eyes. Marsha had told her. Told her what little she knew, anyway. Harley hadn't said more than a handful of words since she'd gotten there.

Lauren's touch, though, seemed to bring her back to the here and now. She wasn't still in San Antonio, still chasing this bastard. She wasn't there still grieving for Travis. She was here, in a new place and a different time. She and Lauren had stumbled into each other's lives by chance, apparently brought together by some deranged killer who was now seemingly playing games with them. Playing games and leaving messages.

She let herself be pulled into an embrace. Lauren probably hadn't recovered from her own ordeal last night, and yet here she was, offering a bit of comfort to her. Whether she was being selfish or not, Harley took the comfort offered her and she relaxed against her. But the reminder that Lauren had had a man in her house last night jolted her. She pulled away, holding Lauren's gaze.

"It was him."

"What?"

"Last night. At your house. I think it was him."

Lauren frowned. "Him?"

Harley's chest felt tight, and she sat down heavily, her eyes going between Lauren and Marsha. Was that the plan? Break into Lauren's house, tie her to her bed? Had he planned to rape and kill Lauren, just like he'd done to Veronica Higgins? Like he'd done to those seven women in San Antonio? Would she have walked in and found her there—duct tape on her mouth and a goddamn smiling teddy bear sitting beside the bed?

"Harley, you're as white as a sheet," Marsha fussed. She turned to Lauren. "What happened last night?"

Lauren sat down too. "There...well, someone broke into my house. It was this morning, actually, about three thirty."

"Oh my god. What happened?"

"I hid in the bathroom and called Harley. He tried to break the door down, but Harley got there and scared him off, I guess."

Marsha gasped and held a hand to her chest. "Oh, my goodness. You must have been terrified."

"Yes, I was." Lauren turned to her, wrapping warm fingers around her arm. "But what do you mean, Harley?"

Harley stared at the hand on her arm, afraid to move, not wanting to lose the touch. But Lauren's touch didn't waver, no. Her fingers wound a little tighter around her as if she could tell Harley needed the contact.

"The scene today," she finally said. "It was identical to the seven in San Antonio. Woman tied to the bed, duct tape over her mouth, throat cut. A stuffed teddy bear on the nightstand." She swallowed, trying to find the words. "The message in the mirror was like at the clubhouse. Written in blood, as before." She met Lauren's gaze. "The message at the clubhouse was meant for me, not you. It was me all along. It had nothing to do with you."

"Oh my god. And you think the guy who broke into my cottage was…was the *same* guy?" Lauren's voice cracked and her fingers squeezed almost painfully against her arm.

"Yes."

Lauren's fingers fell away from her then. "That could have been me," she said in a breathless whisper. "Was that…was that what was going to happen?" She stood up then, moving away from the bar. "You would have gotten there, found me." She covered her face. "Oh my god." She shook her head. "He didn't get me, so he goes and kills this other woman?"

Lauren had tears in her eyes then, and Harley got up too, going to her. "No, Lauren. No. He killed her first." She put her hands on Lauren's shoulders and squeezed. "He's after me, not you. He was using you."

"And the message today? About Travis? What does that mean?"

Harley took a deep breath and sat down again. She buried her face in her hands, trying to make sense of it all. She'd said all along that Travis would never take his own life. She knew in her heart that he wouldn't. That's why it had been such a blow.

That's why she felt such a sense of abandonment. Of betrayal. If he loved her like she loved him, he would *never* do something like that to hurt her. Never.

"The suicide was staged." She looked at Lauren, then at Marsha. "He killed Travis." She shook her head. "Travis didn't shoot himself." She was aware of the relief she felt at saying the words out loud. Relief? Yes. Because she had always felt some blame thinking Travis had taken his own life.

Marsha walked around the bar and bent down, hugging her from behind. Harley touched the hands that were around her neck and she felt another surge of relief.

"He didn't kill himself," she said again.

"You always said you couldn't believe that he would do that. I guess you were right." Marsha straightened. "But Harley, how could this man have killed Travis?"

"The tox report showed his blood alcohol was sky high—he was drunk on his ass, no doubt. For all we know, he could have been passed out. He would have offered no resistance. And now I think this bastard wants me."

"But why?" Lauren asked.

Harley shrugged. "Revenge, I guess. Travis shot his partner."

"I don't know, Harley," Marsha said. "Why wait this long? If he killed Travis, why not try to go after you right then?"

"Maybe he did. Maybe there wasn't an opportunity. Those first few months, I never left my apartment. I lived on the third floor. The only entrance was the door. Maybe after a few months, he gave up."

"But he's here now," Lauren stated. "He had to have been watching you."

"I've been here a year. And not exactly taking precautions. Hell, I ride my bike most mornings and I never carry my weapon with me. If he was watching me, he would have had ample opportunities."

"What does Brian think?" Marsha asked.

"We didn't get to really talk about it yet. He wants me to stay here. We'll go over it all when he gets here, I'm sure."

"I think you should stay here tonight." Marsha looked at Lauren too. "Both of you."

When Harley would have protested, Lauren put a hand on her arm. "You won't get an argument out of me. There's no way in hell I could stay at my place alone."

"I was going to stay with you tonight," Harley said, remembering their plan.

Lauren smiled softly at her. "We were supposed to have a date."

"Well, you can just have that date right here," Marsha said. "I'll plan dinner."

"Don't go to any trouble," Harley said.

"No trouble. You know me, cooking is my stress relief." She eyed the coffeepot. "Anyone want coffee?"

Harley shook her head. "No, thanks."

Lauren, too, shook her head. "I'm sorry, Marsha. I'm pretty much a morning coffee drinker only."

Marsha poured herself a cup. "I'm addicted, I'm afraid."

Harley stood up. "I suppose if we're staying here, I need to run you by your place for a change of clothes and whatever else you'll need."

Lauren nodded. "Yes, thanks. You think it'll be safe, right?"

She nodded. "I think if this guy just wanted to kill me, I'd already be dead. I think he wants to make it personal. It's a game to him. I think he wants me to know who he is, wants to see me when he kills me. Wants to look into my eyes while he kills me." At the look in Lauren's eyes, she gave a sheepish smile. "Let me rephrase that. When he *tries* to kill me."

CHAPTER TWENTY-EIGHT

After a quick trip to the resort and her cottage—which was thankfully uneventful—they'd immediately returned to Brian and Marsha's house. She thought it quite amusing that Marsha pulled them both into tight hugs upon their return, even though it had been less than an hour since she'd last seen them.

"Harley, you know where the spare bedrooms are. Show Lauren."

"Thank you, Marsha, for letting us stay here. I appreciate it."

"Nonsense, Lauren. I'm glad you're here. Neither of you have any business being alone. Now go get settled. I decided on a casserole for dinner. I thought I could bake that up and we could all eat as we wanted. Brian called. He said he'll be later than he thought."

"Yeah, he called me too," Harley said. "Hopefully he'll get here before we crash. I feel like I'm on fumes as it is."

Lauren followed Harley down the hallway. She carried a small duffel bag, and Harley had a backpack hanging off one shoulder.

"Which do you prefer? I think they're pretty much identical. Bathroom is between them."

She hesitated. "Would it be too weird if…well, if we shared?"

Harley's only reaction was a twitch of her right eyebrow. Then she smiled. "Like share the bed?"

"Yes. I know I must appear to be very weak but—"

"We can share. I'll take the side closest to the window."

She let out a breath. "Thank you, Harley. For understanding."

"Are you kidding me? Share a bed with you? I'm not crazy, you know. Who would turn down that offer?" She picked the first bedroom and tossed her backpack on the bed. The smile she'd had on her face disappeared and her expression became serious. "I don't think you're weak, Lauren, or clingy like you said this morning. I want you to feel comfortable and to feel safe. For however long it takes. Okay?"

"Okay."

The smile returned. "Good. Now I could use a drink. I think I'll go raid Brian's liquor cabinet. You want something?"

"Yes. A shot of whiskey or something sounds good."

And it was. They sat on the patio, neither speaking as they sipped on the amber liquid. The ceiling fan was on overhead and an oscillating fan was in the corner. It had been on the hot side at midday, but now a breeze was blowing, and it was quite pleasant sitting outside. A lone birdfeeder hung from a branch on an oak tree, and she watched a bright red male cardinal land there. There were no flowerbeds in the back, but three planters on the patio were filled with colorful petunias. It reminded her of their flowerbeds at the resort and she was glad she'd asked Gerald to take over her watering duties for the next few days. While she may need to go into the office, she'd rather not be out in the open—alone—hauling a water hose around.

"Have you spoken to your grandmother?" Harley asked unexpectedly.

Lauren turned her gaze from the cardinal to Harley. "No. I don't think I should tell her what happened. Do you? It'll scare her, I know. And she'll worry."

"Well, I guess if you don't tell her, she won't find out."

Something in Harley's tone made her question her decision.

"So you think I *should* tell her?"

"That's up to you."

"What about you? Have you told your parents?"

Harley shook her head. "No. I talked to my mom the other day, but I didn't mention it. Like you said, she'll worry. And be pissed later because I didn't tell her."

Lauren nodded. "Yes, if Nana finds out, she'll be pissed, too, that I kept it from her, that's for sure."

"So she's feisty?"

Lauren smiled, thinking of Nana. "Yes. And she thinks you're dashing, whatever that means."

Harley laughed. "Why does she think I'm dashing?"

"Because she watches too much TV. And I've told her a little about you," she admitted. "She wants to meet you."

"Oh, yeah? Do you think she'd like me?"

Lauren met her gaze, matching her smile. "Yes. She'll find you charming."

Harley leaned closer. "Like you find me charming?"

"I like that you can still flirt with me, even after the day we've both had."

Harley sighed and leaned back. "Do I still remind you of your ex?"

"No. Now that I've gotten to know you, you're not really alike at all."

"Is that a good thing?"

Lauren nodded. "I like you, Harley. When we first met, I would have never thought that possible, because yes, you *did* remind me of Leah then. Now? I realize there is nothing superficial about you. You tease and flirt and yes, you have a little bit of a swagger to you, but I like it." She took a sip of her drink, meeting Harley's gaze across the rim. "You are genuine. She was not."

"Maybe I'm just a good actor."

"Are you?"

Harley sighed again. "Maybe. Maybe these crazy shirts I wear turn me into someone I'm not."

"What's that? Happy? Confident?"

"Marsha used to say that I was too serious. That Travis was the only one who could get me to let my hair down, so to speak. He was fun. He was happy, outgoing. I was more reserved."

"She told me that too. Why do you think you've changed?"

Harley held her gaze. "Life is short. Sometimes very short. I always felt like I had this weight on my shoulders, you know. Like I was responsible for *everything*. It was zapping the life from me, that's for sure. With Travis gone, there wasn't anyone to pull me out of it anymore. It was like, I was always dark and gloomy. And I wanted to be bright and breezy, if that makes sense."

"I would never consider you dark and gloomy, Harley."

"No?"

"Not at all."

"No. I haven't felt that in a while now. Moving down here was the best thing. It's like it's always summertime. Hard to be dark and gloomy when the sun's always out and there's a gulf breeze blowing off the bay. So I wear these wild shirts," she said, plucking at her sleeve, "and my cool sunglasses and pretend I'm Magnum, PI, or something."

Lauren laughed. "That's funny. When I first met you, I thought that very thing. Although I think I went with *Hawaii Five-0*."

Harley had a smile on her face now and she looked relaxed again. "You know, after our date tonight, instead of taking you back to your cottage, I was going to suggest a walk along your pier. Maybe try to steal a kiss or three. A proper kiss. In the dark and all."

"Is that right?"

"Uh-huh. But then I remembered the headless body found there in the water and thought maybe that wouldn't be such a romantic setting after all."

"That's what you're shooting for? Romantic?"

"I like you too, Lauren." Once again, her expression turned serious. "Truth is, I haven't really ever dated anyone. I'm not sure I know all the rules and societal norms that go along with it. I think one reason I liked you is because you *didn't* like me. At first."

"Meaning what? I was a challenge?"

"Meaning my relationships with women were usually based on sex and usually one and done. And to be honest, the last year, since Travis, I haven't even given it a thought. Not until you." She met her gaze. "And I'm not saying I expect our friendship to evolve to that, I'm just saying—"

When she stopped talking, Lauren raised an eyebrow. "You're just saying what?"

Harley shrugged. "I don't know what I'm saying. Forget it. We're in no position to explore anything romantic anyway." She laughed a little. "And I'm being presumptuous that you'd even want to go there."

Lauren was amazed how Harley's insecurities came to the surface so quickly. A few moments ago, she was flirty and confident, talking about kissing. Now? Now she was showing a vulnerable side that surprised her.

"I'm attracted to you, Harley. That's shocking to me, really. One, I actually swore off dating after Leah and I haven't even been tempted. And two, you reminded me of her so that was a double whammy against you. Yet, I'm attracted to you. That kiss the other day should have told you that." She set her empty glass down. "But I'll agree with you. Now isn't really the right time, is it? There is a crazy man out there who wants you dead, apparently. And I seem to be in the middle."

Before Harley could reply, the back door opened and Marsha came out, holding a tumbler in one hand and the bottle in the other. It was an unmarked bottle, a decanter, and she had no idea what they were drinking. She assumed whiskey or bourbon but maybe it was scotch. She certainly wasn't an expert.

"I thought I would join you." Marsha sat down and moved the bottle toward Harley. "Figured you could use another splash."

"Maybe a little. Might fall asleep within the hour, though." Harley poured some into her glass and raised her eyebrows at her. Lauren nodded.

"Me too," she agreed. "I think the crazy early start to our day is finally getting to me. I kinda feel like I'm in a daze."

"I imagine so," Marsha said. "We'll finish our drinks, then you can go inside and have an early dinner, if you want. Who knows when Brian will get here."

Marsha chatted away and if she noticed that she and Harley were quiet and not contributing to the conversation much, she didn't show it. Thirty minutes later, after they'd finished their drinks, Marsha stood and announced that the casserole should be ready.

"How about we get something to eat, girls? I think you've both had enough for one day."

Lauren nodded, thankful. While the sun hadn't set yet, the afternoon was giving way to early evening. She imagined that as soon as dinner was over, she'd be ready to crash. It had been a long, emotional day and she was ready for it to be over with.

CHAPTER TWENTY-NINE

Harley was waved out of the kitchen as Lauren helped Marsha clean up their dinner. The casserole—a ground beef and pasta concoction—had been served with green beans and a mixed vegetable medley that she'd slathered in butter. She wasn't certain she'd have enough of an appetite to do it justice, but she'd taken a second helping of the casserole. Lauren, too, had seemed to enjoy the meal, and thankfully, their conversation touched on a range of subjects, none having to do with Travis or the murder.

Now, as she sat on the bed waiting for her turn in the bathroom, she thought about everything she needed to do tomorrow, provided Brian left her on the case. She'd been too numb to do much of anything today. She knew Brian had initiated pulling surveillance videos. A couple of the houses on Water Street had security cameras, as did the motel. The next-door neighbor had a doorbell camera which might be helpful. Even if someone went over them today, she wanted to take a look at them herself. Salazar and Duncan were to interview the neighbors today. She'd want to go over those notes as well. Truth was, she should have stayed there and worked the scene. She knew that. But the whole thing had been such a shock, right down to the damn bear and, of course, the message—she'd been in no condition to act like the detective she was. She was certain that the guys were wondering at her absence. Maybe Brian had explained things to them.

"You look lost in thought. Okay?" Marsha came in and sat down beside her.

"Yeah. Just thinking."

"So you're sharing a room?"

She nodded. "Yeah. Lauren wasn't too keen on sleeping alone."

"I don't blame her, no. Especially since she's in a strange house to begin with." Marsha leaned closer, touching her shoulder. "I like her for you."

She smiled at that. "Now's not exactly the right time for romance," she said, echoing her earlier statement to Lauren. "Don't play matchmaker."

"She likes you. You can tell. There's affection in her eyes when she looks at you."

"Is there?"

"She'd be good for you, Harley. Don't run."

"I'm not running. Actually, I'm quite attracted to her, just the timing sucks right now. Plus, you know, I'm not really good at this dating game."

"I never understood that about you. You're so attractive, Harley. Travis used to say that you had your share of women hit on you, yet you never seemed interested." Then she nudged her shoulder. "Well, nothing long term. I know you had your share of affairs."

"Affairs? Is that what we're calling it?"

"What would you call it? One-night stands?"

"One-*time* stands. Not many lasted until morning. If any." She shrugged. "Lauren didn't like me. She made no secret about it. It was kinda refreshing."

"Oh, I see. Different. She wasn't fawning over you."

Harley laughed. "Women don't fawn over me, Marsha." Was that true? They used to, yeah. But in the last year? She didn't know, really. She simply hadn't paid attention. And it's not like she went out to bars or anything where she could meet someone. She met Lauren by chance, and Lauren had shown exactly zero interest in her. The opposite, in fact. Lauren had dismissed her with only a look. And that, in turn, made her curious as to why.

Marsha patted her knee. "She would be good for you," she said again. "She seems strong. The fact that she's functioning normally after what happened to her last night—well, that in itself is amazing. If that had been me, I'd be hiding in a corner, still in a fit of tears, I'd imagine."

"She's handling it pretty well. Outwardly, anyway. But really, she's only involved because of me. My fault. I can't imagine—in the long run—that she would want anything to do with me."

"Oh, Harley, you don't surely believe that. She is innocent, yes, but so are you. You're not dictating this man's actions. He is."

"It's easy to say—harder to believe. He's after me and he has targeted her, for whatever reason. And she had quite a scare this morning. I don't blame her for not wanting to be alone. I'm not sure I wanted to be alone either," she admitted. "Because I guess we're both targets."

"Let's hope you find this guy and we can end it once and for all and finally put this whole nightmare behind us. And let Travis rest in peace."

"Nightmare, yes." She leaned her head against Marsha's shoulder. "I can't believe he killed Travis."

"I know, honey. But it doesn't change anything. Well, it changes the direction of your anger, but the outcome is still the same." Marsha patted her knee again. "I, for one, am glad to know it turned out this way. The thought of Travis taking his own life was too much to think about. I hate to say this, but it tarnished his memory in my eyes a little."

"I loved him like my brother—more than a brother—and I was so angry at him. Now I feel a bit guilty for that anger, knowing that he was innocent all along."

"Oh, Harley, don't go there. We can only deal with what we know. That was over a year ago. We've all gotten past it, finally. Let's don't go back and revisit it again. As I said, no matter what you do, it won't change the outcome. You've got to remember him the way he was, hold on to that, and get on with your life."

She lifted her head, about to reply when she saw Lauren leaning in the doorway, listening. How long had she been there? Lauren met her gaze, and Harley saw a softness there and yes, affection. She'd been listening for a while, apparently.

"Bathroom is all yours."

Marsha stood with a smile. "Can I get you anything, Lauren? Water for your bedside table, perhaps?"

"I'm fine, Marsha. Thank you. Thank you for everything. Dinner, your hospitality. I so appreciate it."

Marsha waved her thanks away. "If it were up to me, I'd want the two of you to stay here until this is all over with. One less thing for me to worry about." She went to the door, then paused. "Goodnight, girls."

"Goodnight," they said in unison.

Harley met Lauren's gaze, then motioned out the door. "Bathroom. Be right back."

Lauren simply nodded and Harley left, still wondering how much Lauren had heard. Did it matter? It wasn't like she was keeping secrets. And if it made her appear weak that she was still grieving over Travis…well, so be it.

When she returned to the bedroom, the lights were still on, including the lamp on Lauren's side of the bed. Lauren had changed into gray cotton shorts and what she assumed was her sleep shirt, but she was on top of the covers, leaning against the pillows. She stood there, looking at her, then blinked several times. What was she going to sleep in? It hadn't even occurred to her.

"What's wrong?"

She lifted a corner of her mouth. "I was trying to decide what I should sleep in."

Lauren raised her eyebrows. "What do you normally sleep in?" At her silence, Lauren blushed slightly. "Oh. I see." Then

Lauren smiled. "Well, don't let me break you out of your routine."

Harley laughed as she closed the door and turned out the overhead light. "That could be a dangerous game, Ms. Voss."

"What game is that, Detective?"

"You flirting with me."

"Flirting?" Lauren shook her head. "That wasn't really flirting."

Harley went to her bag and took out one of the old, baggy T-shirts she'd shoved in there. "Turn the light out. Let me change."

Lauren laughed lightly. "I would *never* have taken you for the shy one."

Harley arched an eyebrow, then, without waiting for the light to be turned off, she ripped off the shirt she'd just put on after her shower. She smiled as Lauren quickly fumbled with the light, finally plunging the room into darkness.

"God, you're a bit of a tease, aren't you, Detective."

Harley laughed quietly as she pulled the covers back and got into bed. She lay on her back and let out a heavy sigh as Lauren sat up, presumably to remove her shorts before getting under the covers herself. What a day it had been. What a scary, emotional day it had been.

"Thank you," Lauren finally said, her words soft in the quiet room. "And I don't mean that just for tonight, letting me be here with you. I mean for coming to my rescue this morning, for making me feel like I was important to you."

"Lauren—"

"Don't say you're just doing your job, Harley. I know you care about me. I could see that in your eyes when you found me. You were as scared as I was."

What did she say to that? "Yes. When I turned the light on in your bedroom, all of those other murders flashed before my eyes and I was afraid that I would find you tied to the bed, like the others."

"I was so scared, Harley. It was like I could hear the door cracking, could hear the lock trying to give way. I had this crazy thought of being thankful that the door was solid wood—thanking my grandfather for that, hoping it would hold. But he kept banging on it and banging on it and I just knew he would get me." Lauren's hand moved under the covers, finding hers. Their fingers entwined tightly. "I still have a hard time wrapping my head around it all. That…that woman. It could so easily have been me."

Harley recognized the surge of protectiveness that filled her. They didn't know each other that well. Not really. They were new friends and yes, possibly on the verge of becoming more than friends. Yet, the familiarity of their touch seemed to run deep, making her wonder if they were more connected than she thought.

And possibly so. As their fingers tightened even more, Lauren seemed to lose control. Harley heard her quiet tears, and she rolled to her side, pulling Lauren close to her. The tears turned to sobs and Harley held her, stroking her back gently as Lauren cried, all the while whispering words that she knew Lauren didn't hear.

Despite Marsha's comments, she *did* believe that it was her fault. Even if he had picked Lauren randomly—or maybe it was the accessibility of the resort that he picked—it was still her fault that he was in Rockport in the first place. He was after *her*, after revenge. In law enforcement, that came up from time to time. Usually by guys who were behind bars and they used their time to plot their revenge against the cop who caught them or the prosecutor who sent them away or the judge who heard the case. Sometimes even jurors. They plotted their revenge, but it wasn't often carried out.

After a few minutes, Lauren's tears subsided, and Harley let her pull out of her arms. Lauren wiped her cheeks with both hands.

"God, I'm sorry. I'm an emotional wreck."

"Not a wreck, Lauren. You're not weak. Please don't apologize."

"How do you handle this all the time? That poor woman, what she must have gone through."

"I handle it by—" By what? She closed her eyes, picturing Travis in his bed. She shook that away. "I'm not sure. The images, they stay with me. Some are more gruesome than others. The seven women in San Antonio, they were like today. Exactly. Right down to the stuffed bear. That scene isn't something you can easily forget."

"What's your outlet, Harley?"

"Back then? It was Travis. Travis and booze. Now? Here in Rockport? Don't really need an outlet. Life is slow here, crime is nonviolent, for the most part." She rolled onto her back. "Except for these past two months." She turned her head to look at Lauren. "I know you won't say it, but it *is* my fault you're mixed up in this." She heard Lauren draw in a heavy breath before she spoke.

"While I don't want to ever have a man break into my house—ever—I am kinda glad we met, whatever the circumstances." When she would have replied, Lauren touched a finger to her mouth. "Let's just leave it at that, okay? I certainly don't blame you. You seem to be the only one who does."

Harley remained quiet as the soft finger left her lips. She closed her eyes then, feeling Lauren move a little closer to her. Under the covers, their hands met again, and their fingers tangled. The early morning—the long, emotional day—had taken its toll on both of them it seemed. She heard Lauren's even breathing and she relaxed, despite the unfamiliarity of someone sleeping next to her. She decided she liked it.

She liked it a lot.

CHAPTER THIRTY

Lauren stretched her legs out and, after taking a deep breath, opened her eyes. She was surprised to see daylight behind the blinds. She turned her head, even though she knew she was alone in the bed. Her eyes lingered on the pillow that Harley had used. Lauren, in turn, had used Harley's shoulder for her pillow. Oh, how glorious it had been to snuggle up with someone, to feel safe and secure.

She finally leaned up on an elbow, knowing it was probably hours past the time she normally got up. Was she that tired or had it simply been the fact that she'd been in someone's arms that had kept her asleep longer? A little of both, perhaps.

After she'd made up the bed and after a quick shower, she felt wide awake. She found Marsha in the kitchen and as she walked in, she was already pouring her a cup of coffee.

"You slept well?"

"I did. Thank you. I'm normally an early riser. I can't believe it's almost eight."

Marsha slid the sugar bowl toward her. "There's a patrol unit parked out front. Brian didn't want to take any chances."

"Oh? Is he worried?"

"I think it was more to appease you and me than to think this guy would attack here. I, for one, am thankful they're out there."

She sipped from her coffee. "Where is Harley?"

"She and Brian left about seven, I think. They were both up very early, talking police business. She said to tell you that if you wanted to go to the resort, to call her. She'd have someone take you and stay there with you."

"Someone?"

"One of the officers," Marsha explained. "The town is all abuzz about the murder, apparently. The paper wants to interview Brian this morning, and he and Harley are debating whether to let the connection to San Antonio come out or not."

"How can they keep it in?"

"No one knows about it, I'm sure. Brian is afraid if they bring it up, it'll just cause panic. On the other hand, Harley says that maybe people will be more diligent about locking up and taking precautions." She waved a hand in the air. "I have no idea how they'll play it."

"Yes, I can imagine how a serial rapist and murderer would cause panic in town." She met Marsha's gaze. "Not sure how locking up is going to stop him. I had a chain on my gate, a deadbolt on the front door and my window was locked. He still got inside."

"You're handling that so well, Lauren. I would be a basket case, I'm afraid."

She smiled a little. "I had a mini-breakdown last night," she confessed. "I had a good cry. Harley's been the best."

"Harley seems quite fond of you," Marsha said over the rim of her cup.

"It's mutual. I like her a lot." She sipped from her coffee. "I wouldn't have thought that when we first met, but Harley has a way about her."

"You know what, had you two met when Travis was still alive, you probably wouldn't have liked her as much. She's changed.

She's more outgoing now. Travis…well, Travis had such a big personality, it overshadowed Harley. She was content to stay at the edges—the fringe—of Travis's circle. Little did she know, she was the center of his world. That boy would have done anything for her."

Lauren could tell by her tone the fondness she had for both Harley and Travis. "I think she knew. That's probably why his death was so hard for her—and still is. To hear you all tell it, they were as close as two people can be. She must have felt like a part of her own *self* died that night."

"Yes. Especially when she found him like that. She—"

"Oh my god. She *found* him? She didn't tell me that."

"Yes. By the time Brian got there, Harley was inconsolable. Hysterical is the word Brian used at the time. Then she just disappeared into her own shell, needing to grieve alone. Her parents couldn't reach her, her sisters couldn't. We couldn't. We just let her be for a while."

"Until you couldn't any longer? What was it that Harley said to me? You gave her a kick in the ass?"

Marsha nodded. "She was not happy with me, no. Took a week before I got through to her." She surprised Lauren by pounding her fist on the table. "Damn it all, but she wasn't the one who died. So yes, I guess I did have to kick her in the ass," she said with a light laugh. "Oh, but I do love her so. Brian and I never had children. My motherly instinct takes over when it comes to her. If I'd had a daughter, I'd want her to be just like Harley."

"I know Harley feels the same. She called you her second mother."

"She did?" Marsha looked pleased. "Well, I would be a *young* second mother," she said with a laugh. "I know her real mother is only a few years older than me, but I like to think that—despite our age difference—we're more friends than anything."

"Yes. She also said you and Brian were her closest friends. I think that's good to be looked at as both friends and family. Don't you?"

"Oh, yes. Harley is one of those people you can count on, no matter what. Brian and I treat her the same way. No matter what it is, we'd be there for her." She looked at her and smiled. "She treats you the same too, doesn't she?"

"Yes, she does. When we were first becoming friends, I thought it so odd that she—a police detective—had come into my life. Odd. Different." She met Marsha's gaze. "I don't make friends easily. Never have, really. Harley didn't give me a choice." She looked away for a moment, then back at her. "I—I really like her. I hope when this is all over with, we can have some normal time to get to know each other better."

"Maybe you can finally have that first date you talked about."

Lauren stared into her coffee cup, wondering if they still needed that first date. They'd kissed out among the flowers. A kiss that sent shivers right down to her toes. They'd flirted. They'd cried. They'd slept together—cuddled as if they were lovers. Did they *need* a first date?

She looked up, meeting Marsha's gaze, smiling a little. She said nothing, however, and Marsha smiled back at her, giving her a knowing look. No, they didn't need a first date.

CHAPTER THIRTY-ONE

Harley stared at the monitor, watching the surveillance video for the third time. It was dark and shadowy and revealed nothing at normal speed. This time she slowed it down to a crawl, everything now moving in slow-motion.

"Harley, hell, I went over those already."

She didn't take her glance from the monitor as Roscoe hovered behind her. "Won't hurt to look again."

"You got this case? I heard you were AWOL yesterday."

At that, she paused the feed and turned to him, her brows drawn together. "Is that what you heard?"

Roscoe, with his gray hair cut in a short military style, nodded slowly. "The guys tell me you took off after the chief got there. They thought maybe he yanked you from the case."

"Maybe they need to learn to quit thinking so much. Maybe I was checking on something else." She turned back to the screen, resuming the video.

"So where—"

"Roscoe, give me a break, will you? I'm trying to concentrate on this."

"I told you, nothing's there." He finally moved away, going to his own desk.

She'd already heard from Baker that they were all curious about her absence yesterday. Her walking in with Brian this morning and then having a closed-door meeting with him and Commander Lawson seemed to feed the gossip mill more. They couldn't decide if she'd been disciplined or if they'd made her the lead on the case. She didn't feel the need to explain things to them, so she'd told Baker what she'd told Roscoe—she'd had something to check out.

When her cell rang, she paused the video again, smiling as Lauren's name popped up.

"Hey, everything okay?"

"Yes, fine. Just feeling a little…in the way," Lauren said quietly. "Marsha feels like she has to entertain me, I think."

"Is she talking your ear off?"

"She is. I've learned all sorts of things about you. For instance, you hate broccoli but love Brussels sprouts. That's just crazy."

She laughed. "I wouldn't say I *love* Brussels sprouts, but I'd take them over broccoli any day."

"Yes, so, Marsha had mentioned that if I wanted to go to the resort, you'd provide a ride for me. I'm sure everything is okay there, but I wanted to go by and at least check on things."

"Okay, sure. I'll have someone come by and pick you up."

"Good." There was a short pause. "I missed you this morning."

She smiled at that. "You were sleeping like a rock when I got out of bed."

"And was I still using your shoulder as a pillow?"

"You were. I kinda liked it."

Lauren's laugh sounded in her ear. "No, *I* kinda liked it. I'm sure you weren't comfortable in the least."

"I don't think I moved all night, actually." She cleared her throat. "So, I'm going over surveillance video. I should—"

"Oh, of course. You're working, I know. I'm sorry. I didn't mean to—"

"Lauren, I'm glad you called. It was nice to hear your voice."

"Are you okay?"

"Yes. I think I'm over the shock of it all. About Travis, I mean. How about you?"

"Yes. Marsha's been good to talk to. I won't say I'm over it, though. I find myself jumping at shadows."

"Well, just so you know, Brian and I talked this morning. He's in agreement that you don't need to be alone until we catch this guy. He's suggested we have an officer at the resort at all times. At least when you're there."

"How do I explain that to my staff? To the guests?"

"We'll make something up. Say you got a threatening phone call or something."

"And the police are being very accommodating?"

"You can tell them you've sweet-talked a detective into protecting you."

"Have I now?"

She heard the smile in Lauren's voice, and she smiled too. "You have. So I'll send someone over to pick you up. Okay?"

"Okay. Thank you, Harley."

"My pleasure. I'll see you later."

She was still smiling when she went back to the video, but she pushed Lauren from her mind, needing to concentrate. Four or five minutes later, she saw it. A shadow. A shadow that moved. She backed the video up a few seconds, then played it at normal speed. It looked like the palm frond moving in the breeze. She watched it once more, this time slow again.

Yes! The shadow moved behind the palm tree, hiding. Then, as if waiting for the breeze to rustle the fronds again, he moved with them, leaping up and over the fence into Veronica Higgins's backyard.

"Son of a bitch." She turned, finding Roscoe sitting at his desk, feet up, chewing on a toothpick. "Hey, Roscoe. Come look at this."

He flicked the toothpick onto his desk and ambled over. "What?"

"Here."

She played it at normal speed. He watched, then shrugged. "What?" he asked again. "There's nothing there."

"What about now?"

She slowed the video and pointed to the palm tree. "Watch." She could hear his breath catch as he saw the shadowy man leap across the fence.

"How the hell did you see that?"

"So you're seeing what I am? A guy jumping the fence?"

"Yeah. Damn, how did I miss that?"

"I missed it the first two times too." She looked at the file name. "This is the neighbor's security. Is this who found her?"

"No, I think it was the neighbor on the other side. He saw the screen on the ground and went around to investigate. Saw her through the window."

She pushed her chair back. "I'm going out there."

"What for?"

"To talk to the neighbor. Walk around."

"They've already been interviewed."

"So I'll do it again." She paused. "You mind watching the rest of this again? See if you can pick up a shadow like this for when he's leaving. If nothing else, it'll give us a timeframe."

He nodded. "Yeah. Okay." He sat down at her desk, then looked up. "So it's already slowed down for me, right? I just hit this arrow here to make it go?

"Right. I'll be back as soon as I can."

She was out the door before she remembered she'd promised to send someone to pick up Lauren. She pulled her phone out as she walked, calling Commander Deeks.

"It's Harley. I need to have an officer go to the chief's house and pick up Lauren Voss. Take her over to Heron Bay Resort." She got into the SUV. "Can you spare someone?"

"Sure, Harley. The chief talked to me earlier. I'll send Jacobs."

She pulled away, frowning. "Which one is Jacobs?"

"He's one of the new guys."

"A rookie? I'd feel better if—"

"Jacobs can handle it, Detective Shepherd. He's just being an escort, right?"

"He needs to stay with her while she's there and then take her back when she's ready." Damn. Did she trust a rookie?

"Like I said, the chief has already talked to me. We got a handle on it."

"Okay, thanks."

A rookie. She shook her head. No, she didn't trust a rookie, but she supposed he was right. They were just being an escort and a presence.

When she got to the house on Water Street, there was a patrol unit parked out front. She pulled behind it on the street. Instead of going to the neighbor's house, she went inside, finding Craig in the bedroom. He was standing there, hands on his hips, staring at the bed.

"What's up?"

He jumped and spun around. "Damn, Harley, you trying to give me a heart attack?"

"Sorry, man."

He pointed at the bed. "Didn't find a print anywhere on that thing. Didn't find a print anywhere, period. I dusted the whole damn room and not a one that didn't match the woman's."

No, she didn't expect he would. They'd never found one in San Antonio either. "Did they do the post on her already?"

"Haven't heard. I'm no medical examiner, but she looked pretty tore up if you know what I mean. Hopefully he'll find semen or something." He turned from the bed, the bloody sheets now dark and dried. "I hear there was nothing on the surveillance and the neighbors didn't hear or see anything. How the hell do you investigate something like that?"

"The usual step would be to interview the current boyfriend or the ex. Interview friends, coworkers."

"But?"

"But this isn't a usual case." She didn't elaborate, and by the look on his face, she didn't have to.

"Heard a rumor you and the chief think this is some guy from San Antonio. True?"

She nodded. "The scene was identical, right down to the teddy bear."

"Damn. Could it be a copycat?"

She shook her head. "No. There was never a mention of the teddy bear in our reports. It's the same guy."

"So now what?"

"We're going to collect surveillance footage as far back as they have it, especially the motel over there. They've got a good shot of the street. We'll check all the vehicles that traveled down here, weed out the neighbors, that sort of thing. Maybe find a pattern."

"Somebody nosing around?"

"Yeah. He had to do reconnaissance of some sort. You don't just pick someone at random and hope they live alone and don't have a dog or something. But I did find something on the surveillance. He came in from the south side, jumped the chain link fence there into the backyard." She motioned to the door. "You want to come take a look? Might have a shoeprint or something."

"So you found something? Baker said there was nothing. Roscoe was—"

"Roscoe missed it. To be fair, I missed it too at first. Doesn't help us much. He was all in black. Had a ski mask or something on his face." She turned, hearing him following.

The neighbor wasn't home, so they went around to the side of the house. She pointed to the young palm tree that separated the two yards. "He was here. In the shadows of the house first, then he moved behind the palm. From there, he jumped the fence into her backyard."

Craig walked a wide circle, shaking his head the whole time. "The lawn is too thick. There won't be any shoeprints." He went to the fence and glanced over. "Yeah, let me take a look back there. Got some bare spots." He moved past her toward the house again. "I didn't check the backyard at all. The bedroom window is on the other side and there was nothing under there. It was assumed he took off that way."

She stared at the grass behind the palm tree—in her mind, she could see him standing there. With a heavy sigh, she finally turned and followed him into the house.

CHAPTER THIRTY-TWO

Lauren thanked the handsome young man—Officer Jacobs—again when she got out of the police car. He'd seemed extremely nervous on the drive over and she tried to engage him in conversation. It wasn't until they'd pulled in at the resort and he gave a relieved sigh that she understood.

"Did Detective Shepherd threaten you?"

He grinned and nodded. "Yes, ma'am, she did. She said if anything happened to you that she'd...well, that she'd have my ass for lunch."

Lauren smiled at him. "So does that mean you'll be staying here?"

"Yes, ma'am. I'm to stay here until you're ready for me to take you back."

"I see. Well, in that case, I won't stay too long."

She knew she didn't have to be there at all—she was only a phone call away if Jessica had a problem in the office. She hadn't wanted to intrude anymore on Marsha, though. She felt like she'd imposed enough as it was. She certainly didn't expect

Marsha to babysit her while Harley was gone. She supposed she could have gone to see Nana, but she didn't want to chance saying something to her that would raise questions. Maybe after they'd caught this guy, after he was locked up, she might tell Nana what had happened. Maybe. But certainly not now, not while he was still out there somewhere.

Her hand was on the doorknob, but before she could turn it, a loud, shrill scream made her jerk her head around. Gerald was out among the flowers and he tossed down the hose, running toward the clubhouse.

Now what? What else could possibly happen? She headed in that direction, only to be stopped by Officer Jacobs.

"Ms. Voss, Detective Shepherd said I shouldn't let you—"

Another scream and she locked eyes with Officer Jacobs. "Come with me, please."

They found Angela standing with a hand clamped over her mouth. Paula was beside her, hiding her face against Angela's shoulder. Gerald was standing at the edge of one of the flowerbeds, bent over.

"What's going on?" she asked quickly as she came up beside them. "Who screamed?"

"Me first," Paula said. She pointed. "There's…there's a man's head…in there."

"A *head*?"

Officer Jacobs moved Lauren out of the way. "Sir? Do you mind stepping back, please?"

Gerald's face was pale as he stood up, his eyes wide with disbelief. Lauren looked where he'd been and gasped as she glimpsed a man's head partially obscured by the red hibiscus flowers. Lauren jerked her glance away and drew Gerald out of the flowerbed, then tugged all three of them to the side. She absently saw Jacobs pull the radio from his belt, heard him talking, but she wasn't really listening to his words. A head? In her flowerbed? Was it Christopher Bryce? Or—god forbid— had someone else been killed?

"Let's go over to the laundry room." She felt exposed standing out there, even with the others around her.

"Do you think it's real?" Angela asked. "I mean—"

"It's real," Gerald supplied.

"Please say it's not one of our guests," Lauren said.

"A man. I don't recognize him," Gerald said.

"What's going on?" Paula asked in an almost accusatory tone. "Why is there a police officer here anyway?"

"I...I kinda caught a ride with him." Should she tell them what happened? "You know I've become friends with Harley—Detective Shepherd—ever since the vandalism in the clubhouse and—"

"So you were with her last night?" Angela arched an eyebrow. "Is it serious?"

"No, no. I wasn't with her. Not like that. Well, we—" She sighed. "Look, someone broke into my house Wednesday night. Well, during the early morning hours Thursday."

"*What?*" Angela and Paula asked at the same time.

"I called Harley and she came over and scared him off, I guess. Anyway, I wasn't around much yesterday, as you probably noticed and I was afraid to stay here by myself, so—"

"So you stayed with her?"

"Sort of, yes." Should she tell them she was at the police chief's house? No. That would only bring more questions. "I mean, yes, I stayed with her." That wasn't technically a lie. "The point is, she thinks it's all related to that break-in we had in early July."

"What about the man found out by the pier?"

"We didn't think that was related, but if that's his head over there," she said, pointing to where Officer Jacobs was, "then, yes, it's probably the same guy who broke into my house."

"Oh my god. What is happening here?" Paula asked. "And that poor woman they found murdered out on Water Street. It's like we're living in a big city or something."

"I know. It's been awful lately, hasn't it?" That was an understatement, she thought.

"Do you think we should be worried?" Angela asked.

"You mean here at the resort? Harley doesn't think so. Not for you, anyway. She seems to think this guy has fixated on me, for some reason." She wouldn't tell them that the guy was after Harley. She wouldn't tell them what Harley had said, that he was using her to get to Harley. "I think—especially during the day—that everyone is perfectly fine. I just don't want to cause a panic with the guests, you know."

"Well, having police cars coming and going has raised a few questions," Paula said. She pointed down the driveway. "Here comes another one."

She let out a breath. "Yes. Let me go see what's going on. Just go about your business. Hopefully they can remove the... the head without causing a big scene."

"Yeah, good luck with that," Gerald said.

He motioned with his head to where a small crowd of five or six were standing. She recognized Bret Blevins among them. She'd forgotten he'd checked in yesterday. She'd been so disconnected with the resort lately, she wasn't sure who all was there. As she headed back to where Officer Jacobs was, Bret separated from the crowd, walking toward her.

"You seem all shook up, Ms. Voss. Is everything okay?"

Something about the way he said the words—the smugness of his tone—made the hairs on the back of her neck stand up.

"Yes, fine. Excuse me," she said, intending to move past him.

"Is your girlfriend coming? I understand there is a...well, a body part amongst your flowers. I'm sure she'll want to pop over and make sure," he laughed, "well, that it's not *your* head out there." His eyes met hers and for the first time, Lauren recognized the coldness of them. "So much happening in town this summer, she's been very busy, hmm?"

The frostiness of his eyes seemed to penetrate her very soul, and she felt the chill all over her body. Without a word, she hurried over to Officer Jacobs. When she got there, she turned back around, but Bret Blevins was nowhere in sight.

"Harley? Is she coming?" she asked quickly. "Have you called her?"

"She heard it on the radio, so she called me. And, yes, ma'am, she's on her way." He motioned to where Gerald was still standing. "Was he the one who found it?"

"No, one of my staff did. Do you need to talk to her?"

"Harley may want to, yes." He looked past her down the driveway and she followed his gaze, relief filling her as she saw Harley pull up. A man got out of the passenger's side carrying a black kit of some sort. Harley locked gazes with her for a long second as she walked over.

"Where is it?"

"Over here," Jacobs answered, pointing to her once lovely hibiscus bed, which was now being trampled.

Lauren stood back, out of the way, watching as Harley held up her phone, looking at something—a picture, perhaps. She then nodded and turned to the other man.

"It's Christopher Bryce. I'll call CCPD and let them know." Harley came over to her then. "You heard?"

"Yes. And who is that man with you?"

"Oh, that's Craig Schobert. He does our forensics." Her voice lowered. "You okay?"

"I suppose."

"Gonna need to take a look at your surveillance video, Lauren."

"Of course." She was about to mention her encounter with Bret Blevins, but Harley was already on her phone.

"Need to call the detectives over in Corpus," she explained, then turned away, already speaking to someone.

Lauren nodded, wondering if she should stay there, close to Harley and the officers or if she should go to the office to wait. She looked around, seeing a few guests still milling about, talking among themselves. Angela and Paula were loading clean towels onto a golf cart and Gerald had resumed his watering, all acting as if nothing was out of the ordinary. Well, almost. All three of them glanced frequently toward the officers—and the flowerbed where a man's head was resting.

She folded her arms across her chest, tucking each hand under her armpits, still indecisive, but Harley turned around, motioning for her. She fell into step beside her as they headed to the office.

"Craig says it looks like it's been frozen. The lab in Corpus will tell us for sure."

She didn't know if that required a comment or not. When she said nothing, Harley nudged her arm.

"Did you find it?"

"No, no. Paula did. Her scream brought Angela and Gerald over. And me. I'd just gotten here." She opened the door to the office and Jessica looked at her expectantly.

"Is something going on? The police…"

"Yes, something's going on." She motioned to Harley. "You've met Detective Shepherd."

"Yes, I have."

"We're going to need the office. I'm sorry. I know it's a little early, but maybe take a lunch break?"

Jessica nodded without question. "Sure, Lauren. That's actually good because I didn't get breakfast and I'm starving."

She grabbed her purse and was gone in an instant. Lauren gave Harley a tentative smile. "I'll be lucky if my whole staff doesn't quit on me. Not to mention guests packing up and leaving, never to return."

"I know you're worried. It's been a little crazy."

"To say the least." She sat down at the computer and clicked on the surveillance icon. "Do you want the clubhouse feed or this one here at the office?"

"Both. The clubhouse camera will catch the flowerbed, but this one hits the driveway and the open space. And did you remember to call about adding a couple more cameras?"

"Yes. They're coming out next week." When she brought up the security feed from the office camera, she got out of Harley's way, letting her sit down instead. She leaned against the wall, watching her. A rather tame blue and white shirt today, sunglasses shoved on top of her head like normal. She really was an attractive woman. It was ridiculous, really, the way they'd met; events put in motion by a killer and rapist who wanted revenge. If—when—this nightmare ended, would they be able to be friends—more than friends—without all of this shadowing them? Or would it always be there? Would they always think about the reason they'd met?

"What's going through that pretty head of yours?"

Harley asked the question without turning around. Lauren shoved off the wall, going to stand behind her. She paused only a second before resting her hands on top of Harley's shoulders.

"I was thinking about us, actually."

At that, Harley turned her head and looked up. "Us?"

Lauren squeezed her shoulders and nodded. "Yes. Us. Like in the future. Wondering if this guy will be a part of it. Hovering around, you know."

Harley turned her attention back to the monitor. "We probably wouldn't have met if not for this guy."

"Yes. I know. That's a little creepy, isn't it?"

"That a serial killer introduced us? Maybe we should—there!" she said excitedly. "There he is. The bastard."

Lauren leaned closer, feeling tense as she watched the screen. He was dressed all in black, head to toe. There was no way to identify him. Black face mask, black gloves. "Looks like he came from back here." She pointed to the side wall of the office, indicating the back fence.

"The subdivision? Yeah. But how the hell did he scale a ten-foot privacy fence carrying a goddamn head?"

They watched as he moved slowly in the shadows, never totally coming out into the open until he moved toward the clubhouse. Harley minimized that window then clicked on the clubhouse feed, fast-forwarding it. She slowed it down, then pointed as he came into view. He went directly into the flowerbed, pausing only a few seconds to look around in all directions. Then he opened the bag he held and took out the man's head. Lauren stared in disbelief as she watched, her fingers digging into Harley's shoulders unconsciously. He posed the head, leaving just enough of it showing so that someone would see it—that unlucky person being Paula. Then, quick as a cat, he ran back the way he'd come, disappearing out of the camera's view. Only then did she take a breath, unaware that she'd even been holding it. She relaxed her hold on Harley and moved away.

"What time was that?"

"He first showed up on camera at, let's see…" Harley went back to the office feed. "Three thirty-three."

Lauren nearly gasped. "Coincidence?"

"What?"

"That's when I called you that night. Or morning. I looked at my phone, seeing the time, thinking that nothing good could possibly happen at three thirty-three." The witching hour, she remembered thinking.

"I don't think it's a coincidence, no. We've got a brief glimpse of him from a surveillance camera that Veronica Higgins' neighbor has." She pointed to the monitor, the video now paused. "Dressed identically."

"So the same guy who killed that woman was the same guy who broke into my home. Same guy who vandalized the clubhouse. And the same guy who killed Mr. Bryce and brought his…his head back here to me." Lauren shuddered. "God, it's a freakin' nightmare." She wrapped her arms around herself. "It hasn't hit me yet, I think. How close I came to being one of those women. If—"

Harley stood up quickly and pulled her into an embrace. "It's easy for me to say don't think about it, because I know that's impossible to do. But Lauren, you *weren't* one of those women. And I promise you, you *won't* be. I won't let that happen."

Lauren unfolded her arms and slipped them around Harley's waist, sinking against her, letting Harley hold her for however long she wanted. It would never be long enough.

"I wish we could have some normal time together," she said quietly against Harley's neck. "I feel so close to you. I can't explain it." She pulled away a little, meeting Harley's gaze. "Maybe it's not real."

"What do you mean?"

"Maybe I'm projecting my affection for you because you saved my life."

Harley smiled at that. "It can't possibly be so. We had a very lovely kiss before that." Her voice softened. "I don't remember ever kissing anyone before. Not like that." At her questioning gaze, Harley pulled away. "I've never really dated before."

Lauren nodded, remembering what she'd overheard between Harley and Marsha. One-night stands. No. One-*time* stands, Harley had called it. She supposed that, no, there wasn't much real kissing involved if all they were doing was having sex. Most likely emotionless sex.

"I'll need a copy of the surveillance," Harley said, getting back to business. "Can you email it to me? Both feeds?"

"Of course."

Harley opened the door, then turned. "I can have Jacobs take you back to Marsha now, if you'd like."

"Yes. I think so. I'll wait until Jessica gets back."

Harley paused one more time. "You're okay with staying there again tonight or—?"

"I want to stay wherever you're going to be."

As their eyes held, Harley closed the door and came back to her. Harley didn't hesitate and neither did she. Their kiss was almost fierce—intense, possessive. For a breathless few moments, everything faded from her mind as she pressed close against Harley, their breasts touching, their hips, their thighs. The moan escaped before she could stop it, and Harley pulled her even closer, then abruptly released her. There was a fire in Harley's eyes that made her knees weak, and she had to grip the countertop to keep from stumbling.

"So I think it's real, Lauren."

Lauren nodded. "Yes. Yes, I think so too."

She leaned fully on the counter as she watched Harley walk away. Sweet Jesus, but that was some kiss. For the few seconds they'd touched, she'd forgotten everything that was going on. There was no murder, no headless body, no madman on the loose. No, it was just her and Harley, touching and kissing like everything was perfectly normal in the world.

But then, of course, that wasn't true, was it? No, the multitude of police cars outside her window said otherwise.

CHAPTER THIRTY-THREE

"They can work the case all they want, but let them know I don't plan to stay out of their way. We've got our own victim." She paced in front of Brian's desk. "Do they know about San Antonio yet?"

"No. And without sharing that with them, they have no reason to believe we're both after the same suspect. The deaths of Christopher Bryce and Veronica Higgins are completely different. They're not convinced it's the same killer."

"Does CCPD know about the break-in at Lauren's house?"

"No. And we have absolutely zero evidence that it was him, Harley."

Harley met his gaze. "We both know that it was."

"I'm in agreement, yes." He tossed the pen he was holding onto his desk. "I requested copies of the old files from San Antonio. I know you probably know them word-for-word, but…"

"I used to know them, yes." She sat down in front of his desk and leaned back in the chair. "You heard we got no surveillance from that subdivision, right?"

"Yeah. A few doorbell cameras, that was it."

She nodded. "I checked them myself. Nothing on them."

He shrugged. "It wouldn't have helped us anyway, unless he didn't mask up until he climbed the fence."

"Found where he crossed over. There's a small oak there, low limbs. Easy climb. Hell, I think even I could have jumped the fence."

Brian leaned forward. "What are we going to do, Harley? Our suspect is a masked man dressed in black."

"Yes. He's very good at what he does. Seven times in San Antonio. Not a sighting. Not a print. Just blind luck on our part that someone spotted them at three one morning." She tilted her head thoughtfully. "That must be his favorite time. When he broke into Lauren's house, it was three-thirty when she called me. Same time he jumped the fence to drop off the head. Three or three-thirty in the morning, your nighttime folks have already gone to bed and your daytime ones aren't up yet."

"Why do you think he stopped? In San Antonio, I mean."

"I assumed it was because his partner was the brains behind it. When Travis shot him, well..." She shrugged and shook her head. "I thought this guy just went into hiding. Maybe he was grieving. Maybe he was plotting his revenge. On me, I mean. He got Travis within four days. If he'd been able to take me out, too, then maybe he would have gone back to his killing spree. Who knows? We were of the mindset that the partner did the killing, and this guy did the raping. That may have been true in San Antonio, but Veronica Higgins begs to differ."

"Marsha said you thought he may have tried—or at least wanted to—get you right away but you were holed up in your apartment."

"Yeah. Four months. I think he got tired of waiting."

"So he follows you here and takes a whole year to put things in motion?"

"Like I told her. I don't think he wants to just kill me."

"He wants to look into your eyes while he does it." He nodded. "Yeah, she told me. She's worried about you. Hell, I am too."

"I can take care of myself."

"And what about Lauren? You going to take care of her, too?"

"I am."

"Marsha said I was to tell you that you're both welcome to stay with us for however long it takes."

"I appreciate that, but no, I don't think so. I don't want to stay at my RV, but I'm thinking her place at the resort should be safe now. I don't think he's crazy enough to come back there. Besides, she's got a business to run."

He nodded. "Figured that would be your plan. And don't argue with this, but I'm going to have a unit parked there each night."

She stood. "Won't get an argument from me." She pointed to the closed door. "Gonna give CCPD a call, see if the lab found something on the head that might help us."

And she needed to call Lauren. She'd indicated that they would stay with Brian and Marsha another night, but she felt like they would be fine at Lauren's place, especially if Brian had an officer posted outside. Revenge or not, she didn't think this guy was that crazy to make a move with a patrol unit on the site.

Then again, she almost hoped he was. Because she'd be ready. The son of a bitch wasn't going to walk away this time.

CHAPTER THIRTY-FOUR

Lauren was thankful that the police presence at the resort was rather brief—if you could call almost two hours brief. A few of the guests had come in, asking questions and she'd answered them truthfully—yes, a man's head had indeed been found in the flowerbed, and no, he was not a guest at the resort. She was amazed by the nonchalance most of them showed and even more surprised that not a single one had checked out early.

Now, though, she was on her way to Marsha's, courtesy of Officer Jacobs. Harley had called, proposing that they stay at her place tonight. She'd been shocked by the suggestion, but Harley thought it would be safe there—their guy surely wasn't crazy enough to try something with a police cruiser parked out front—and it would save them running back and forth to Brian and Marsha's place.

"Would you like me to come inside with you?"

She shook her head. "I won't be long. Sorry you're having to babysit me."

Officer Jacobs smiled at that. "It's not a problem, ma'am."

Marsha seemed to be waiting on her; she opened the door before Lauren rang the doorbell. The look on her face indicated she was not happy with Harley's plans.

"She thinks she's intruding on us by staying here. I know her. She's so stubborn sometimes."

"She seems confident that we'll be perfectly safe there. Besides, I believe Brian will have an officer parked at my house." She shrugged. "I think we'll be fine, Marsha."

"Well, Brian seems to think so too, but I would still feel better if you both stayed here at least for one more night."

Lauren went back into the bedroom they'd shared, intending to pack their things. Marsha followed.

"This thing could drag on for days or even weeks. One more night isn't going to make a difference," she reasoned.

Marsha gave her an exaggerated sigh. "I see she's convinced you as well."

Lauren smiled at her. "She said you would call her stubborn."

Marsha smiled too. "I just worry, that's all. And to hear Brian tell it, they are no closer to IDing this guy than they were in San Antonio."

"Yes, I know."

Marsha followed her into the bathroom while Lauren collected their things. "You weren't the one who found it, were you?"

"No, thankfully." She paused. "Although I did see it." She closed her eyes and shook herself. "I still can't believe it."

"That poor man's family. What they must be going through."

"I know. It's awful." She glanced at her. "And I can't believe that I'm involved in it all. He was found tied to our pier. The break-in. Now his head…"

"We've got to think that it'll be over soon. Rockport is too small of a town to be terrorized by a crazy man. People will be wary. I'm sure if there's anything suspicious going on, someone will call the police."

"We can hope."

"Well, not to sound like a mother hen, but if you could call me first thing in the morning to let me know all is well…"

"I will."

"And what about dinner? I've got some of that casserole left over. I could—"

Lauren laughed. "Marsha, don't worry. We'll probably pick up something. I do cook, it's just living alone, I don't make the effort very often, therefore my pantry and fridge are a little bare."

"Well, you don't seem as affected by all of this as I'd be. I admire you for that."

Lauren glanced at her before zipping up her bag. "I'm not sure if it's so much that I'm not affected by it or if it's just that I feel safe with Harley. If we hadn't become friends and I wasn't getting this level of personal attention, then yes, I'd probably be a basket case as you said."

She met her gaze for a moment. "I don't have anyone I could turn to. My grandmother is eighty-six and lives at The Oaks. I have no close friends in town. If not for Harley, I…" What? She'd be all alone? Yes, she would be. For the first time, that really hit home. She hadn't bothered with finding—and nurturing—friendships. She'd simply immersed herself in the running of the resort, the interactions with the guests and her staff taking the place of meaningful relationships. Then Harley unexpectedly came into her life, with her wild shirts and her flirty smile. Where would she be if not for Harley?

"Lauren, if you *ever* need anything—Harley or not—you don't hesitate to ask me. I'd like to call you a friend if you don't mind. Other than my family and a few of the ladies I've met at the museum, I don't have a long list of friends here either."

Lauren smiled and touched her arm affectionately. "Thank you, Marsha. That's sweet of you."

Marsha led them back into the living room. "When this is over with, I hope you and Harley will come over for dinner again. I have a freezer full of fish and I think a good, old-fashioned fish fry is in order. Maybe you could bring your grandmother over too. I'm sure she'd love to get out for an afternoon."

"Oh, she would love it. Thank you, that's kind of you. She's dying to meet Harley as it is."

"Well, let's plan on it. Hopefully it'll be sooner rather than later."

Lauren nodded. "I should get going. I promised Officer Jacobs that I wouldn't be long."

"And where is Harley? I didn't even ask."

"Oh, she went over to her place for some clothes. I'm supposed to meet her back at the resort."

As expected, Marsha drew her into a hug before she left. "You'll call me in the morning? Let me know y'all are okay?"

"I promise."

Then Marsha winked at her. "Give Harley a kiss for me."

CHAPTER THIRTY-FIVE

Harley parked in her usual spot in front of her RV. When she got out, the dog down the way started barking, as usual. She heard the normal sounds of the RV park—a radio playing country music, voices and laughter from a group of men gathered a few trailers over, the roar of a boat's engine as it left the boat ramp and headed into the bay, and the sounds of gulls as they flew overhead. All familiar sounds she heard as she headed to her door.

She paused, though, as she approached her rig. Everything seemed normal, yet she had a gut feeling that everything *wasn't* normal. She slid her gaze to her bike which was chained to the corner jack on the camper. It was as she'd left it, but not. Before it even registered that both her tires were flat, she'd pulled her weapon from its holster at her side. A closer inspection showed the tires had been slashed.

Her eyes went to the door, eying the lock. The door was closed and there was nothing to indicate the lock had been jimmied with. Instead of standing on the step, she stood to the side of the door. She pulled out the handle, not really surprised to find it unlocked. She stood back as she swung the door open, half expecting someone to be waiting for her inside.

All was quiet, though, and she paused on the step, listening before going inside. Other than in the tiny bathroom or the bedroom, there was no place to hide. She turned the lights on, nearly gasping at the mess she saw. Her normally neat camper had been trashed—vandalized much like Lauren's clubhouse had been that day.

She moved slowly toward the bathroom that separated the bedroom from the rest of the camper, her eyes glued to the door. She ignored the mess around her as she opened the door. It was dark and quiet. Even though she had no sense of another's presence there, she didn't dare relax.

She pushed open the second door into the bedroom. The light was on in there—a light she'd most surely turned out when she'd left—and the sight of her clothes strewn about caused her to take a shaky breath. All her colorful Hawaiian shirts and neatly pressed khaki pants were slashed to pieces and tossed haphazardly on her bed.

"That son of a bitch."

She glanced to the small closet where not a single shirt hung. They were all ruined. All slashed to pieces on her bed. She stared at the mess, feeling an odd sense of loss. She brought a hand to her chest and pressed it hard against her heart, trying to ease the ache there. The shirts were her lifeline. The shirts made her feel close to Travis and they chased away the pain.

She holstered her weapon, then sat down heavily on the bed. She grabbed a fistful of the ruined garments and buried her face in them, shocked to feel tears in her eyes. *Damn.* She stood up quickly, blinking the tears away as she tossed the shirts down. It wasn't the shirts she was crying over, she knew, but she still felt foolish. Instead, she opened one of the drawers, pulling out four or five of the Rockport Police Department T-shirts she had. She paused to wipe the tears from her face, then she grabbed two pairs of jeans, a couple of sports bras, some socks, and a handful of underwear. She'd left her backpack at Marsha's, so she shoved all the clothes into a plastic trash bag, then looked around for whatever else she might need. The only thing that caught her eyes were her flip-flops and she tossed them in as well.

Back in the living room, she looked around, her gaze landing on her book, which was on the floor. She bent down to pick it up, then sucked in her breath as the photo fell out. It had been torn in half. This time she couldn't stop her tears as she stared at the torn photo, the book landing back on the floor with a thud. She held the two pieces together—she and Travis.

She wiped at her tears with the back of her hand, trying to collect herself. She didn't have time for a breakdown. Not now. She picked up the book again, intending to put the torn photo back inside. Marsha had given the book to her, thinking it would help her accept Travis's death, help her heal. She hadn't read the damn thing, though. She kept it out, beside the sofa, and on occasion she'd open it up and scan a page or two. Mostly she'd just sit and think about Travis and look at the photo. It had been taken on her birthday, the last one they'd shared together. They were at a bar and he'd handed his phone to a friend, getting them to take the picture. A week or so later, Travis had made a couple of prints of it. While he kept his on his desk, she took hers home, saying she was too embarrassed by the shirt to display it. Even so, she ended up sticking it on the fridge where she looked at it each day. And it never failed to bring a smile to her face.

She looked at it now—torn in half like it was. Even so, a tiny smile formed. As she stared into his eyes, she smiled a bit broader. It wasn't the book that had helped her heal. No, it was this photo, a reminder of their friendship and love. Sure, Travis was gone, but her memories were still bright and vivid. No one could take that from her, torn picture or not. So she tossed the book onto the sofa without tucking the photo back into it. Instead, she pulled her wallet out of her back pocket and carefully slipped the torn pieces inside.

CHAPTER THIRTY-SIX

"Oh my god. *All* of your shirts?"

"Yep. The only two survivors are this one," she said, pointing to the one she wore, "and the one I had at Marsha's. That one was your favorite, I believe."

Lauren laughed at that. "I'm not sure if it's the parrots that push it over the top or the pineapples." Then she shook her head. "And I'm sorry. It's not funny."

"Well, it kinda is. And if that's all the damage I incur, then I'm okay with that." Harley motioned to her bedroom. "So, do you mind if I shower? Then I guess we need to see about dinner. Don't know about you, but I'm starving."

"Go out for something or delivery?"

"Delivery. With all that's going on, I don't think we need to be out."

"Good. That would be my choice too." She waved her hand. "Feel free to shower. You don't have to ask, Harley."

"Thanks. And order whatever you want. I'm not picky."

For having had her RV trashed, Harley seemed to be taking it all in stride. She appeared almost *too* unconcerned with it. Was it forced cheerfulness for her benefit? Maybe. But at this point, after all that had happened, the vandalism at Harley's camper seemed tame in comparison. Maybe that's why they were both taking it with a shrug.

Still, she must feel violated. This guy—this killer—had been inside her home, had invaded her personal space, had destroyed her belongings. Had violently destroyed them. He must be eaten up with anger, with revenge, to take a chance like that. According to Harley, though, none of her neighbors had seen— or heard—a thing.

She picked up her phone, trying to decide on dinner. They could always do pizza, but she wasn't in the mood. The barbeque place down the way delivered, but that didn't sound good either. What she was really in the mood for was a burger from The Pub, but they didn't do delivery. There was always seafood. There were two places that she knew would deliver and she knew Harley liked it. So, two seafood platters it was.

"Hey, Lauren?"

She turned, finding Harley peeking around the bedroom door, her hair damp. "That was a quick shower."

"Yeah, I'm not much for lingering." Then she raised her eyebrows teasingly. "Well, unless I have company. Then I might linger."

Lauren smiled at her. "Are you flirting with me?"

"Of course not. So, other than some Rockport PD T-shirts, I'm kinda low on clothes. Do you have a T-shirt I can borrow? Maybe one of those cute ones you wear with the resort logo?"

She stood up. "Of course. For as many Hawaiian shirts that you had, I have an equal number of Heron Bay T-shirts, I think."

She found Harley in nothing but khaki shorts and a dark blue sports bra. She stopped and blatantly stared. Harley stared back for a long moment, then crossed her arms, as if hiding herself. Lauren smiled at that.

"Really? Gonna be shy? After you mentioned showering together?"

Harley dropped her arms. "Okay, no. I won't be shy. Besides, this thing covers more than a bikini top would."

"I can't see you in a bikini."

"No, but I can see you in one."

Lauren moved closer to her. "I haven't worn a bikini in years. The Speedo you've seen me in is it."

"I like that too. I'm just saying I can *see* you in one. Like, I've pictured you in one. Or out of it." Then Harley laughed and shook her head. "Okay, yeah, so it's a poor attempt at flirting." She motioned to the chest of drawers. "So...a shirt?"

"You're too cute." She opened the bottom drawer. "What color?"

"Some kind of blue."

She held up a bright royal blue and a navy.

Harley grinned at her, then took them both, tossing a "thank you" over her shoulder as she went back into the bathroom. Lauren's gaze followed her, noting her straight back and squared shoulders, trim waist, and the loose-fitting shorts that hung rather low on her hips. She took a deep breath, then turned away, conscious of the smile on her face. How lucky was she to have made friends with a police detective—a rather attractive police detective—who was also serving as her bodyguard?

"Pretty damn lucky."

A few minutes later, Harley came out wearing flip-flops and looking quite at ease in her borrowed shirt—the navy one, not the royal blue.

"I ordered seafood. I hope that's okay."

"My favorite. Thanks."

"Would you like a glass of wine? I'm afraid I don't have anything else."

Harley shook her head. "I'm technically on duty, you know. Better stick to water."

She hesitated. "Do you mind if I have a glass? It's been one of those days."

"I don't mind at all. In fact, I guess I will have a glass with you. Because you're right, it's been one of those days."

They sat at the table across from each other, both twisting their wineglasses with their fingers. Harley had a faraway look in her eyes.

"You want to talk?" she offered quietly.

Harley brought her gaze up, then sighed. "You've seen my RV. There's not much personal stuff there."

"I know. Are you one of those people who doesn't have a lot of material possessions?"

"Yeah. I'm pretty low maintenance. Now. When I lived in San Antonio, I had a house full of furniture and all the clutter and stuff that goes along with it. I pretty much sold everything or gave it away. There were a few things I wanted to keep. Some memorabilia—mementos—that I held dear, I left with my parents." She took a sip of her wine. "There was one thing that I kept with me, though. It was a picture. A picture of me and Travis."

"I saw it. You had it tucked into the pages of a book. A book on grief."

Harley met her gaze and nodded. "Yeah. Marsha gave me that book."

"Did it help?"

Harley lifted one corner of her mouth in a smile. "I haven't actually read it. I'd open it up, scan a page, then end up staring at the picture, remembering good times. And at first, the thoughts of those good times were very painful, knowing I'd not get to have them again. Then it finally hit me that I needed to be thankful that I'd even had those good times in the first place. So then that picture had a different meaning to me. It became a symbol of happiness, not pain."

"When was it taken?"

"My birthday. The last year before…well, before he died."

"Where's the picture now?"

Harley's face hardened. "The son of bitch tore it in half."

"Oh, no." She reached across the table and squeezed her arm. "I'm so sorry."

"Travis printed two of them. He kept one at his desk. I had the other—this one—stuck on my fridge. After he died, I took the one from his desk. It's with my things at my parents' house. So it's not like it's destroyed. It's just that he was in my house, touching my things. And to know that he picked up this picture, that he looked at it, saw Travis…and ripped the damn thing in half—I want to put a bullet in this guy." Then she shook her head. "I'm a cop. I'm not supposed to say things like that. I'm supposed to say I want to arrest him, let him go to trial, and hopefully spend the rest of his miserable life behind bars. Or better yet, on death row awaiting a lethal injection."

"You're only human, Harley. I don't think it's out of line to have those thoughts."

"I shouldn't even be working this case. It's personal. If this was San Antonio and all of this was happening, I wouldn't be anywhere near this case. If Commander Lawson knew all the details, he'd probably insist I back down."

"Would Brian allow that?"

"I don't think so. It's imperative that we catch this guy. He wants me. How he plans to do that, I have no idea." She met her gaze. "Or maybe I do."

"What do you mean?"

"I think he goes after you."

"Well, that's comforting," she said dryly, then nearly jumped at the loud knocking on her door.

"Moon Dog Delivery," a young woman called from outside. "Dinner."

When she would have gotten up, Harley stopped her. "Let me."

* * *

"Wednesday is my weekly dinner date with Nana. And I usually go see her on Sundays."

Harley bit into a shrimp and shook her head at the same time. "Absolutely not."

"I can't stay locked up here."

"You can. You will."

Lauren put her fork down. "What am I supposed to tell her?"

"Tell her your dashing police detective has you under house arrest."

Lauren smiled as she picked up a piece of fish. "Yes, that's all fine and good, but she'll want to know why. And I don't think I want to tell her why."

"Okay. So maybe we'll go visit her together. You said she wanted to meet me."

"And what will you tell her? That some guy wants to kill you and I'm in the middle?"

"Let's tell her the truth, Lauren. There's no sense omitting stuff or lying to her."

"She'll worry."

"No doubt." Harley popped the rest of the shrimp into her mouth. "Better that than to keep her in the dark. Don't you think?"

"I don't know. She's all I have. I'm all she has. If she thinks I'm in danger, then—"

"Lauren, I promise you, I won't let anything happen to you." Harley met her gaze. "In case you didn't know, I'm kinda attracted to you. So call me selfish or whatever, but I'm not going to let anything happen to you."

Lauren held her gaze. "We've known each other...what? A couple of months?"

"Are you wondering if you should put your faith in me?"

Lauren didn't blink. "If there is anyone I would put my faith in, it would be you, Harley. I guess I'm wondering why you would be willing to put your faith in me?"

Harley leaned her elbows on the table, looking at her. "Not to scare you or anything, but that very first morning when we met, when I looked at you and you laughed at my Hawaiian shirt—I think I started to...to fall for you at that very moment."

Lauren felt her heart jump into her throat, nearly choking her. That statement, she was not expecting. Fall? What did she mean? Fall in *love*? She didn't know what to say. Harley smiled at her, then reached over and stole a shrimp from her plate.

"So that rendered you speechless? Should I apologize? Take it back, maybe? Because I've never really fallen for someone before. What do I know? I may be way off base."

Harley's demeanor was relaxed, not overly serious, and she didn't feel the need to delve further into her comments. Not now. Because yes, she *was* shocked speechless. So instead, she kept things light between them.

"You can start by apologizing for stealing a shrimp." Lauren picked one up and held it between them. "Because I'll fight you for them."

CHAPTER THIRTY-SEVEN

Lauren moaned quietly. Was it only a delicious dream or was she really being cuddled like she was someone's lover? She blinked her eyes open.

"I thought I was dreaming," she murmured in a quiet, sleepy voice.

She rolled to her side, facing Harley. She was immediately pulled close, close enough so that their bodies were touching. She closed her eyes, savoring the contact. How long had it been? How long had it been since her body had hummed with life like this? She felt Harley move, and she lifted her face, finding Harley's lips. Their kiss was slow—breathtakingly so—and she let her mind drift away to nothingness as Harley's lips moved with hers. A long kiss, mouths and lips moving achingly slow. Who knew such a leisurely, drawn-out kiss could set her on fire?

But oh, it did. Her hips moved—their lower bodies now flush. They pressed together with an almost urgent need, and the kiss changed, their tongues meeting for the first time. They moaned simultaneously, and Harley's hands moved around her hips, pulling her even closer. Lauren arched into her as, yes, the fire had turned into a raging need.

But good god, how far were they going to take this? They were in nothing but T-shirts and panties. She could feel her wetness between her legs and imagined Harley was the same. That thought made her groan and she deepened the kiss, pressing even closer to—

"Oh god no," she said when loud ringing interrupted their kiss. "No," she groaned.

Harley rolled away from her, blindly reaching for the offending phone. "Shepherd," she said, her voice thick and husky.

Lauren closed her eyes, not even hearing Harley's words. No. She was simply reliving their heated kisses, letting her body slowly come down from the high it was on. Yes, if they hadn't been interrupted, she knew exactly how far they would have taken it. The thought of Harley touching her, being inside her—oh, what a glorious feeling that would have been. She squeezed her legs together, noting the throbbing ache that hadn't diminished.

"I'm sorry."

Lauren turned her head toward her and smiled. "Not as sorry as I am."

"I couldn't resist any longer."

"Are you apologizing for kissing me or because we were interrupted?"

"Both, I guess."

She reached out, touching Harley's face gently. "You have to leave, don't you?"

"I do."

Disappointed, she let her hand fall away. "I don't think I've ever been woken up quite so wonderfully before. What time is it?"

"Five thirtyish."

She brushed the hair away from her face. "I'm usually up before five. I seem to sleep like a rock with you."

Harley leaned down and kissed her again. Whether Harley intended it to be quick and short, she didn't know, but when their lips met, their passion flared again. Lauren pulled Harley to her, relishing the feel of her weight on top of her. It was a mistake, of course. She wanted more. So much more. The arch of Harley's hips into her told her that Harley wanted more too. With a near growl, Harley rolled away from her. Lauren kept her eyes closed, listening as Harley got dressed in the darkness.

"I'll be back in an hour or so, hopefully."

"Okay," she murmured without opening her eyes. Then they popped open as Harley's words sunk in. "Wait. You're leaving me? But—"

"I'll get Officer Monroe to come inside. I'm sure he would love some coffee anyway."

Officer Monroe had relieved Officer Jacobs last evening. Jacobs was due back at seven, Harley had said. She sat up then and ran a hand through her hair. Were they really just making out minutes ago or *had* she been dreaming?

"Why are you leaving? Did something happen?"

"Big Al found blood in his freezer at his bait shop. Another detective got the call, but he said there was a message there. Had my name on it. So…" she shrugged.

"What was the message?"

"Oh, something about counting down the days or something. I'm just going to take a look. If I had to guess, that's where he kept Christopher Bryce's head, buried in Al's freezer."

Lauren turned the lamp on, finding Harley already dressed and clipping her holster to the waist of her jeans. Instead of one of her normal Hawaiian shirts, she was wearing a black T-shirt with Rockport Police Department embroidered on the upper left side. Lauren walked over to her.

"You look cute."

"Cute?" Harley ran a hand through her hair. "I have bed head."

"I've seen your bed head before." She touched her cheek. "I like it."

Harley motioned to the bed. "About earlier. I shouldn't have—"

"Please don't apologize. I'm not sorry you started that. I'm only sorry you have to leave."

"I'll be back as soon as I can. If you need to go to the office, wait until Jacobs is back on duty and have him take you there. Okay?"

"Yes. Trust me. I don't plan to be alone." As Harley turned to leave, she called after her. "Be careful."

CHAPTER THIRTY-EIGHT

Harley parked along the marina—the lights of Big Al's bait shop not quite as pronounced as dawn approached. She sat for a few moments, watching as he spoke to a customer at the outdoor counter. Her mind wasn't on him, though. No, it wasn't. It was on the dark-haired beauty she'd been in bed with. As she'd told Lauren, she simply couldn't resist a second longer.

They'd talked some after dinner, both pretending that she'd not told Lauren she was falling for her. *Good lord, what were you thinking?* Well, at the time, she really hadn't been thinking at all and the words had tumbled out much too easily. She was only thankful she hadn't said "in love," because how the hell could she back out of that? And really, she didn't know the first thing about being in love or what it felt like. She only knew that being around Lauren made her feel good, made her happy inside, regardless of the circumstances. She found she wanted to be around her, with her. That certainly had never happened to her before. But god, couldn't she have kept her mouth shut?

It hadn't spoiled the evening, though. Yes, they pretended she hadn't spoken the words, but it wasn't awkward between them. Their conversation flowed as easily as always. By nine, they'd both been fighting yawns and—after offering to sleep on the sofa, which Lauren had said a firm no to—they'd fallen into bed and had been asleep within seconds, it seemed.

Perhaps unconsciously on both their parts, they'd gravitated together, drawn to each other. She'd drifted in and out of sleep, finding Lauren wrapped around her or her wrapped around Lauren. And finally, the last time, when Lauren had rolled toward her, she couldn't resist.

And damn Big Al, but if she'd not gotten that phone call, she would have slipped Lauren's sleep shirt off. She could imagine Lauren pulling hers off as well. They wouldn't have stopped, no. They would have made love. They may have fallen back into a tangled sleep again, for a few minutes. Then she could imagine waking, touching, kissing—

She shook her head and got out, slamming the door a little harder than necessary. With a sigh, she walked up to Big Al just as he bagged a scoop of bait shrimp. The sun was now up, the red glow shining across the bay. Whereas a few minutes earlier, the marina had seemed quiet and deserted, except for the few early morning fishermen, it now was alive with activity. Shrimp boats were both coming and going, and pelicans and gulls followed their progress.

The marina smelled damp and fishy, and she wondered if Al or those who worked the shrimp boats ever got sick of it. Most likely, they didn't even notice it any longer.

"About time you show up. That other detective has been here an hour already." He had on the same dirty baseball cap he always wore—a cap stained with God knew what. The normal two-day stubble was missing however, and he was clean-shaven for once.

"You get those security cameras installed yet?"

"I'll tell you like I told that Lawson fella, I ain't payin' for no damn security cameras."

Another customer came up behind her and she stepped out of the way.

"Morning, Al."

Al wiped his hands on a dirty rag. "What you need this morning, David? Shrimp? Crabs?"

"I'll take some crabs," the man said. "I heard that drum have been hitting on them."

"Oh yeah. Had a guy come back yesterday and he showed me a huge black drum he pulled in."

Harley motioned to the shop. "Norton still back there?"

"Yeah. Go ahead on."

She started to go, then stopped. "Where's your help this morning? Carlos and what's the other guy? Rocky?"

"Bucky. I ain't heard from him. Carlos went out on the boat earlier."

"Who found it?"

"Hell, I did when I went to get some shrimp out. I was digging around in the big freezer and saw blood."

"Did you touch anything?"

"Hell, no. I didn't even get the shrimp. Sold him live ones instead."

She nodded, then went through the open door. She wrinkled her nose up at the smell as she moved past the open tanks. She glanced over at them, seeing *things* swimming inside. The bait shop was a small, square building with live holding tanks in front and the coolers and freezer in the back. An old, wooden door centered the back of the building—which opened to the dock of the marina—and there was a window on each side. The four glass panes in each window were dirty and smudged, except for one. The one that normally got broken during a break-in.

She turned the corner, finding Brad Norton standing at the side door. He nodded at her, then came back inside.

"Morning, Harley. Sorry to call so early."

"No problem." She glanced at the freezer. "Is Craig coming out to dust?"

"I haven't called him yet. I wanted you to take a look, get your feel. Al says that's not fish blood. Everything is boxed up before it goes in the freezer."

She opened it up, seeing assorted plastic tubs of frozen bait shrimp, some small fish that looked like sardines or something and...tiny squid? She wrinkled up her nose again.

"You fish, Brad?"

"Not so much, no. My dad drags me out sometimes, but it's not a passion of mine."

She looked at the empty spot in the back corner where a pool of blood had frozen. She reached in, fingering the white plastic that was stuck to the side.

"What do you think?"

"I think he had that man's head in a white plastic trash bag and hid it under all this bait." She glanced over at him. "You?"

"Honestly, that never occurred to me. I guess when we get a blood sample to the lab we'll know for sure." He motioned for her to follow him. "Here's the message. Don't think Al saw it."

The message—written in blood again, it appeared—wasn't on a mirror this time. It was written on a cardboard box.

I'm counting down the days, Harley. Are you?

"What the hell does that mean?"

With a deep breath, she turned to him. "You heard about the message over on Water Street?"

"Yeah. Salazar said you turned white as a ghost when you read it."

"Travis was my partner back in San Antonio."

"And this guy killed him?"

"So he claims."

"I mean, you verified it? He's dead?"

"Yes. He died before I moved down here." She took out her phone and snapped a picture of the message. "I'll call CCPD, let the detectives there know we'll be sending over a blood sample. Not sure how much good it'll do to learn that he kept the head here."

"There are some security cameras about. Maybe we—"

"Not here. Al's had a few break-ins in the last several months. This is a blind spot right here and he refuses to get a camera." She tilted her head, then glanced back toward the back door and the two windows. "How did he get in? The glass was always busted before."

"Not sure. Al didn't say."

"So he kills the guy, brings the head here to hide. Comes back to retrieve it and then dumps it at Heron Bay Resort. He dumped the head about three thirty in the morning. It was midmorning when it was found. It was still mostly frozen when I got there, so we can assume he broke in here, say three o'clock, maybe a little earlier."

"So you're saying this guy has broken in here before?"

"Can't be sure. Each break-in, there was always the window busted out and stuff taken from the freezer. I guess it could be a coincidence that he picked Al's to store the head, but highly unlikely."

"There's no busted window," Brad said, pointing to the back wall.

"Maybe that was for show. Maybe he was doing some kind of reconnaissance or something. Scouting out a place where he could hide a head for a few weeks." She nodded. "In fact, I think the busted window *was* for show." She walked over to the side pane that had been replaced. "He busts out this window. Then what? Is he able to reach all the way inside to unlock the door?" She stood there, moving back a little to account for being outside. She reached as far as she could and was still six or eight inches away. "Each time, the door was unlocked afterward. If it's our guy, he doesn't need to break in. Locks are apparently no match for him." She knew this firsthand from the seven crime scenes in San Antonio, from how easily he'd gotten into Lauren's cottage and her RV.

"So you're saying he busts the glass out just for fun, then picks the lock? That makes no sense."

"It makes perfect sense. If he didn't bust the glass out, how was anyone going to know he'd been in here?"

Brad frowned. "Why would he want anyone to know?"

"I think maybe he was just setting it up. I've been out here five times. Each time the window was busted. So now you've got Al conditioned. The window is broken, he goes to the freezer and checks his inventory. The window is not broken, no worries."

"So when he brings the head, he doesn't break the glass. He hides the head, buried beneath that shit," he said, pointing back to the freezer, "and no one is the wiser."

She nodded. "He comes and gets the head with the same intention. Maybe he didn't mean for the bag to leak blood. So when he dug the head out and saw the mess, maybe that's when he decided to leave a message. He knew we would trace it back to him anyway, so why not play this game with me a little longer?"

"And what game is that?"

"He intends to kill me. That game."

CHAPTER THIRTY-NINE

Lauren felt a sense of peace—normalcy—as she stood with the garden hose in her hand, mindlessly giving the flowers a drink. Well, not really mindlessly. She glanced around often, making sure Officer Jacobs was still leaning against his car. He was, his gaze locked on her every move. Gerald was also about, putting out mulch in the hibiscus bed where the…the head was found. He didn't normally work on Saturdays, but she'd asked him to come in.

Everything seemed to be routine today, back to normal. And oh, she wished that were so. However, having a police officer watching you wasn't exactly normal. She moved along the flowerbed, drizzling water as she went.

Inevitably, her thoughts went to Harley—again. But it wasn't the wonderful scene in bed that morning that popped into her mind this time. No, it was the words that Harley had uttered last night.

Was Harley falling like she'd said? Falling in love? Is that what she meant? And she wasn't sure which of them had been more surprised. She'd been—as Harley had said—rendered speechless. Harley had no experience with love. But *she* certainly did. And she wasn't sure she wanted to go there again.

She flicked her eyes to the sky in a mocking roll. It had been three years. Surely her scars had healed. She wasn't even sure why she had scars to begin with. Yes, it was a bitter breakup but one that had been coming on for more than a year. Ego perhaps, but she wished she'd been the one to initiate it, not Leah. She did learn quickly, however, that not only were they not still in love, but they also no longer even liked each other. She could readily admit that now.

Is that why Harley—and her words—frightened her? Relationships ended and there was always pain involved. Why go through it in the first place? Yes, she liked Harley. Yes, she was attracted to her. Did love have to be a byproduct of that? Couldn't they simply enjoy each other's company? Like their little make-out session in bed. Now that had been nice.

She sighed almost wistfully at the thought. They had a chemistry, an attraction, that she felt down to her toes when they kissed. And they'd done so much more than kiss that morning. If Harley hadn't gotten the phone call, would they have made love? Would they have gotten naked and touched and—

She closed her eyes for a moment, then moved along the flowerbed. What about tonight? Would they finish what they'd started that morning? Did she want to? It would definitely change their relationship. But damn, yes, she wanted to.

"You're going to drown them, I think."

She spun around, finding Harley standing beside her. She only barely missed spraying her with water again.

"How is it you can sneak up on me so easily?"

Harley tilted her head, studying her. Then she smiled. "Lost in thought?"

Lauren felt a blush light her face and Harley laughed quietly. "What were you thinking about? You look kinda dreamy."

"None of your business."

"No?" She took a step closer. "Did it have anything to do with me...and this morning?"

"Don't get a big head. It has been well over three years since—"

"Since you've been intimate with anyone?"

Harley's voice had taken on an almost sweet tone with none of the earlier teasing. Lauren met her gaze, nodding. "Yes."

Harley's expression softened so much so that Lauren wanted to toss the water hose down and gather her into an embrace.

"It's been forever for me, Lauren," came Harley's quiet reply. "I've never made love to anyone before. I couldn't name you a single person I've been with that I would consider it anything other than just a physical, emotionless act. Ever. Yet, I find myself wanting that with you. I want you to be my first."

If she didn't know Harley as well as she did, if she didn't know her past history from Marsha, Lauren might think that Harley was handing her a line. But she did know her, and she could see the sincerity in her eyes and it simply melted her heart. She tossed the hose down onto the grass and—without caring who might be watching them—moved closer to Harley, initiating the kiss before Harley could.

Harley pulled her into a far too intimate embrace for out here among the flowers and sunshine. Lauren didn't care. She pressed her body as close as she could, feeling each point of contact as they kissed. Her earlier thoughts—fears—vanished as if they'd never been there. She was attracted to Harley and Harley was attracted to her and that was all that mattered. She wouldn't let her past influence her future. If she did, she'd die a lonely, bitter old woman. So she held Harley tighter, deepening the kiss, wishing to god they were alone and could finish this in private.

But they weren't alone, and they most likely came to that conclusion at the same time as they drew apart almost simultaneously. They looked at each other and she could see the throbbing pulse in Harley's neck. It surely matched her own, for she felt her thundering heartbeat still. Then Harley smiled and she did the same. They both took a step away and she bent to retrieve the hose that was soaking the grass. She turned the nozzle off but held it between them. Harley shoved her hands into the pockets of her jeans.

Lauren cleared her throat before speaking. "I think I miss your Hawaiian shirts."

"Oh, yeah? Well, as you know, I'm down to two. Gonna have to space them out a bit, I think."

She looked around them, finding only Officer Jacobs observing them. As she glanced at him, he looked away and she was certain he sported a blush on his face.

"So? Anything at Big Al's?"

Harley's expression turned serious. "Yes. We'll take a blood sample to the lab, but I'm certain it'll match Christopher Bryce." She paused. "And yes, there was another note for me."

Lauren raised her eyebrows questioningly.

"Let's see. This one said 'I'm counting down the days, Harley. Are you?'"

"Do we have a plan?"

Harley smiled at her question. "Other than staying secluded in your bedroom?"

Lauren laughed. "That could be a good plan."

Harley's smile faded a bit. "Yeah, so, no, there's not really a plan. The marinas in Rockport and Fulton are managed by the Aransas County Navigation District. They have security cameras placed out there and they employ a security guard and whatnot. Anyway, I've looked at all the security feeds—this time and on past break-ins at his shop—and Big Al's is in sort of a dead zone. A blind spot. It's like each camera's vision stops just short of his shop."

"Which is why you suggested he get his own camera?"

"Yes. But I see his point. No one else out there has to provide their own security. Why should he? He's paying a fee to keep his shop there, he should be afforded the same security. But regardless, I think our guy picked Al's shop because of that. I walked around and looked at the cameras. It's obvious that he's in a blind spot."

"But that doesn't help you."

"No, not at all. There's never prints. The only visual we have of him in on your security cameras from the other morning and the brief glimpse of him on Water Street."

"Well, I think—" She stopped, seeing Bret Blevins come out of his cabin and walk rather briskly toward his rental car. She groaned. "I'd forgotten he was here."

Harley turned to see what she was looking at. "Has he been bothering you again?"

"No. Actually, when he came to check in, he barely spoke to me. Jessica was working and I just happened to be outside the office." Her eyes widened. "Oh, but I forgot to tell you. That morning when the…the head was found. He came out to watch. He made a point to come over to talk to me. Something about his words, the look on his face—" She nearly shuddered, remembering the coldness of his eyes. "He asked if my girlfriend was coming over. Then he made reference to how busy you've been this summer. Something like that." She grabbed Harley's arm. "Wait. He said something else. It just now dawned on me. No one had seen the head except my staff. When the police came, that's when some of the guests came outside to watch, but still, the head was hidden in the flowers and Officer Jacobs was standing there, blocking any view."

"What are you saying?"

"Bret said he figured you'd want to be there to make sure it wasn't my head out there. That might not be verbatim, but that's the gist of it." She met Harley's eyes. "How would he have known it was a head?"

Harley nodded slowly and Lauren could almost see the wheels turning in her mind. Then Harley took the hose from her hand and let it drop.

"Come on. We need to take a look at your guest register." They headed toward her cottage and not the office. "How far back can you go?"

"Well, the register itself, that gets dumped after each quarter, when the final reports are done for taxes and stuff. But each quarter's reports are kept. We keep that in case we get audited. There are so many different taxes we have to collect and then dole out to the county and city and—" She waved her hand. "Never mind. Anyway, yes, I can access as far back as you need. It just won't be as easy as the daily register."

She fumbled with her keys to unlock the gate, then they hurried inside her cottage. Harley stood behind her as she opened her laptop. "What is it you're looking for?"

"Let's see if he was here during any of the previous break-ins at Big Al's." Harley leaned on her desk, scrolling through her phone. "The break-ins at Al's were always on Thursday nights or Friday morning before daylight. Let's try June 24th."

"Okay. That's just last quarter. I haven't dumped that yet." She quickly pulled up the register and her eyes widened. "Oh my god. Yes. He checked in that morning. Stayed only one night, which is unusual for him."

"Then let's check April 8th."

"That's also in the last quarter, so…" She pulled up April, scrolling to the 8th. Her heart hammered just a little quicker when she saw his name. She pointed to it. "Yes."

"Son of a bitch," Harley muttered.

"But what does this mean, Harley? What does Al's Bait Shop have to do with it?"

Harley moved away, pacing in front of the sofa. "I have a theory as to why but it's just that—a theory. A hunch." She stopped pacing. "Each break-in, there was a broken windowpane on one of the side windows by the back door. Same pane each time. It was assumed the guy reached through the pane, unlocked the door, and went inside. The freezer is back there. The only thing missing would be some boxes of frozen bait." She started pacing again. "So I'm thinking all along, who steals bait?" She shook her head. "No one. So then I thought maybe they were moving drugs. Maybe one of Al's guys was in on it. They go out in the boat very early to catch bait fish and shrimp. I thought maybe they were meeting another boat out there, offloading the drugs, then bringing it into the shop. Al says the guys don't have keys to that door, so I thought maybe one of them just broke the glass to get inside. Or maybe whoever they were working with." She shrugged. "All just speculation."

"I still don't understand what that has to do with what's going on now."

"So say our guy planned Christopher Bryce's murder all along. Not necessarily Bryce, but someone. He planned to cut his head off and he needed to store it. So he does reconnaissance, finds Al's place, determines the cameras won't catch him and he breaks in. When he breaks in, Al does an inventory, finds the bait missing. This happened five times. So if there's no break-in, Al doesn't do inventory." Harley leaned against her desk again. "I always just assumed the busted-out pane was how he got in. But today, I measured it. Unless he's got an abnormally long arm, he couldn't reach the door."

Lauren frowned, still not understanding. "So it was staged?"

"Yes. We know our guy doesn't need to break glass. He got into your house easily. He broke into Veronica Higgins's place easily. He broke into my camper. Stands to reason he could break into Al's back door." Harley smiled. "So he broke in, left the head buried beneath all the frozen bait. Al didn't see a busted-out window, so he didn't do inventory. Never found the head. Then, weeks later, when our guy wants to leave you a present, he breaks in again. Only then did he realize that his bag had leaked blood out. He takes the head, but there's all this blood in the freezer. So he leaves a message for me, knowing that Al will call the police when he sees the blood."

"But there was no broken window?"

"No."

"Forgive me for not getting the big picture, but if you do, that's great."

Harley nodded. "All speculation as I said, but that's my theory." She pointed to the laptop. "The fact that Bret Blevins was here on those previous break-ins is circumstantial only."

She leaned her elbows on the desk. "Do we really think that he might be the guy? I mean really?"

"When did he check in this time?"

"Umm, Thursday. It was right after you'd left."

"A guy broke into your house Wednesday night. Well, Thursday morning."

"Your place is trashed on Friday."

"And Christopher Bryce's head is found here at the resort."

Lauren met her eyes. "Oh my god. So it *is* him?" She wrapped her arms around herself. "Can it be true?"

"Like I said, circumstantial evidence, that's all."

"So what are you going to do?"

"Run it by Brian, first of all. Then see if we've got enough to request a warrant. Then I'd like to see if we can place him in San Antonio during any of those murders. If we can, then I think that's way past circumstantial."

Harley motioned her up and Lauren closed her laptop. "You're not going to leave me here, are you?"

"Not out there, no. But here in your house? Yes. With Jacobs."

"But—"

"He can stay inside with you, Lauren. I'll be back as soon as I can."

"What if Blevins comes back?"

Harley drew her closer and they embraced. She closed her eyes as she pressed her cheek against Harley's.

"I'll have Jacobs bring his patrol unit back here. He stays inside with you."

"It kinda freaks me out to think it might have been Bret Blevins all along. To think that I talked to him, was around him. That he was in the pool with me that one morning." She shook herself, as if to ward off the image. "Intuition maybe, but there was always something odd about him. From that very first time I saw him, he just gave me the creeps."

"And if it is him, it's going to piss me off that he was right under my nose the whole damn time." Harley moved toward the door. "Lock the door behind me. I'll have Jacobs lock the gate when he comes inside."

"Harley?"

"Hmm?"

"Can we make love tonight?"

She stayed where she was at the desk and Harley stayed by the door. Across the room, their eyes met and held.

"I would like that very much. Of course, you'll have to show me how."

Lauren smiled at her. "I can do that. It'll probably take me several long hours to show you, though."

Harley smiled back at her, then opened the door and left. Lauren let out her breath, still smiling. But that smile vanished as Bret Blevins's face popped into her mind. Could it really be him? Sure, he was annoying and creepy, but was he a killer and a rapist? Was he the man who had broken into her home and scared her half to death? Had he killed Christopher Bryce? Veronica Higgins?

She looked around, startled. A noise of some sort. In her bedroom? The door was closed. Had she closed it?

She didn't wait to ponder the question. She bolted for her front door and flung it open, about to call to Harley, but she was already out of sight. She stood at the gate, looking behind her, expecting to see someone—Bret Blevins—coming out of her house.

A slamming of a car door made her jump and she turned, seeing Officer Jacobs heading her way. She let out a relieved breath, smiling as he approached.

"I'm so glad you're here."

"Yes, ma'am. Harley said—"

"Please call me Lauren." She drew him through the gate. "And would you mind very much checking my bedroom?"

He stopped and a slight blush lit his young, handsome face. She shook her head quickly.

"I mean, I heard a noise in there and the door is closed, and I can't remember if I'm the one who closed it or not," she said in a rush. "I'm being a little paranoid. I'm sorry."

"Oh, I see. Sure, I'll check it." He paused. "You should come with me. Harley said I wasn't to let you out of my sight."

"Good. Because I don't plan to let you out of mine."

Her fear was unwarranted, it turned out. There was nothing out of the ordinary in her bedroom and nothing looked disturbed. She apologized to him.

"I'm sorry. As I said, I'm a little paranoid."

"No problems, ma'am."

He followed her back into the kitchen. "Would you like some coffee?"

"Oh, that'd be great. Thank you."

She pulled out a medium roast for him. "What's your first name?"

"It's John."

She smiled. "John Jacobs. Have you been on the force long?"

"A little over six months." Then his expression changed. "I feel confident in my ability, ma'am. You don't have to worry."

"I'm not worrying, and please, call me Lauren."

He shrugged. "Habit."

"Well, I'm sure you'll be glad to get off of this assignment. You must be terribly bored."

"Not at all. I was the first on the scene when the head was found. That was pretty cool." Then he quickly held his hand up. "I'm sorry. That sounded—"

"It's okay, John. It added a little excitement to everyone's day, I'm sure." She took the cup from the Keurig. "Sugar? I'm sorry, I don't have any cream."

"I like it black. Thank you."

"Dare I offer you some breakfast? I've got some frozen burritos."

"No, I'm fine. It's a short day for me anyway. I get relieved at noon. I'm switching to nights, so I'll be back on at seven Sunday night."

"Here?" She put her own pod into the Keurig to brew.

"I don't know. I haven't been told yet."

"That's only like one day off. Is that normal?"

"My shift is switching, so yeah. Then I go to twelve-hour shifts with four on and then three off."

"Oh, okay." She added a little sugar to her cup. "Do you have a partner?"

"You mean on patrol? No, not anymore. I rode with someone the first month. I've been on my own since then."

She smiled at him. "So, I don't see a ring. Not married?"

He blushed slightly. "No, ma'am. Not yet."

"Seeing someone?"

He nodded. "Ashley. We've been engaged forever, but she's not crazy about my job."

"I imagine not."

"We're a small town. I keep telling her, there's never been an officer killed in the line of duty here."

"Well, maybe she'll come around."

"Maybe so. I've always wanted to be a police officer. She knew that in high school."

"Oh, so you're high school sweethearts then?"

He blushed again. "We started dating when we were sixteen."

"And you're what now?"

"Twenty-four."

She patted his hand. "That must be nice. I hope she does come around then."

"What about you?" he asked unexpectedly.

"Me?" She raised an eyebrow. "Are you asking about Harley and me?"

"Well..."

She nodded. "You saw us kiss," she stated, remembering belatedly that he'd been a witness to that. "Yes, we're...new friends," she said carefully.

"She's staying here," he stated as well.

She smiled. "She's protecting me." Then she laughed. "Sorry. Don't mean to be so vague, John. I assume it's not exactly protocol to have her staying with me. Or for us to be involved," she added. "I'm sure it's been a topic of discussion."

"I'm kinda new so I miss out on a lot of the gossip." He set his cup down. "I like Harley. Haven't been around her much before this, but she's been nice to me." He smiled quickly. "Well, other than her threatening me if anything happens to you. But I like her."

"Yes. She is nice. And I like her too."

CHAPTER FORTY

Brian nodded. "Yes, circumstantial. And if we were in San Antonio, I wouldn't try to get a warrant with what we've got. But here? After what's happened in the last two months? I don't think Judge Cannon would even blink at a request."

"But you know I did that background check on him. Found credit card receipts on Port A during the time Christopher Bryce would have been abducted and killed."

"I remember your timeline. But you said this Blevins guy has a boat—a yacht. From Port Aransas to where Bryce was last seen is a quick trip across Corpus Christi Bay. Not hard to pick up Bryce, hold him on his yacht, continue to use his credit card to establish an alibi, then go take care of him."

"So he steals another boat, kills the guy, takes him up Aransas Bay to Rockport? Dumps the body, dumps the boat." She nodded. "Possible. My gut says he's the guy. When I met him, there was something about him that was familiar. It was weird. And he had such cold eyes. I thought, at the time, it was because he was trying to score a date with Lauren and I was there, getting in the way." She met Brian's gaze. "Now, I think that look in his eyes was pure hate—anger—directed at me for a completely different reason." She shrugged. "Still circumstantial."

"Yeah, it is. But we'll get a warrant for phone records, but I don't know if that'll help us in San Antonio. Depending on who his carrier is, the phone records may already be dumped so we won't be able to track him. It's been what, a year and a half since the last murder there?"

"Yes, just about."

"Okay. I'll give Judge Cannon a call. You'll do the paperwork?"

"I'm on it." Before she left his office, however, Commander Lawson came in. She was surprised he was there. "Got everyone working on a Saturday, huh?"

Lawson ignored her statement. "Harley, we got a call from the Lamar Volunteer Fire Department. They were looking for you. There was a fire out at St. Charles RV Park."

Her eyes widened. She could tell by the look in his eyes that he wasn't just passing on news. "My camper?"

"Afraid so. I'm sorry. Your neighbor told them that you owned it. They said it's a total loss."

She sat down heavily, her eyes meeting Brian's. "Christ."

"What are you thinking?"

"I'm thinking that the son of a bitch is a dead man."

Lawson looked between them. "What? You don't think it was an accident?"

"Don't jump to conclusions, Harley."

"You think it's a coincidence?" She ran a hand through her hair. "It can't be."

"What's going on?" Lawson demanded.

Harley glanced at him. "My place was broken into yesterday. Trashed."

"I didn't hear about that. Did you file a report?"

"No." She looked at Brian. "Have you told him about San Antonio?"

Brian shook his head. "No. Go on out there, Harley. I'll take care of the warrant." Brian motioned for Lawson to sit. "Sorry. Things were happening too fast. Sit down. I'll fill you in. Harley? You take a unit with you. Get with Deeks. You don't need to be out there alone."

She stood up, her legs feeling shaky. Goddamn. The son of a bitch burned down her house. She left without another word, feeling numb as she walked outside.

Why the hell would he torch her camper? What purpose did that serve? He'd already trashed the place. He had to know that she'd been there, had seen it. What the hell was his reasoning? It was Saturday. Did he think she was inside? No. There was no vehicle there. Besides, he must know that she'd been with Lauren. Then what was his reasoning?

Didn't have to be a reason, she knew. It was all a game. The goddamn fucker was playing games with her. She stared up into the sky, her jaw clenched. And when she found the bastard, she was going to put a goddamn bullet in his brain.

* * *

The fire department was still on site when she got there. A lot of the residents were gathered nearby, and she motioned to Salazar—who had followed her out there—to stay back. She saw Tommy Butcher, her neighbor. His trailer had suffered damage too. How could it not? They were crammed together like sardines. She imagined the RV on the other side of her was damaged as well.

But her camper? Damn, it was practically burned to the ground. She stood there, staring at what was once her home. Smoke still rose from the rubble, nothing at all recognizable any longer. Her gaze landed on her bike—a charred stick-figure of a bike—then on the little table and chairs that had served as her patio. They were all scorched as well.

"Harley?"

She turned slowly, seeing Tommy coming over to her. "I'm sorry, man. Looks like the fire did some damage to your camper there."

"Hell, Harley, we're just glad you weren't home. What do you think happened? Electrical? You know they say these RV fridges aren't worth a damn."

She nodded. "Yeah. Probably. Say, you didn't see any strangers around, did you?"

"No. But I went out fishing about three this morning. I crawled back into bed when I got here. Heard all the commotion outside. We couldn't do anything with yours, but a bunch of us sprayed water on my rig and Gerald's over there."

"I've got insurance. It'll cover the damage done to your rig, Tommy." She blew out a breath, then walked closer to the camper. She wasn't sure how she felt. In shock? Yeah. But she put it in perspective for the here and now. It had already been trashed from the break-in. She had nothing inside that was irreplaceable. Hell, he'd ruined her clothes already. There wasn't anything personal in there anyway. She slid her glance to her bike again. Yeah, the bike was probably the only thing she'd miss.

She turned away from the sight and pulled out her phone. She paused just a second before pushing the number. Lauren answered on the second ring.

"Hey. How's it going? Are you coming back soon?"

Harley closed her eyes for a moment. "It's going okay." She cleared her throat. "Jacobs still there with you?"

"No. He got relieved at noon. There is an Officer Baker here now."

She nodded. "Good. Baker's good." She watched as smoke still drifted around her camper. "I was thinking maybe I could order some Mexican food for dinner. Maybe fajitas or something. I'll pick it up."

There was a long pause before Lauren replied. "What's wrong, Harley? You sound, well, not yourself."

She let out a heavy breath. "Yeah, so, there was a fire."

"A fire?"

"My RV. Up in smoke."

"Oh my god. Was it...was it him?"

"No way to know, really. Could be arson. Could be an accident." She sighed. "So? Dinner?"

"Honey, are you okay?" came the quiet question.

Harley closed her eyes, letting the question wash over her. "I'm not sure. I feel kinda numb, I think."

"Then come here, would you?"

She paused. "Do you have any booze?"

"You mean other than wine? No. I'm sorry, I don't."

"Do you mind if I pick something up?"

"Of course not. After the week we've had, I think I'll join you."

"Okay. And fajitas?"

"That's sounds good."

She nodded. "See you in a bit."

She turned her back on the wreck that was her camper and walked over to where Salazar was leaning against the patrol unit

"Gonna make two stops. At Spanky's Liquor and then at Jalisco's. Follow me?"

"You okay, Harley?"

She shrugged. "It is what it is." She looked back to the black heap. "Nothing I can do here."

She was crossing over the causeway with Salazar following close behind when her phone rang. She smiled at the ring tone.

"Hey, Marsha."

"Oh my god, Harley. Brian just told me. Are you okay?"

"I guess."

"Why don't you and Lauren stay with us tonight? You could—"

"I appreciate the offer, but no. I wouldn't be very good company, for one. I'm going to buy a bottle of expensive scotch, pick up some fajitas, and lock myself in Lauren's house for the night."

"Was there anything salvageable?"

"No. Burned to the ground."

"Oh, Harley. I'm so sorry."

She nodded as she passed the resort, glancing over there for a second, then driving past and on into town. "I think it'll be over soon, Marsha. Once way or the other."

Marsha took in a sharp breath. "You talk like that, Harley, and I'll send Brian over to haul your ass back here."

"Sorry. I'm just tired. Like I said, I wouldn't be good company."

"Okay, dear. Well, you call us if you need anything. And I mean anything."

"I will. I'll touch base tomorrow."

She disconnected before Marsha could reply. She loved Marsha, but she wasn't in the mood to talk. She wasn't even in the mood to think. So she called Jalisco's Bar and Grill and ordered a platter of fajitas, both beef and chicken. Then, with a long sigh, she headed to the liquor store.

CHAPTER FORTY-ONE

Lauren had been shocked by the lost look in Harley's eyes. It was something she had not seen before. Her words, however, were spoken matter-of-factly. "I imagine they'll rule it as accidental unless there is an obvious sign of an accelerant used." Harley wasn't hysterical, as she most likely would have been. She wasn't even very emotional. If not for the look in her eyes, Lauren would have thought Harley was completely unaffected by it.

That is, until she took out a glass. Not a small tumbler, no. A tall tea glass. Lauren watched as Harley opened the scotch, sniffed it, then poured enough in the glass to go way past the halfway mark. She wouldn't have been surprised if she'd guzzled it down. But no, she took only a small sip, then sighed before reaching into the cabinet for another glass.

"I'll take about half what you have."

Harley smiled but said nothing as she added scotch to another glass. The fajitas, along with rice and beans, were in the oven warming. The smell was enticing, but she imagined Harley was in no hurry to eat.

"You want to talk?" she asked quietly.

Harley took another sip before looking at her. "I'm not great company. Sorry."

Lauren moved closer. "You want to talk?"

When Harley looked at her this time, there were tears in her eyes. Lauren drew her into her arms, holding her tightly. But Harley didn't cry. Lauren felt her relax against her, heard a quiet sigh. When Harley pulled back, the tears had been blinked away.

Lauren picked up her drink and took Harley's hand, leading her to the sofa. Harley sat down beside her, but she didn't lean back as Lauren was doing. She sat up, her forearms resting on her thighs, the glass held between her hands.

"I feel a sense of loss, but I'm not sure why. As I said last night, you've seen my place. There wasn't much there to begin with."

"It was your home," she said gently.

"It was a place to sleep," Harley countered. She glanced over at her. "My bike got fried too. I moved there so that I'd be by the bay. Having access to the state park turned out to be the best part of it all, I think. Now that's gone too." She took a swallow of her drink. "It's the shirts. It's the damn shirts. I didn't tell you, but when I found them all torn up, I nearly cried." She glanced at her again. "Okay, so I did cry. A little. The shirts...they are what kept me sane this last year. And they're gone. So now I'm afraid I won't be able to...well, keep my shit together, if you know what I mean."

"You're afraid you'll go to that dark place again?"

"Yes. The shirts—"

"The shirts were only a symbol, Harley. That's all. Yeah, I miss you in them but not because they are what define you. You are you, whether you're wearing a gaudy Hawaiian shirt or not."

"Gaudy?"

Lauren smiled. "Yes, gaudy. Or should I say colorful?"

"They made me happy."

"You don't need them to make you happy. They were a reminder, that's all." She leaned closer, touching her arm. "Do you need a reminder of him, Harley?"

When Harley looked at her, she had a faraway look in her eyes. "Don't I?"

"Do you? Isn't he in your heart? In your mind—your memories?"

Harley nodded. "It's the picture. He tore it in half, and I felt violated. Now, I'm thinking, what if he hadn't torn it in half? I would have left it there, in the book. And it would have burned up with the rest of my stuff."

Lauren nodded, her fingers still touching Harley's arm. "What if it had?"

"That damn picture was my therapy. My link to him."

She was no therapist, and she didn't know if her words were helping or hurting, but she stated the obvious. "You were living your life still mourning for him, Harley. The shirts were a symbol. So was the picture. But now the picture is torn in half. You on one side and Travis on the other." She squeezed her arm. "Symbolic, but maybe you should take it to heart."

"Meaning what? That we're torn apart?"

"Separated. He's gone, Harley. You're still here. Your Hawaiian shirts are just window dressing. Whether Travis is here or not, that doesn't define you. You are still you."

She saw a tear run down Harley's cheek and she just barely resisted wiping it away. Were her words too harsh? Too blunt? Hell, what did she know about it? She should have kept her mouth shut. She let her hand slip away from Harley's arm, thinking she'd overstepped her bounds.

"I'm sorry, Harley. I had no right to—"

"No." Harley wiped a tear away impatiently. "You're right. I'm hanging on to him like he's coming back or something. The picture—we're both in our Hawaiian shirts." She leaned back against the sofa with a sigh. "Yeah, that's why I wore them. That picture. I look at that picture and it makes me smile. It was such a damn fun, happy night. We were carefree. The murders were already happening then, of course, but for that night, we pushed them away."

She didn't say anything, she just sat there quietly beside her, letting Harley gather her thoughts. Thoughts that she would either share with her or not.

"That case, it wore on us both, but Travis—he started drinking more and more. That's how he coped. We'd go out some nights and have a few drinks and he was his usual happy self. But then he'd go home and keep drinking. And I knew it. I'd call him sometimes, you know, to try to talk to him. He'd be so drunk, he couldn't carry on a conversation. And the next day at work, he wouldn't even remember that we'd talked." She rolled her head to look at her. "When I found him that morning—at first, I was so angry with myself because I hadn't called him the night before. I thought he'd done it. I was...I was hysterical really. Out of my mind."

Yes, Marsha had told her that very thing. Harley had been inconsolable, she'd said. She leaned closer now, letting their shoulders touch.

"The more I thought about it, my heart told me that he hadn't done it, though. That wasn't him. Now if he'd died from alcohol poisoning or something, yeah, I could believe that. But put a goddamn gun to his head? No way. Didn't matter. That was the official cause of death. Suicide. It was his weapon, his prints on the gun—GSR on his hands. Gunshot residue," she explained. "I kept telling Brian that he didn't do it, but it didn't matter. The case was closed. I finally had to let that seed of doubt in. Hell, maybe he had done it."

Harley sat up again. "None of it mattered anymore, though. I moved down here, I wore those damn stupid shirts and plastered a smile on my face." She took a deep breath. "Eventually, I convinced myself that I was happy again. And at night, I'd sit there and pull out that picture and...and reminisce and smile and I *was* happy. For a little while, at least." She stood up suddenly. "I was living my life in the past. Hell, I knew I was, I just couldn't stop it." Harley turned to her then. "That day I met you, I felt something change. I didn't know what it was at the time, but I felt it. I felt drawn to you."

Then Harley held her hand up and shook her head. "I'm sorry, Lauren. That sounds like I'm putting pressure on you and I'm not. We've only known each other a couple of months. I don't expect you to sweep in and take me to a place where Travis is truly in the past and I'm—"

Lauren stood up too, interrupting her. "We've known each other a couple of months, yes. And a hell of a lot has happened in those months. Here we are, thrown together unexpectedly, forced to become closer than the time on the calendar warrants." She met her gaze. "Because I do feel close to you, Harley. You know I'm attracted to you—I've told you so. And I can say and think all I want that I don't want this case—this guy—to define us and our relationship. But right now, it is. Because of this guy, we met. Does that make it wrong? Only time will tell and I'm willing to give it a go if you are." She moved to her then, taking the glass from her hands and setting it down blindly. "Travis is in the past. He's gone." She touched above Harley's left breast. "But he's in here. You don't need his Hawaiian shirts to be happy. You don't need a picture of him to be happy." She moved closer, touching Harley's face gently. "Let me make you happy. Give me a chance to do that, Harley. Would you?"

She wasn't sure what she expected but more tears weren't it. Harley couldn't blink them away this time. She met her damp eyes, then pulled her close, holding her tightly. Harley's arms slid around her waist and she felt them tighten against her. "It's just all been too much," she heard Harley whisper.

Yes, it had been. While it had been traumatic for her, it hadn't been an emotional roller coaster like it had been for Harley. And even though Harley had been a near rock through it all, it appeared that she'd reached her limit. She looked—and sounded—broken.

"Let's go to bed. Let's make love."

She pulled out of Harley's arms, not waiting for a response. She took both of their glasses and placed them on the kitchen counter, then turned off the oven. Harley didn't protest when she took her hand. She also didn't say anything. Her eyes had a faraway look to them, and Lauren gently nudged her down onto the bed. She undressed her slowly, methodically, all the while noting that Harley's expression hadn't changed. She was beginning to worry. Was she in shock? Had she simply given up?

"Sweetie?"

Harley looked at her then, blinking several times as if to bring herself back to the here and now. She smiled then. "I think I'm nearly naked. How did you manage that?"

Lauren returned her smile. "I'm sneaky that way." She bent down, kissing Harley gently, pulling back when Harley would have deepened the kiss. "Do you want to talk some more or…"

"No. I'd rather we do the 'or' if you don't mind." Then Harley's expression turned serious. "I'm about spent, Lauren. I'm kinda on overload."

"So you want to disappear for an hour or so? Make love? Block out the real world?"

Their eyes held and Harley's darkened. "Can we? Please?"

Lauren smiled at her. "Seeing as how I've almost got you naked…"

CHAPTER FORTY-TWO

Harley couldn't remember the last time—if ever—that she'd let someone have control. Actually, she couldn't remember anyone ever trying to take control. But Lauren guided her into her bed, and before she knew what was happening, Lauren's naked body was on top of hers, her mouth kissing her passionately for long moments. Long enough for Harley to nearly melt beneath her. Then lips were at her ear, whispering softly, then moving across her face to her mouth again.

She kept her eyes closed, letting her mind go blank. She let out a tiny moan when Lauren shifted, moving enough to put some space between them, her fingers brushing lightly across her nipples. Then she gasped when a warm mouth kissed across them gently, finally pausing long enough to bathe them, a soft tongue swirling around one, then the other.

She was having a hard time catching her breath, and when Lauren lifted her head away from her breasts, Harley opened her eyes, finding dark ones looking back at her. She saw a question there, but she simply closed her eyes again, letting Lauren do as she may. She supposed Lauren got the answer she was seeking because her mouth returned to hers and soft hands played upon her breasts. The kisses were no longer measured—they took on an urgency that made her moan into Lauren's mouth.

She finally moved, letting her hands glide up Lauren's body, cupping her hips and pulling her close. When she spread her thighs, Lauren slipped between them, echoing her moan as their tongues danced and battled. It was a glorious feeling—one she'd not experienced before. It was almost a relief to feel herself responding to Lauren's touch, to feel her body let go and simply enjoy the immense pleasure that Lauren evoked.

She lay back, hands lightly resting on Lauren's skin as Lauren's mouth and fingers seemed to be everywhere at once. With eyes still closed, she thought of nothing but Lauren's touch, a touch that ignited a fire at each pass. Then all thoughts ceased as a mouth settled over her breast and fingers slid into her wetness. She seemed to be floating in the darkness—a hot, searing blackness that enveloped her at every turn.

The blackness faded into a blinding white light in a matter of seconds, it seemed. She cried out and lifted off the bed, squeezing her eyes tightly against the brightness that flashed in her mind's eye. She lay there limply, feeling Lauren gather her close, feeling quiet lips moving across her skin again, hearing murmurs that she couldn't decipher.

She was aware that she was smiling, aware that she was being held protectively, aware of the warmth surrounding her. Nothing else. Her mind was blessedly blank.

And it felt so very good.

CHAPTER FORTY-THREE

Lauren was amazed at the difference in Harley this morning. Gone was that lost—troubled—look in her eyes. She seemed to be back to her normal cheerful self—playful and teasing as they'd showered together. A rather late shower, to be sure. Because it had been a rather long night.

They'd gotten out of bed at ten thirty to finally eat dinner. Harley had been almost shy then. Lauren hadn't commented on it, but she wondered if Harley had been embarrassed by the need she'd shown. One time, Harley had clung to her almost desperately after she'd climaxed, and Lauren had to remind herself that Harley wasn't used to making love. She was used to having sex. One and done. No emotions involved and probably not much passion.

That hadn't been the case last night. They'd showered after their late dinner and had gotten back into bed. Sleep came intermittently, though, as they'd wake to touch again. She remembered seeing the awe in Harley's eyes as Harley brought her to orgasm once again. They'd touched and pleasured each other at will, long into the early morning hours. Then Harley had pulled her close and covered them with the sheet. She'd fallen into a deep sleep, not waking until the sun was already high in the sky. Harley had still been asleep, her arm resting across her waist in an almost possessive pose. Lauren quite liked it.

Now, after their shower, they were on their way to pick up tacos for a very late breakfast. Or early lunch. Harley had surprised her by offering to take her to visit Nana. While she did normally see her on Sundays, she didn't know how she could possibly tell her all that had been happening out at the resort. As she'd told Harley, Nana would worry.

"We don't have to go, you know."

She looked over at Harley, noting the smile on her face. A relaxed, contented smile. She reached over and took her hand, their fingers entwining easily.

"No, we should go. I just think maybe we should temper some of the news, that's all. She'll probably be more interested in meeting you anyway."

"Should I tell her that you had your way with me last night?"

"Don't you dare! She doesn't need to know *everything*."

"And did I thank you for having your way with me?"

Lauren smiled at that. "I think you thanked me quite thoroughly in the shower this morning."

Harley squeezed her fingers. "Would you believe me if I said I'd never showered with anyone before?"

"I would. Because it was a first for me too."

"Really? You and Leah?"

"No. Never."

Another squeeze of fingers. "It was nice."

"Yes, it was."

Their fingers separated as Harley turned into the drive-thru at Jalisco's. "Should we get your grandmother something?"

"No. They usually have a large breakfast on Sundays. Then she and her friends gather for lunch and afternoon cards. My visiting window closes at noon."

"So we won't even have an hour with her."

"Plenty of time for her to inspect you."

"And what's on your agenda for this afternoon?"

Lauren smiled at her, wondering if staying in bed all day would be acceptable. Harley must have read her mind because she laughed and shook her head.

"I've got to go in to work. Or at least I think I do. I'll need to call Brian. I forgot to tell you that he was working on getting a warrant for Bret Blevins's phone records, going back as far as we can. We'll try to trace his activity, his whereabouts. See if we can place him at any of these scenes."

"Going back to San Antonio too?"

"Yes." She pulled up to the order board. "What would you like?"

Lauren peered past her, scanning the breakfast items, then looking over the lunch choices. "I think I'll have a ground beef and rice taco and a chipotle chicken and rice. Green salsa," she added before Harley could ask.

Harley gave their order, then pulled up to wait. There were two cars in front of them at the pickup window.

"How long will it take to get the results? Of the phone records, I mean."

"A day or two. It depends."

"Do you have to wait? I mean, can't you bring him in for questioning?"

"We can ask. He doesn't have to agree to it." She pulled up another spot. "Marsha wanted us to stay with them, by the way."

"You mean last night?"

"Yeah."

Lauren smiled. "Well, I'm certainly glad you declined that offer. I doubt we would have had nearly as much fun." Then she paused. "Was it odd for you?"

"Odd?"

"I don't imagine you're used to waking up with someone. After sex."

Harley met her gaze. "It didn't feel like sex. Not what I'm used to anyway. You made me want to cry."

"Cry in a good way though, right?"

Harley nodded. "I felt…loved. I felt emotionally connected to you. It was wonderful and scary at the same time."

Before Lauren could ask what she meant by that, Harley pulled up to the window. Lauren took out some money from her purse, but Harley stopped her. "I'll get it."

"You paid for dinner last night."

"And you're letting me stay at your house."

Lauren laughed. "Letting you? Is that what I'm doing?"

Harley murmured a thank-you to the girl who handed her a bag. Lauren took it from her as Harley pulled away. She was going to suggest they wait until they got to Nana's to eat but her stomach rumbled at the enticing smells coming from the bag. She pulled out a taco, seeing "chorizo" scribbled on the front. She handed it to Harley. She took one of hers—the beef and rice—and unwrapped the foil, taking a huge bite out of it.

"I didn't realize how hungry I was," she mumbled as she chewed.

At the light on Austin Street, Harley unwrapped more of hers, taking another bite. "We barely touched our dinner."

"That's because we were more interested in bed."

They'd both finished their first tacos by the time Harley pulled into the parking lot at The Oaks Retirement Village. It was aptly named as the townhomes were crammed between the trees much like the cottages were at the resort.

"To the right," she directed. "She's in Building Six." There were four homes in each building. Nana and her friend Mary were both in Building Six.

"Is there like a cafeteria or do they have meals delivered to their rooms?"

"There's a dining hall in the main building that serves as the community center. Those who are still able walk over. Of course, most of the units have small kitchens and Nana cooks some. It's just easier to go over for her meals, especially since it's already factored into the price."

Harley glanced at the watch on her wrist. "I guess I'll wait to eat my other one after we visit. Your window is closing."

As they went toward the door that would let them into the building, Lauren nudged her arm. "Thank you for doing this. If I missed a Sunday visit, she would be curious but not concerned. But I think you're right, we should probably let her know what's been going on." She paused before opening the door. "To a degree. Let's don't tell her a man was in my house, okay."

"I'll follow your lead. I'm just your chauffeur this morning."

"Is that what you are? My dashing police detective is only a chauffeur today?"

"Well, at the moment," Harley said with a smile.

Lauren knocked on Nana's door. "It's me, Nana."

The door jerked open a few seconds later. "You're late." Then Nana's eyes widened. "Oh, you have company."

"Yes. This is Harley."

Nana actually brought a hand to her hair as if to primp, fluffing it up a bit on each side. Then she gave a broad smile. "This is your policewoman?"

"Yes, she is. Harley, this is Nana, my grandmother."

Harley held her hand out. "Pleased to meet you, Nana. May I call you Nana?"

Lauren was surprised by the blush that lit her grandmother's face as she took Harley's hand. Of course, she didn't let it go. No, she covered it with her other hand, then tugged Harley inside, unmindful of her.

"You may call me Nana. That's so sweet. Come inside, dear." Then Nana glanced back at her. "Oh, Lauren, close the door, would you?"

Harley gave her a wink and she nearly rolled her eyes as she followed them into Nana's small living room. Instead of sitting in her recliner—like she always did—Nana sat down on the sofa beside Harley, still holding her hand.

"It's so exciting. A real live policewoman, right here in my living room. Now, Lauren's told me so much about you. She says you're dashing, just like on TV."

At this, Lauren *did* roll her eyes. She had said no such thing. "Nana, I think you're exaggerating, aren't you?" She sat down in Nana's recliner, noting the amused expression on Harley's face.

"I've been asking Lauren to bring you around. She's been so secretive about your relationship." Nana leaned closer to her. "I think my Lauren is quite taken with you."

"Nana!"

Nana ignored her, so much so that she didn't even look her way. "She says you reminded her of Leah, her ex."

"Yes, she told me that too."

"I, for one, don't see it. She did say you always wore Hawaiian shirts. I think they're very fashionable, Harley."

Harley glanced at her and grinned. "See? My shirts are fashionable."

"So they are," she agreed. She turned her attention to Nana. "There's something I—we—wanted to tell you."

Nana's eyes brightened. "You're getting married?" She clasped Harley's other hand now as well. "I knew it. I could see it the minute you walked in here."

Lauren held her hand up. "No. No, no, no. We are *not* getting married." *Good lord, where had that come from?* "Nana, it's—" But Nana was staring at Harley, still holding her hands.

"Why aren't you wearing one of those colorful shirts that Lauren loves so?"

Harley glanced at her with a smile. "Did she love them?"

Lauren returned her smile. "I told you, they grew on me."

Harley turned her attention back to Nana. "Well, I'm afraid I'm down to two shirts. There was a fire. At my place. I kinda lost everything."

"Oh my goodness. When?"

"It was yesterday. I lived at an RV park over on Lamar, by St. Charles Bay."

"That was you? They were talking about it at dinner last night. Oh no." Then she slid her glance to Lauren. "So where did you stay?"

"She stayed with me, Nana."

"Yes, Lauren was kind enough to offer her place."

"I bet that was cozy." Nana smiled coyly at her. "There's only one bed."

"Okay, that's enough," she stated. "We really did come over to…well, to fill you in on what's been going on. I thought you had a right to know."

Nana frowned. "What do you mean?"

Lauren looked at Harley, wondering where to start. "Well, you know about the vandalism at the clubhouse, of course. And the body that was found by the pier."

"The headless man, yes. That poor family. How awful."

"You heard on the news about that woman found over on Water Street?"

"Of course, how terrible was that? Which reminds me that I meant to tell you to be extra careful, Lauren. Crazy times we live in." Then Nana looked at Harley. "Of course, you seem to have protection, don't you? Having a policewoman staying with you and all."

"About that," Harley said. "It seems that this guy is using the resort—and maybe Lauren—to get to me."

Nana frowned. "I don't understand."

"Nana, there was a man's head—*the* head—left at the resort Friday morning," Lauren explained. "Well, we found it Friday morning. He came early that morning and left it."

Nana's eyes were wide as she looked between the two of them.

"We saw it on the security camera," Harley supplied. "We think it's all related. The same guy is responsible for it all. Including the fire at my place."

Nana turned to her as if for confirmation. "Lauren?"

Lauren nodded.

"And that poor woman? Her too?"

"Yes. It all appears to be related," Harley said. "It goes back to my time in San Antonio, I'm afraid. So there's been a lot happening and Heron Bay has been at the center of it, so to speak."

Nana looked at Lauren sharply. "Why didn't you tell me?"

"Oh, Nana, I didn't want you to worry, that's all. And besides Harley staying with me, there's been a police car parked there too, so I feel safe."

"A police car? At the resort? What are the guests saying about that?"

She shrugged. "A few have asked. I say it's a precaution because of the vandalism and all. Of course, finding that man's head, well, a few guests were aware of that. Even then, most don't seem too concerned."

Nana turned to Harley then. "You are keeping her safe?"

"Yes, ma'am. I promise."

"And she won't be left alone?"

"Not for a minute."

Lauren still saw the worried look on her face. "Should we not have told you, Nana?"

"Ignorance is bliss sometimes, isn't it?"

Lauren smiled warmly at her. "I don't want you to worry, Nana. I feel safe. It's a pretty good deal to have a police detective as a friend."

"Yes, I guess it is." Nana seemed to relax again as she took one of Harley's hands. "Now, tell me, what are your intentions with my granddaughter?"

"Nana!"

Harley smiled at Nana. "Right now, my intentions are to keep her safe. Now, after we catch this guy, my intentions will probably change."

"I would hope so." Then she leaned closer. "So you're sharing a bed. What did you—?"

"That's enough." Lauren stood up quickly. "Don't you have lunch and a card game to get to?"

Nana laughed. "Why, Lauren, I believe you're blushing. I can't wait for our Wednesday dinner date. You'll have to fill me in. It's been years since we've talked about sex."

"Oh, good lord, Nana. Must you?"

Nana patted Harley's hand. "I'm serious now. The thought of my Lauren being involved in…well, all of this, is very scary to an old woman like me. You take care of her. She's all I have."

"I promise. I'll protect her, no matter what."

Lauren and Nana exchanged a tight hug and Nana kissed her cheek when they parted. "Thank you for bringing her by. She's cuter than you let on."

Lauren flicked her gaze to Harley, who was waiting by the door. "She is kinda cute, isn't she?"

Nana hugged her again. "Oh, Lauren, do be careful. I love you so. I don't know what I'd do—"

"I love you, Nana. I'll be very careful. I promise."

As they walked back outside, Harley said, "I think she took that pretty well, don't you?"

"She did. Or she pretended to. The death grip hug she gave me said otherwise. But as she said, I'm all she has. And she's all I have."

"Your brother?"

"No. He's currently not speaking to Nana ever since he found out about the will. And me? Our relationship is rather frosty as well. He didn't bother coming down here for my grandfather's funeral. I can't imagine he'd be someone either of us could count on in a time of need."

She was surprised when she felt Harley's fingers touch hers as they walked. "You can count on me, Lauren."

Lauren turned to her, meeting her eyes. They were the same warm brown that they always were. The same, yet something was different today. The eyes were more open to her, yes, because she saw the genuine affection Harley had for her. But different, as if Harley were hiding something from her. Or trying to hide it, she supposed. She stared into them for a long moment, imagining she saw love there. She squeezed Harley's fingers.

"I know I can. And that makes me feel very, very good."

CHAPTER FORTY-FOUR

Marsha hugged her tightly, just as she'd done Lauren. "I trust you had an uneventful night?"

Lauren glanced at her with an impish smile and Harley felt a blush on her face. "No problems, no," she said as nonchalantly as possible.

Marsha gave a hearty laugh and hugged her again. This time, her words were for her ears only. "I like her for you. Don't run."

Harley wanted to tell her that, no, she had no intention of running. She only hoped Lauren wouldn't be the one to run. She wouldn't blame her if she did. She'd been a real trooper through it all, but at some point, it would get to be too much. Then, after the case was over with, would they drift apart? Or would the case be a stain on their relationship that Lauren couldn't overlook?

Marsha released her with a kiss on her cheek, then she felt a warm hand slide into hers. Lauren's fingers tightened and Harley looked at her, surprised by what she saw there. Without thinking, she leaned closer, kissing her lightly on the lips. Lauren was the one who deepened the kiss, if only for a second.

"I'm ready to go back home," Lauren whispered. "I'm ready to get you alone."

Harley smiled at her, then bumped her shoulder playfully as they followed Marsha into the kitchen. Brian was at the bar, adding seasonings to ground meat.

"We thought we'd grill some burgers. I hope you haven't eaten," he said as he plunged his hands into the mixture.

"We had a late breakfast so, no, we've not had lunch." In fact, after they'd left Nana, they hadn't even eaten their second tacos. Brian had called when they'd been pulling away and they'd simply headed right over.

"Good," Marsha said. "I know y'all have business to talk about. I'll get Lauren to help me in here."

Harley was about to protest. There was no reason that Lauren couldn't be privy to whatever they needed to discuss. She knew, though, that Marsha was probably trying to protect Lauren from all the details of the case. Didn't matter. She'd fill her in anyway.

"Sure, I'll be glad to help," Lauren said. "In fact, a burger sounds good."

After Brian had washed his hands, he motioned her out of the kitchen. She glanced back, watching as Lauren was already cutting up a tomato. Brian paused, then turned back.

"Lauren? Do you happen to know what time Bret Blevins checked out of the resort this morning? Or if perhaps it was yesterday?"

Lauren looked up sharply, meeting her eyes and not Brian's. She shook her head. "He usually leaves early, like at seven or eight. Sometimes earlier than that, before I'm even at the office. He leaves the keys in the box then."

"Can you check?"

"Of course. I'll call Jessica."

She wiped her hands on the towel Marsha gave her before pulling out her phone. Harley looked at Brian questioningly.

"Trying to get a timeline," he explained. "We know he made his flight out of Corpus this morning. But we lost his phone signal somewhere over Corpus Christi Bay."

She frowned. "I'm assuming he didn't toss it out of the plane. Off the causeway while he drove?"

Brian nodded. "Most likely."

Lauren slipped her phone back in her pocket. "Jessica said the keys were in the box when she got there. So no way to know if he put them there last night or early this morning. Well, I guess we could check the office security camera if you needed an exact time."

"Thanks. I don't suppose it matters much one way or the other. His flight was this morning."

Harley followed Brian out into the living room, but he didn't stop there. He went out the sliding doors to the patio. "You want a beer?"

She raised her eyebrows. "Are we not working?"

He pulled out two from the fridge. "I've been working since five this morning." He used the bottle opener attached to the side post to pop the caps off. He handed her a bottle, then clicked the necks together before taking a drink.

"You have the coldest beer." She took a long swallow. "Beer on ice isn't even this cold."

"That's because we keep it one notch above freezing." He pulled out a chair and sat down. "We've been working the phone records since yesterday. Recent ones, anyway. We probably won't get past history until tomorrow sometime."

"Why didn't you let me know? I could have—"

"To be honest, Harley, I thought you needed a break. A one-day break isn't much, but you've had a hell of a lot happen to you in the last week. Emotionally. Not just the thing with Travis, but your RV too. I thought you needed to take a step back."

She stared at him. "Are you pulling me from the case?"

"You know damn well if we were still in San Antonio you'd be off the case." He took another swallow of beer. "But I need you here. So I just wanted to give you a little break."

"So what did you find?"

"Phone tracking puts him at your RV both Friday and yesterday. We've got him at Lauren's house early that Thursday morning. We've got him at Veronica Higgins's house at two thirty that same morning. Got him at the resort on Friday morning at three thirty."

"When he left the head."

"Yeah. And we've got him at Big Al's about an hour before that."

Harley felt a surge of excitement. "So we've got him. All of that is not circumstantial. We can place him at every scene."

"Right. We've issued an APB and put out a photo of him to CCPD and our guys, of course. He dropped off his rental car and got on the plane in Corpus. It was a flight to Austin. That's it. No phone, no hits on credit cards, nothing. We have no idea where he is." Brian held his hand up. "And yes, I've alerted Austin PD."

"So on his way to the airport, he tosses his phone in the bay. That means he knows we were tracing him. Or knew we would at least try at some point." She nodded. "Smart. He kept his phone with him at all times, so we'd know it was him. But when he felt we were getting close, he tosses it."

"How would he know we were getting close?"

"I think he wanted us to get close. He spoke with Lauren that morning when they found the head. She said he was, well, a little creepy. Making innuendos about me and making reference to there being a head in the flowerbed. Lauren said at that point, no one knew it was a head. The guests couldn't have seen it from where they were."

Brian nodded. "So he should have had no way of knowing unless he's the one who put it there."

"Right. And I think he told her that, hoping she'd tell me. Like the last message, he's counting down the days. I think he's ready for it to be over with too."

"Then why disappear?"

"Because without a phone, we have no idea where he is. He could have landed in Austin, then turned around and headed right back here. It's a little over a three-hour drive."

"No hits on credit cards. How'd he rent a car?"

She leaned back in her chair, her mind racing now with possibilities. "He's the son of a very rich oil man. A man who has business holdings and offices in San Antonio, Odessa, Houston, Pleasanton, and, yes, Austin. How hard would it be for him to arrange to have a car at his disposal?"

"I know you did a background check on him. What did you find?"

"Nothing popped out. His father made a fortune in oil and gas. He's had everything handed to him all his life. He's listed as an employee of his father's company, but I couldn't tell if he actually did anything. He flies into Corpus, but his flights out are to different places—Dallas, Houston, San Antonio. There didn't seem to be a pattern."

"So we've got a guy with a rich daddy, a guy born into privilege without any responsibilities…so what does that mean? He's got time on his hands? He turned to rape? To murder? For what?"

She shrugged. "For fun?"

"What was his partner's name? Radisson?"

"Thomas Radisson, yes."

"So we ran everything we could on him. Are we sure there was no link to Bret Blevins?"

She closed her eyes, trying to remember. They'd only had a couple of days. Once Travis died, she completely shut down. She didn't do another thing with their case.

"Thomas Radisson was from Michigan. According to his mother, he moved to Dallas. She had no idea what he was doing in San Antonio. The driver's license he had on him was from Michigan. That's how we ID'd him. As far as I remember, we never found a current address in San Antonio or Dallas." She looked at him. "Of course, after Travis, I—"

"I pulled you from the case. And that's where it died. So let's assume he and Bret Blevins met up somewhere. Maybe a bar. Hell, maybe Radisson applied for a job with his father's company. Regardless, they met. They found they had an affinity for killing."

"That's crazy. If you're Bret Blevins, are you going to trust some kid you just met with that? You risk losing everything."

"Maybe he had something on Thomas. Maybe Thomas confessed to another killing or something. So Bret can now use that as blackmail or something."

Harley shook her head. "Makes no sense. You don't just wake up one day and decide to rape and murder some random woman. And seven times, no less."

"But nothing showed up in his background check."

"No." She arched an eyebrow. "But what if his records were sealed?"

"Juvenile record?"

"Yeah."

He nodded. "I'll have Craig check on that. If he's got a record that's sealed, I'll get a warrant from Judge Cannon. I'll give her a call too, just to make sure she's available on a Sunday."

Harley only halfway listened to his conversation with Craig. She was picturing Bret Blevins's face. Yeah, a rich kid who got everything he wanted. His daddy's only child, stood to reason he would have been spoiled rotten. So what happened? Did he get bored? Bored enough to kill? No. If a rich kid gets bored, he buys a race car or something. Maybe he buys a jet and learns to fly. These guys don't become serial killers.

They don't become cop killers.

CHAPTER FORTY-FIVE

"Harley looks relaxed today. So do you," Marsha mused. "After the hell you've both been through the last week, I wouldn't have thought it possible."

Lauren paused her slicing, smiling at Marsha. She knew the older woman was fishing for information. She didn't see the point of ignoring it—or trying to hide it. She and Harley were both grown women. There was no need to act otherwise.

"We had a very...a very lovely night." She smiled a bit broader. "And morning."

It was Marsha who blushed, and with her platinum blond hair, her red face was quite a contrast. "I suppose you both needed that."

Lauren laughed quietly at that statement. "Did we?"

"A release, if you will."

Her smile tempered a bit. "Harley was, well, emotionally drained, I think. She'd reached her limit. She was almost impassive. Her eyes were blank, emotionless. I was kinda worried about her, actually. About her mental state, I mean."

"I guess it was too much for her. First a man breaks into your house, then the woman on Water Street and the message about Travis. That alone would have been enough to do me in. But it kept going. The head is found, her place gets broken into. Then worse. Burned to the ground." Marsha shook her head forcefully. "I was worried about her too. I wanted you both to stay here last night. But Harley was insistent that she would be fine at your place." Then Marsha smiled. "Maybe she knew if you two were here…"

"I think her reasoning for wanting to stay at my place had little to do with sex. I think she wanted to just drift away for a while and not talk about it. That's not to say that we didn't talk. We did. Quite a bit, actually. About Travis. About her feelings for him then and now. About why she wore the shirts, how she was trying to hold on to him. We talked about all of that."

"She was better this morning?"

"Yes. Back to being Harley again. Well, the Harley that I know. You'd said once that she changed after Travis."

"I say changed because she became more outgoing." Marsha shrugged. "Who knows? Maybe she was that way all along, but Travis stifled that. As I said, Travis had such a gigantic personality, he overshadowed her."

"And so she stayed in the shadows?"

"I never knew Harley without Travis. Brian met them when they were fresh out of the academy and he was a sergeant. As he moved up—lieutenant, then captain—they moved along with him, both making detective at the same time. Brian was torn as to whether to make them partners or not. They were too close, he thought. But because they were that close, they were damn good partners. Half the time, they didn't even have to talk—they knew what the other was thinking." Marsha slid a jar of pickles toward her. "After Travis died, after Harley was so distraught, Brian kicked himself for them being partners."

"If they were as close as you say, I doubt them not being partners would have made much difference."

"I told him that very thing." Marsha washed her hands at the sink. "I'm glad Harley has you, Lauren. If not, I wonder how she would be handling all of this. Or even if she could."

Lauren opened the jar and took out a pickle to slice. "And I'm thankful that I have Harley. If not, I wonder how *I* would be handling all of this." She felt Marsha's eyes on her, and she looked up, meeting them.

"Are you falling in love with our Harley?"

The words were spoken quietly, gently. Lauren put the knife down. "Oh, Marsha…" She glanced toward the living room. "I think I am, yes. And I'm terrified of getting my heart broken."

Marsha patted her hand. "Says every woman who's ever fallen in love."

Lauren smiled at that comment. "In other words, there are never any guarantees?"

"Relationships aren't effortless. Falling in love is much easier than staying in love. I do worry that Harley may not recognize it, though. She has had zero experience."

"So she's told me." She picked up the knife again to finish with the pickles. "I think—"

But she stopped talking as Harley came into the kitchen, holding two beer bottles. She set them down on the bar. "Didn't want to get ahead of you." Harley eyed her. "Everything okay?"

"Yes. We've just been visiting."

Harley glanced at Marsha. "Telling tales?"

"None of your business." She picked up her beer and took a swallow. "Thank you. Are y'all out on the patio?"

"Yes. Join us?"

"Yes. Everything is ready in here. Have you finished your discussion?"

"He filled me in. We're waiting on Craig to check on something for us now." Harley turned to her and stole of pickle slice from the cutting board. "Come on out?"

She nodded. "And a beer sounds good. It'll be nice to sit and relax for a bit."

And they did. They sat on the patio and chatted. Harley told them how she'd met Nana and Marsha had been full of questions. There'd been no mention of the case—or Bret Blevins—until Brian got a phone call. He stepped off the patio, just out of earshot. The call lasted only a handful of seconds. Then Brian had turned to Harley.

"You were right. There were two incidents when he was a juvenile. Records are sealed. I'll get a warrant. Judge Cannon is out of town, but she said she'd be available by seven in the morning."

"Having his juvenile records won't really help us, other than providing some information or background on him."

"You're talking about Blevins?" Lauren asked.

"Yes. He's our guy," Harley said. "Unfortunately, he flew to Austin this morning and has since disappeared."

That brief discussion seemed to take the luster out of the day for all of them. Brian lit the gas grill and Marsha went inside to get the meat patties. Lauren accepted another beer, but conversation was rather sparse, despite Marsha's attempts to keep it going. She was suddenly very tired and wondered if Harley was too. Their long night of only intermittent sleeping seemed to be taking its toll on her.

She got her answer as soon as they finished eating. "I'm beat," Harley announced. "Thanks for the burger, but I think we're going to head back."

Lauren's offer to help clean up was met with a firm "no" from Marsha and after hugging them both, she sent them on their way.

"Don't forget," she called after them. "When this thing is over with, we'll have a fish fry out here. Invite Nana. I can't wait to meet her."

"She really likes you," Harley said as they backed out of the driveway.

"I like her too. I feel like we left in a rush, though."

"That's because we did. I think I saw your head bobbing."

Lauren leaned her head back now. "Yes. I could take a nap, I think." Then she smiled. "Or something."

Harley laughed but said nothing. Lauren closed her eyes, then felt Harley's fingers entwine with hers. She sighed contentedly, knowing that she was indeed on the brink of falling asleep. She didn't try to fight it. She was with Harley. And she was safe.

CHAPTER FORTY-SIX

Harley was too spent to care about outside noises, but the horn that honked for a second time finally registered. She opened her eyes, blinking against the darkness. Lauren was curled against her, one arm resting across her waist and the other clutching her forearm from beneath. She forgot about the horn as she rolled to her side, feeling Lauren's naked body slide against her own. She heard Lauren moan, even in sleep, as they touched.

What an amazing night it had been. Their hands had moved more surely, their kisses were deeper, longer. It wasn't lost on her that it was the first time she'd ever slept with someone more than once. Even now, as tired as she was, the feel of Lauren's body against her own sent shivers along her skin.

The horn honked once again, and she rolled to her back, listening. What time was it? She reached over, fumbling for her phone.

"What is it?" Lauren mumbled against her neck.

"There's a horn honking." She stared at her phone. It was three thirty-two. Damn. "I should check it out."

Lauren sat up sleepily and rubbed her eyes. "What? Like go outside?" She flipped on the lamp beside the bed. "Harley, no."

She got out of bed. "Let me just take a look. Jacobs would have called if something was going on." The horn sounded again, and their eyes met. "Let me check it out."

Lauren got out of bed too, both of them naked. They pulled on T-shirts and underwear, nothing more. At the front door, Harley flipped on the outside light. She could see the gate clearly and it was still locked, the chain secure.

She opened the front door, listening. There was no sound at all. No insects calling, no breeze. A thick fog was hovering overhead in an eerie pattern, the full moon illuminating it from above. The sidewalk was damp and glistening, as if it had rained. The horn this time was but a short burst and she knew it had come from just behind the fence. Where Jacobs should be.

"Where's the key to the gate?"

Lauren opened a drawer at the edge of the kitchen and pulled out a ring with a single key on it.

"You stay here. Lock the door behind me."

"But—"

"I'll be right back. Just gonna check on Jacobs."

"Okay," Lauren said weakly as she ran a hand through her hair.

Harley saw the fear in her eyes and touched her cheek gently. She didn't want to leave her alone, no. But if someone was out there, she certainly didn't want her exposed. It was best she stay inside the house. "I won't be gone long. But lock the door."

She went out into the damp fog hearing the deadbolt slip into place. She stopped at the gate, listening. There was nothing out of the ordinary.

"Jacobs?" she called. Again, nothing.

She hesitated, holding the key loosely in her hand. She should go back inside. She should call Jacobs, make sure everything was all right. She turned, planning to do just that when the horn sounded again—another short burst by the fence, where Jacobs was parked. She grabbed the lock at the gate and inserted the key, letting the chain dangle free as she went through. She grimaced as her bare foot landed on a small rock. She walked along the fence, seeing Jacobs's patrol car. The light was on inside, the door open.

She hurried to it, seeing him slumped back against the seat. Her eyes widened as she saw a knife sticking out of his neck. Blood oozed from the wound and had soaked his shirt. She wouldn't have thought he was conscious if not for the hand resting in the center of the steering wheel.

"Jacobs?" He opened his mouth to speak but no words came out. "Christ, man." She saw the radio in his lap and wondered if he'd managed to call it in. She grabbed it, but it was no longer attached. The cord had been cut. "Son of a bitch."

She saw his cell lying on the passenger's seat, then raced around the car, jerking open the door and grabbing the phone. It required a passcode, so she simply touched "emergency" and waited only a moment before the 911 operator picked up.

* * *

Lauren paced nervously in her kitchen, her eyes glued to the front door. It had been too long. Where was she? She went to the door and unlocked it, but before she could open it, she locked it again. Harley had said to wait.

But what if she was in trouble? What if she needed help?

"Like I could help." No, she needed to stay put. Jacobs was out there. Harley would be fine.

So she resumed her pacing, her steps becoming faster and faster as she anxiously—and unconsciously—chewed on a nail. She had a bad feeling, that was all. She felt alert, aware of every little thing, every sound. The problem was, there was no sound. The horn had stopped. But if it had stopped, then surely Harley would come back already.

She'd barely registered that thought when there was a hurried tap, tap, tap on the door. She nearly jerked it open, so relieved that she was back. It wasn't Harley who stood there, however.

She attempted to slam the door shut again, but a strong arm easily blocked it. "No!" She turned to run, but he grabbed her hair, yanking her back against him. She screamed as he reached for her, but it was the gun held to her face that cut off the scream.

"I gotcha now."

He wrapped an arm around her neck, but instead of closing the door and locking it—which she imagined him doing before dragging her to the bedroom—he hauled her outside, pulling her along with him as they went toward the gate. She yelled for Harley and got a hard punch to the side of her face with the gun. She stumbled, swearing she'd seen stars. She blinked several times, hoping she didn't pass out.

"I will indeed shoot you if you yell out again."

Oh god, Harley. Where are you?

Once outside the gate, he backed up, going toward the bay. He pressed the gun to her temple. "Call out for her now."

"What?" she asked with a shaky breath. "But you said you'd shoot if—"

"And now I'm saying to call out for her." He pressed the gun tighter. "Now!"

CHAPTER FORTY-SEVEN

"Hang on, Jacobs. They'll be here in two minutes."

He lay back limply, his arms having collapsed by his sides. He'd opened his eyes once, and she saw relief in them as it registered to him that she was there. He had a weak pulse, but a pulse, nonetheless. Finally, she heard a siren in the distance. She squeezed his hand. "See? They're almost here. You hang on."

"Harley!"

She jerked her head up. *What the hell?*

"Harley!"

"Oh my god."

She dropped Jacobs's hand, heading in the direction of Lauren's scream. She reached to her side without thinking, but obviously there was no weapon there. She turned back to the car, reaching around Jacobs to pull his gun from the holster. Then she hurried around the fence, stopping up short as she saw them.

She calmly pointed her gun. "Let her go!"

He had Lauren held in front of him—like a shield. They were too far from Lauren's porch light to be able to see her expression, but she could only imagine. His response was a laugh as he backed up along the path, pulling Lauren with him.

"Nowhere to go, Blevins!"

"I know where I'm going, Harley. I also know where you're going. Straight to hell!"

"Let her go, man. This is between us. Not her."

"Now why would I let her go? You won't shoot me with her here." He laughed. "You should thank me, Harley, for setting you two up. Best I could tell, you hadn't gotten laid in over a year. Hope it was good for you. It'll be your last."

She followed along with them as he backed up. He was at the bay road now. One arm was around Lauren's neck, the other held the gun to her head. As he crossed the road toward the pier, the soft green lights were bright enough to finally see Lauren clearly. Her eyes were pleading, begging, and swimming in fear.

I'm so sorry, baby.

She looked past him, wondering what he planned to do. He wanted her dead, that was for sure. But then what? There was no vehicle parked along the road. No. But there was a boat tied to the end of the pier. It was a bay boat, and she wondered if he'd stolen it. Maybe he had his yacht anchored offshore. Maybe that was how he planned his escape.

When he got to the steps of the pier, it was only then that she saw that the gate was unlocked and propped open with a rock. Of course, he'd been a guest at the resort. He would know the combination to the lock. He pulled Lauren up the steps with him. Harley followed along, wondering how she could take a shot. Lauren was shielding his body, but one of his legs was exposed as they walked. Could she take a chance? If she shot him, then what? Would he shoot Lauren? Or would he take a shot at her?

"We're almost there, Harley. What a great night for fishing, isn't it?"

"Does your daddy know what you've been doing? Does he know about those women in San Antonio?"

His laugh could only be described as evil. "Did you not know about the two in Odessa? Or the three in El Paso? Or what about the five in Dallas?" He laughed again. "Now one in little bitty Rockport. When I leave here, I'll be out hunting again. You won't be around to stop me, Harley. As if you could."

"Even if I don't shoot your ass, the game's up. We got a warrant for your phone records. We'll place you at the crime scenes. You'll—"

"Oh, please. You think I'm stupid enough to have carried a phone with me?"

"You did here."

"Of course. I wanted you to find me. Doesn't matter anyway. My daddy has the best lawyers. I won't be spending any time in jail. I never do."

She gave him a humorless smile. "No, I don't suppose you will. Because I'm going to put a bullet in your head. Just like you did Travis."

Another laugh and this time he peeked around Lauren to look at her. She almost—*almost*—took the shot.

"Man, he was so drunk. I had a hard time waking him up. But I wanted him to know he was about to die."

"What took you so long to come after me then?"

"I wanted you to suffer. I wanted his death to eat at you, just like Tommy's ate at me."

"Do you think it did?"

"I know it did!" He yelled. "I've been watching you. You're nothing but a shell of what you were."

Harley could see the desperation in Lauren's eyes. They were but twenty feet apart. The fog seemed to be dissipating and the moon was finally showing itself. The green glow of the lights seemed to dance around them. She could hear the waves lapping at the pylons. High tide.

They were now near the end of the pier. She could see the boat clearly as it bobbed in the water. Whatever he planned to do, it would happen soon.

"Let her go," she tried again. "Just me and you. Let her go."

"Or what? I don't care about her, Harley. I'll shoot her where she stands."

"And I'll drop you half a second later."

She stared into Lauren's eyes, willing her to do something. All she needed was a little window and a fraction of a second. That's all she needed. Because if she didn't do something—and soon—then she had no doubt that he would shoot Lauren. As he'd said, he doesn't care about her. So she stared into Lauren's eyes, silently begging her to turn her head enough for her to take a shot.

She was breathing fast, hard, and she knew in her gut that time was running out. There were sirens all around it seemed. Blevins knew that time was short as well. What was his plan? But she knew the plan, didn't she? She could see his finger tighten on the trigger. He would shoot Lauren, but still hold her up in front of him as he fired at her.

"Lauren," she said quietly as she met her gaze.

Their eyes locked together, and she nodded slowly. Then Lauren closed her eyes and rolled her head to the left. Harley fired, then stared in shock as his weapon fired too. The force of it sent Lauren over the side and into the bay. Without thought, Harley fired again, twice more, three times, sending him careening off the side as well.

"Lauren!" she screamed.

She dropped the gun and ran, blindly jumping into the bay. It was deep, eight or ten feet with high tide. She surfaced, frantically looking around. "Lauren! Lauren!"

They were near the fishing deck on the side where there were no lights. She treaded water, her head jerking in all directions, looking for her. "Lauren! *Lauren!*"

There, closer to shore, she saw it. A body. Her heart nearly stilled in her chest as the tide carried it to shore. She swam toward it, spitting out salt water as she went. As she got closer, the lights illuminated the bay. The water was red with blood, the high tide washing Bret Blevins's body toward the stone breakwall.

She spun around, her feet touching bottom now. She was crying, she knew she was. Oh, Lauren. *God.* She swam back out, her eyes blurry from the water and her tears.

"Lauren," she called again, this time weakly, softer. There was no one to hear her, she knew. She could feel it. There was no one. She was alone out there in the bay. Alone.

Despair washed over her, and she felt herself sinking under the water as the tide carried the waves in. God, no. She couldn't go through it again. She just couldn't. She couldn't be left all alone again. She'd never survive this time. She tried to keep her head above water, but a wave splashed her, and water gushed into her mouth.

She felt no panic. Not really. Because she simply didn't care anymore. She went under water, not intending to come back up. It would be easier this way. Her lungs were burning, but she still held her breath as she sunk against the tide. Then she felt hands on her, touching her, propelling her upward in a fierce rush. She surfaced and took gulps of air. She looked around, but she was still alone.

She lay back, floating, feeling the tide carrying her toward the shore. Then she heard it. Or she imagined she heard it.

"Harley?"

She touched bottom now, the water a little over five feet deep where she was. She looked across the blackness of the bay. "Lauren!"

"Harley!"

Oh dear god. She swam back toward the fishing deck, fighting against the tide. "Lauren? Where are you?" she called.

"At the boat," came an answering voice from across the water.

The boat still bobbed where it had been, but the tide was nearly slamming it against the pylons. Another wave drenched her, and she came up coughing. There, against the back, she saw Lauren clinging to the motor, her head just barely above water. Harley swam toward her, amazed at how strong the tide was in the bay. She felt like she was moving in slow motion.

She swam up beside her, putting a hand on the edge of the motor to steady herself. When their eyes met, they both smiled with relief. Harley moved one of her hands to cover Lauren's, needing some contact with her.

"I'm freezing," Lauren said through chattering teeth.

Harley spit out water. "I'm waterlogged." Then she saw the gash on Lauren's forehead. "You're injured. Oh Jesus, did he shoot you?"

"I hit the boat, I think. I'm not really sure what happened. I found myself out there," she pointed, motioning away from the pier. "I saw the boat and swam toward it. I didn't know if you… well, I didn't know what had happened."

Then the tears came, and Harley moved closer, holding her as best she could as high tide surrounded them.

"It's over now, honey. All over." She wrapped one hand around Lauren's waist. "Come on. Let's get out of here."

They left the safety of the boat and swam toward the steps at the fishing deck. The same steps she'd used to haul Christopher Bryce's body out of the water in early summer. They held on to the lower steps and rested.

"I've never been in the bay before," Lauren said.

"No? Well, this is my second time. I don't really recommend it."

Lauren smiled. "Maybe we should take up fishing."

"We'll talk about it."

She urged her up the steps, then turned back around, looking over the water. The waves still splashed against her. Over by the shore, where the lights were brighter, she saw Bret Blevins's body, now lodged between the large rocks of the breakwall.

"Harley?"

She looked up, meeting Lauren's eyes in the moonlight. "I thought you were dead. And I thought I wanted to be too. I couldn't go through another loss."

Lauren's expression softened as she shook her head. "No. God, no, Harley." She motioned her up. "Come out of the water."

Harley was almost afraid now, afraid of what Lauren must think of her. Did she find her weak? But she climbed up and

Lauren was there, pulling her into her arms. They were wet and cold, and it didn't matter. Lauren held her tightly and Harley did too. She wasn't sure if she felt like laughing or crying. She did neither. They were standing there in next to nothing. Wet T-shirts and underwear. *God.*

"Come on. Let's get out of here."

They made it to the end of the pier before the flashing lights of a police unit pulled up. It was Baker.

"Jesus, Harley. What the hell happened?"

She pointed to the breakwall where Bret Blevins was lodged. She stared at the body. He was facedown, the water all but covering him now.

"Probably need to call a dive team in. His gun is in the bay. So is mine, I guess. Or Jacobs's gun. I kinda borrowed it." Baker stood next to her, looking at the body. "How is Jacobs, by the way?"

"He was unconscious but alive. They left the knife in. That was a sight. He's just a kid, you know."

Lauren gasped beside her. "What happened to Jacobs?"

"Blevins stabbed him in the neck." She turned to Baker. "They take him to Corpus?"

"Yeah. It's four in the morning and the whole department is up and about. I think Deeks was going to Corpus to be with him."

"What about his fiancé?" Lauren asked.

Baker shrugged. "Don't know nothing about that." He pointed to the body. "Is that the bastard?"

"Bret Blevins. Besides the seven rapes and murders in San Antonio, he confessed to others. El Paso, Dallas, and Odessa."

"Damn."

"Yeah. He was a monster, all right." She clapped his shoulder. "You'll handle it?"

"I'm on it, Harley." Then he smiled. "You might want to put some clothes on."

She gave him a weak smile. "Thanks."

CHAPTER FORTY-EIGHT

Lauren knew that Brian was on his way over. She'd heard Harley on the phone with him. But she wanted to talk. Before Brian got there, she wanted to talk. Harley had showered first—a quick, hurried shower that she'd rushed through in less than ten minutes. Then she dressed and went outside to "tend to things" as she'd told her. Lauren had taken a much longer shower, letting the hot water warm her chilled body.

She'd stood at the mirror, staring at herself. The gash on her head was only an inch long, and it was no longer bleeding. A small knot had formed there, though. She really didn't remember what had happened and that scared her a little. When she'd looked in Harley's eyes, she knew...she knew that Harley was going to take a shot. She had to. Lauren knew that as well. There was such calmness in Harley's eyes—and confidence—that she no longer had been afraid. Well, that was a lie, wasn't it? Yes, she'd been terrified, to be sure. The gun barrel was against her temple, his arm was wound tightly around her neck, yet she relaxed. He planned to kill her, one way or another. She knew that. And she knew she had to give Harley a chance. So she'd looked in her eyes, taking strength from what she saw there.

Then gunfire. She could still hear the loud bang in her ear as his gun went off. She saw the flash. It was right at her head. For a long second, she wasn't sure if she'd been shot or not, she wasn't sure if she were dead or alive. Then he pushed her, and she went flying. Flying in slow motion, it seemed. She remembered closing her eyes as the black water got close. That was all. The next thing she knew, she was out in the darkness, seemingly far away from the pier and its lights. She'd panicked then, feeling disoriented. The water was deep and cold, and wave after wave seemed to equally push and pull at her, forcing her toward shore then back out into the bay. She couldn't see Harley. She couldn't see him. She heard nothing but the splashing of the water around her. She felt all alone, and she panicked, splashing frantically as she tried to swim.

When she made it to the boat, she called for Harley. She'd been so afraid he'd killed her. Afraid he'd won after all. Afraid he was looking for her. When she finally saw Harley in the water, coming toward her, the relief was so profound, it nearly choked her. But Harley's words—she'd wanted to die—God, that had sent a dagger to her heart.

So she wanted to talk. She hoped Harley would be up for it.

She made a second cup of coffee. It was still dark out and a glance at the clock on the microwave told her it wasn't yet five. She'd glanced out earlier, seeing that most of the police vehicles had left. She could still see flashing lights by the bay and wondered if they'd already taken Blevins's body away.

She sipped from her coffee, thinking of Officer Jacobs. He was such a nice young man with his whole life in front of him. Then she thought of his fiancé, the woman he'd been dating since he was sixteen. How must she feel? She hated him being a cop in the first place. Now this? She wondered if they would be able to get past it.

She turned when the door opened. It was Harley.

"I'm sorry. I didn't think it would take that long. Everyone wanted a play-by-play, it seems."

"It's okay. Is there any word on Officer Jacobs?"

Harley shook her head. "Nothing yet. I called Brian. Told him I was fine. Told him he didn't need to come around to check on me."

Lauren smiled at her. "Told him to go be with Jacobs instead?"

"Yeah." Harley came closer. "How are you holding up?"

"I'm okay. It's kinda surreal, I think. Almost like it happened to someone else, not me." She met Harley's gaze. "Do we have some time to ourselves?"

"We do. Do you want to talk?"

"I do." She put her cup down and took Harley's hand, leading her to the sofa. Harley had a wary look on her face, and it occurred to her that Harley had no clue as to what she wanted to talk about. She squeezed her hand.

"First of all, thank you for saving me. Again."

"Did you know I was going to take a shot?"

"Yes. Even then, I was prepared for it to go so very wrong. His gun was pressed so hard against me. I didn't know how he *wouldn't* shoot me, you know."

"Yes. That thought crossed my mind too. But we were out of options, out of time."

She folded Harley's hand inside both of hers. "Tell me what happened, Harley."

Harley didn't pretend to not understand the question. She had a haunted look in her eyes. "After he threw you into the bay, I shot him three more times. He fell in too." She swallowed. "I ran to the spot where you'd fallen and jumped in. But I couldn't find you. And I called for you and called for you but..." She swallowed again. "I saw Blevins." She closed her eyes. "I saw a *body*," she clarified. "I was so afraid it was you. When I saw it was him, I kept calling for you and looking for you, but it was so dark out there and the waves, the tide was getting so high and..."

"And what?" she asked gently.

Harley met her eyes, holding them. "It was over my head. I was going under and I...I just let it happen, Lauren. I couldn't go through it again. I just couldn't. So I thought, just let it happen."

Lauren moved closer so that they were touching. "But it didn't happen. Did you hear me then? Hear me call for you?"

"No. I was under water. I couldn't hold my breath for another second, then...then I felt hands on me, pushing me up. Forcefully pushing me up. Then I was above the water and gasping for breath and...and then I heard you." Harley looked away. "I know that sounds crazy. Maybe I imagined it. But it was so real."

"Oh, Harley." She leaned her head on Harley's shoulder, not sure how to respond to that. "I don't care if it's real or not. Just know that I would have been devastated if...well, if you hadn't swum over to me."

"I'm sorry. You must think I'm pretty pathetic."

"I think no such thing. It's been a very emotional week. It's been a rough two months, to be honest. Having you in my life is the positive in it all." She lifted her head, looking at Harley. "You *are* going to stay in my life, aren't you? You're not going to drift away, right?"

"I was afraid you would drift away, actually."

"I'm falling in love with you, Harley. It's a little scary and not something I expected to happen to me when I moved to Rockport. But I'm awfully glad you came into my life. I kinda want you to stay."

CHAPTER FORTY-NINE

"He had two juvenile records that were sealed," Brian said as he pulled two bottles from the patio beer fridge. "When he was fifteen, there was an attempted rape of a thirteen-year-old girl. The girl first refused to cooperate and then later recanted. And when he was seventeen, still in high school, a classmate accused him of attempted rape and assault. Same outcome."

"Daddy paid them off?"

"Most likely. Both in Harris County."

"Well, I contacted the other cities. They were all glad to possibly close the books on those open cases."

"They're taking your word for his confession?"

She shrugged. "The similarities to our cases in San Antonio were too numerous, right down to the teddy bear. And all of the murders took place during the same timeframe as ours."

"So during the same thirteen months, he was preying on women in Dallas, Odessa, and El Paso? Not just us? Why didn't anything pop up in the database if the cases were so similar?"

"We checked it after the second one to see if there were similar crimes where a teddy bear was left. There was nothing. The closest we got was the Raggedy Anne Killer in Tucson, I think it was."

Brian nodded. "The other cities hadn't logged theirs in yet because he was killing at the same time."

"Yes. And the killings stopped after Radisson was taken out."

"Then that suggests that Radisson was the catalyst then. Unless there are some that Blevins did on his own that we're not aware of yet."

"I think the two of them meeting up was the perfect storm. Blevins liked to rape them. Radisson liked to kill."

He nudged her arm and motioned to where Lauren stood talking to Marsha and Nana. "How's she holding up? I have to say, she looks perfectly fine. Of course, it's been a week now."

"She's doing good. I think her staff was more shook up about it than she was. He'd been staying there with them since early spring. They all knew him or had seen him around."

"What about the resort itself? I'm sure that caused quite a stir."

"As she told me, Sunday nights in late August aren't exactly a draw. The weekend crowd had checked out and I think they only had four cabins booked that night."

"And what about you? We haven't talked much this week. You okay?"

"Yeah. I'm really good, to be honest. I feel great."

"Good, Harley. Do I need to ask where you're staying or if it's any of my business?"

She smiled at him. "You know where I'm staying."

"Is it permanent?"

"I don't know. We haven't actually talked about me staying or going. I'm just there. For now. I'm just there." She pointed at her T-shirt. "And I'm wearing her clothes. I guess I do need to do something about that."

"You know you're welcome to stay with us, if you ever need to."

"Yes, Marsha has already offered. Thanks. But I'll see how it goes with Lauren."

"Oh, I heard you two went to see Jacobs the other day."

"Yeah, he was doing okay, considering. Lauren wanted to see him. I guess they kinda bonded or something."

"Well, he got out of the hospital yesterday. He's damn lucky to be alive."

"Yeah, he is. You think he'll stay on?"

"Hard to say. A rookie cop—he doesn't have a lot invested in the job yet. This might make him reconsider his career."

Harley nodded. "I think he'll stay on. Something in his eyes. He had a fight to him, that's for sure."

"Are you two talking police business?" Marsha demanded as she came over. "I thought we had an agreement. Fish fry, beer, and no police talk."

"We hardly saw each other this week. It was a whirlwind."

"I'm sure it was, but it's over with." Marsha linked arms with her and drew her away from Brian. "Nana is an absolute delight." She leaned closer. "She thinks you're quite the catch, by the way. She had poor Lauren blushing crimson." She paused. "I take it she doesn't know anything about what happened? To hear her tell it, Lauren ran into a tree limb at the resort and cut her forehead."

"Yeah. She knows what the paper reported, that's all. Lauren didn't want to tell her about her involvement. I don't blame her."

"No, I don't either. The paper was quite glowing about you. Maybe that's why she thinks you're a good catch," Marsha laughed.

"The paper went a bit overboard, didn't they?"

Lauren looked over at them, meeting her gaze. She smiled at her and Harley returned it. That got her another laugh from Marsha.

"You two seem perfect for each other. It's so nice watching you fall in love, Harley."

Harley blushed. "I like her an awful lot."

"Oh, Harley, who are you kidding? Your eyes light up when you look at her."

Yeah, she knew they did. When she looked at Lauren—when Lauren looked back at her—she felt all warm and gooey inside. Here they were, a week removed from "the thing at the pier" as they'd been calling it. And yes, she'd slept at Lauren's every night. The first night, Lauren had woken up from a dream and had thrashed at the covers, screaming out in fright. Harley had held her, and Lauren had been shivering so, fighting back her tears.

That was the only night, though. Since then, she'd slept soundly, although she'd had a death grip on Harley's arm each night. Not that she minded. It was rather nice to have someone cling to her like that.

And it was rather nice to wake up with someone. Like this morning when she'd been awakened by a warm, wet tongue bathing her nipples. By the time she was cognizant of what was happening, Lauren had been kissing across her stomach and by the time her eyes fluttered open, Lauren's mouth had settled between her thighs. Yes, it was quite wonderful to wake up with someone.

She stared at Lauren now, thinking of their time in bed that morning. Lauren had been nearly insatiable, and it had been after nine before they'd finally collapsed back into a deep slumber. An hour and a half later, with the sun shining in, she'd found herself alone. The smell of coffee roused her from bed, and she found Lauren in the kitchen, attempting to make an omelet. While it looked nothing like an omelet—it fell completely apart when she tried to flip it—it was delicious. Of course, as Lauren had said, they were ravenous and would have eaten shoe leather at that point.

She nearly laughed at the memory, and when Lauren walked over to them, she smiled back at her. "What's so funny?"

"Thinking about omelets."

Lauren laughed. "Oh, Marsha, you should have seen it. I was trying to surprise Harley and my omelet was an epic failure."

"I can't make an omelet to save my life," Marsha admitted. "I sauté all my veggies first, then scramble eggs with them and call it good. Now, do you think your grandmother would drink a glass of wine?"

"Oh, I'm sure she would. I'll get it, though, Marsha."

"Okay. There's a chardonnay in the fridge and one of those red blends out on the counter. They've both been opened so whichever she'd prefer."

"Nana's favorite is chardonnay. Thank you." Lauren turned to her and winked. "Want to help?"

Harley grinned. "Sure."

Marsha laughed and pushed them toward the house. "Yes, go steal some kisses or something. I'll keep Nana occupied."

She was surprised when Lauren took her hand and tugged her inside. But instead of going into the kitchen, she led her down the hallway and into the bedroom they'd used that one night. She found herself pinned against the door.

"I lied, Harley. I thought I was falling in love with you, but I was so very wrong."

Harley stared at her in disbelief as her heart fell in her chest. It had felt too good to be true and it apparently was. And now she was going to get her heart broken. But Lauren kissed her, a sweet, slow kiss that made her moan. Should a broken heart feel this good?

"I should have worded that differently." She kissed her again. "What I mean is, I'm already in love with you."

"Jesus, Lauren, you about ripped my heart out."

Lauren met her gaze. "When we made love this morning, the way you touched me, the way you looked at me, I knew you were in love with me. It filled me up so, I thought I was going to burst with it. But you didn't say the words."

"I thought maybe it was too soon or maybe you didn't want to hear them yet."

"Couldn't you tell, Harley?"

Harley nodded. "I wanted it to be true, yes. But…"

"But you were afraid?"

"It's like, maybe I'm not supposed to be this happy."

Instead of kissing her, Lauren pulled her into a tight hug. Harley closed her eyes as she felt Lauren's lips at her ear.

"I love you, Harley. You make me happy too."

Harley was smiling as they kissed. "Does this mean I can continue to steal your clothes?"

Lauren pulled back, meeting her eyes. "You don't want to replace your Hawaiian shirts?"

She shook her head. "No. I don't think I need them any longer."

One more slow kiss, one that made her melt just a little inside. Then Lauren stepped away from her, entwined their fingers, and led her back into the hallway.

"I think you should get one or two. I'll admit it now, I thought they were kinda sexy."

She laughed. "Sexy? You *hated* my shirts! You called them obnoxious."

"So I changed my mind." Lauren stopped suddenly. "I fell in love with you, obnoxious shirts and all. You say you don't need them any longer and maybe that's true. You don't need them for the purpose that they served. But maybe you could get a couple of them…just for fun."

Harley held her gaze, seeing love in her eyes. "Can I get you a couple too? Maybe matching shirts. We'd be so cute together, Ms. Voss."

Lauren laughed loudly. "Not on your life, Detective Shepherd."

Before Lauren could pour wine into a glass, Harley stopped her. Lauren looked at her questioningly. Harley thought she'd stumble over the words. They were words she'd never said to another woman before. But she didn't. They came out clearly. Sincerely.

"I love you."

Lauren put the bottle down, her eyes smiling into her own. Then, as if forgetting where they were, Lauren moved into her arms, pressing their bodies tightly together as they kissed.

A clearing of a throat behind them drew them apart. It was Marsha, with Nana standing beside her. Harley felt a blush on her face, but Lauren didn't seem fazed at all.

"We were getting you some wine, Nana."

"So I heard. It was taking you so long, I thought maybe you had to go stomp the grapes first."

"Aren't you the funny one," Lauren teased her. She picked up the bottle again, pausing to glance at Harley. Her smile was slow and sweet, and Harley felt it all the way to the tips of her toes.

Love. She felt love. And it was pretty damn awesome.

Bella Books, Inc.

Women. Books. Even Better Together.

P.O. Box 10543
Tallahassee, FL 32302

Phone: 800-729-4992
www.bellabooks.com